CANDARA'S GIFT

THE KINGDOM OF GEMS TRILOGY

THE KINGDOM OF GEMS TRILOGY

- BOOK 1 -

CANDARA'S GIFT

Jasper Cooper

Illustrations by Jasper Cooper

SILVERWELL PUBLISHING

For more information about Jasper Cooper and his books, visit:

www.JasperCooper.com
or
www.TheKingdomOfGems.com

Published in 2006 by SilverWell Publishing,
PO BOX 948, Canterbury, Kent. CT1 9BH

1 3 5 7 9 10 8 6 4 2

ISBN 0-9551653-0-X
ISBN 978-0-9551653-0-6

Printed and bound in Great Britain by
Bookmarque Ltd, Croydon, Surrey

CONTENTS

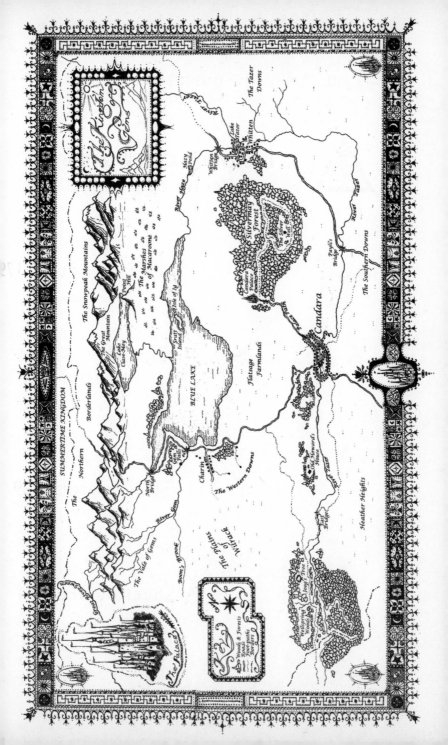

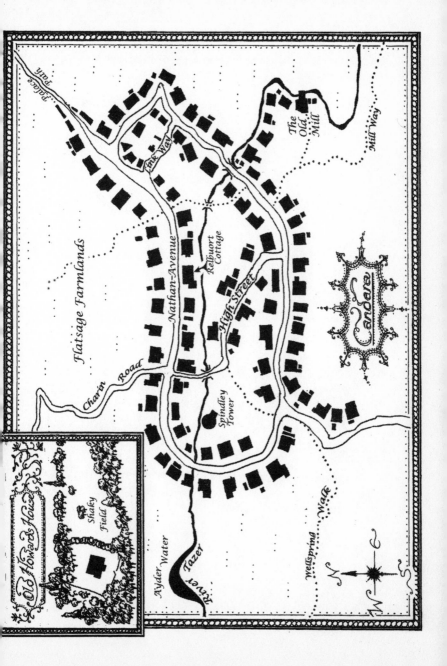

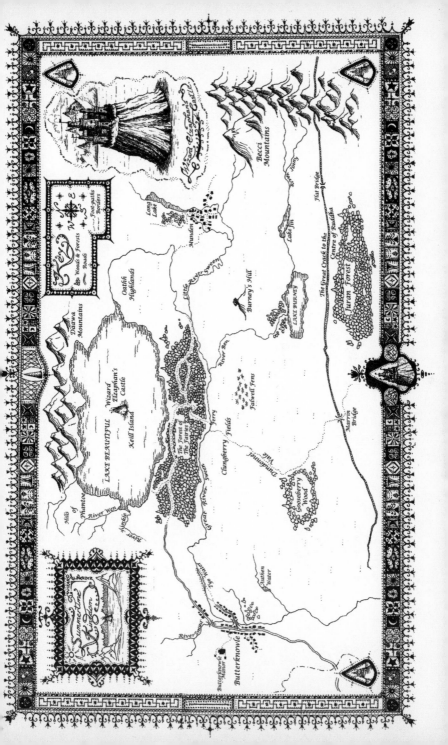

This book is dedicated to Jeremy Pickles.

Introduction

The Accounts of

Candara

Candara's Gift is the first book in the trilogy called The Kingdom of Gems. The events described in this book take place mainly in two kingdoms; the Kingdom of Gems and Summertime Kingdom. This first trilogy describes the extraordinary things that happened over a short period of time, things that were linked to the past and were to have considerable impact on the future.

The history of these kingdoms, and the others in the surrounding lands, were inextricably bound together not only by the events that trickled through them like the sand in an egg timer, but also by the workings of the powerful forces of good and evil.

Over five hundred years before the events described in this book the Great Wizard Candara lived in the Kingdom of Mardice in the north. These were troubled times in which terrible danger abounded everywhere originating from Gugeol. Wizard Candara travelled extensively in an attempt to help the threatened kingdoms. He was largely successful although he was unable to completely defeat the enemy, and seventy years after his death the forces of Gugeol regrouped and the Dark Ages began. These Dark Ages, also known as the Thousand Seasons of Night, smothered most of the kingdoms for almost two hundred and fifty years.

During his travels Wizard Candara bequeathed magical gifts to some of the kingdoms he visited and helped. The King and Queen of the Kingdom of Sanseem were fortunate to have a gift of three magical gems bestowed upon them and they were so thankful that they renamed their main town and called it Candara after the great wizard. Their royal palace became Candara Palace and the kingdom became the Kingdom of Gems.

The gems provided an energy of protection and goodness, so much so that the kingdom remained completely free and unscathed throughout the Dark Ages. Even at the time of the Great Invasion, when the evil force of Gugeol was finally resisted and pushed back and the Dark Ages came to an end, the inhabitants of the Kingdom of Gems were not involved in these troubles. Throughout all this, due to the gift they had received, they lived peacefully.

Unfortunately, over the passing years, the people and creatures living in the Kingdom of Gems forgot to be thankful for their blessings. They even forgot about the gift that they had received and they began to believe it was just an ancient legend which made a good story but was not true. They became disinterested in the welfare of the surrounding kingdoms. Even when Gugeol arose again to attack Summertime Kingdom, their neighbours to the north, they felt no urge to help.

So the inhabitants of the Kingdom of Gems lived peacefully and, on the whole, honestly. They took joy in much goodwill between each other, but they had become complacent in their contentment and cut off from the other kingdoms. Whether it was this that made them vulnerable or the hand of fate, or just chance is hard to tell, but the peace which they enjoyed was to be suddenly snatched away from them. This book tells the story of how this happened.

Chapter 1

~ The Troubler ~

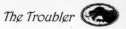

The tall figure approached the woods with powerful strides. Just behind him, held on a metal chain which he shook every so often to keep it moving, was a great creature. As the darkly cloaked man and the creature moved, the plants nearby withered, their leaves falling to the dying grass, and flowers, so bright and beautiful the day before, drooped as if touched by invisible poisonous vapours.

Close by, and high up in an old oak tree, perched a snowy owl called Joog. He clutched a branch with his powerful talons as he slept soundly amongst the swishing leaves of the swaying tree. A powerful gale blew over the hills and through the valleys of the kingdom and ruffled his beautiful white feathers, but even this could not wake him tonight.

Joog was meant to be watching. He was always particularly vigilant during nighttime as it was his job to guard the kingdom, but tonight, however, he had slipped into a deep and absorbing slumber leaving the kingdom unprotected and open to intruders.

The wild wind whistled and sighed through the trees. It swept across the kingdom from the west, like a curtain drawn at the end of the day and now it persisted deep into the night, swirling across the whole kingdom with a groaning presence. It seemed to herald the arrival of something unusual, bleak and unwelcome, something that forewarned of danger. In spite of this howling wind, however, Joog slept soundly and so did every creature in the Kingdom of Gems. Even the nocturnal animals were sleeping which was strange because during the dark hours of the night they were usually busy.

Then, as the dawn approached, the air seemed to grow weary of its swirling movements and the driving wind collapsed, like an exhausted wild animal that finally runs out of energy. But this was not a peaceful stilling, it was as if the air grew too heavy to be in motion any more, too thick to stir and its dreadful weight fell upon the land. This utter stillness that filled the kingdom, seeping into the very earth, was a brooding expectant atmosphere. The whole kingdom seemed to be wrapped in a weighty darkness, grave and intense, that awaited the arrival of something uninvited and unwanted.

Joog was still absorbed in a deep sleep.

Then a rustling sound, at first distant in the still air, but soon growing louder, broke the heavy silence. The shadowy figure, with the great creature following, was moving into the woodlands and striding steadily over the spongy leaf-strewn earth. Joog did not hear these approaching footsteps. He did not feel the strange sinister chill that had suddenly filled the air. He did not see the dark-cloaked figure far below him cross the border and enter the Kingdom. A Troubler had arrived.

It was growing lighter as the night began to soften into day, although the sun had not risen yet. The great creature looked in some ways like a massive crocodile but was in fact a Komodo Dragon. It had a rugged appearance and was covered with small smooth scales of dark green and brown. Its legs were short and looked exceptionally sturdy and strong and each leg had a five-toed foot with sharp claws. Its body was a muscular bulk and dragging behind it was a long tail which tapered to a point and rustled across the dried leaves. Its ferocious looking head was long and flat with a rounded snout. As it walked its body twisted to the rhythm of its steps. It gave every impression of being savage and vicious.

Around them as they moved, the oppressive heaviness hung in the air most strongly. The gentle early light, which normally wakes up the many colours of plants and flowers in the woods, was having no effect. Everything remained painted with the shadowy grey of night. They were well past Joog's old oak tree now and heading towards the town, leaving a path of dying plants and bushes behind them. The woods were so unnaturally quiet that their footsteps, rustling on the blanket of leaves and the shaking of the metal lead echoed amongst the trees and the Troubler's low mutterings could be heard some distance away... but there was no one awake to hear them.

The sinister looking duo followed a path, called Wellspring Walk, which led out of the woods. The path dropped south across the River Tazer where there was just enough room on the wooden East Bridge for the Komodo Dragon to cross. The path turned east again to follow the river towards the town of Candara. When they were in sight of Candara they left the path and walked into a small group of trees. It was just before dawn.

The Troubler tied the dragon to a tree by the metal lead and it immediately sank down to the ground to rest with a low groan that resounded in its massive leathery-scaled body. Its mouth dripped with bacteria-filled saliva that could infect anything that it bit, bringing a quick and certain death to the unfortunate victim. The Troubler sat down nearby on a moss-covered log to rest and look at the scene. As the sky began to grow lighter he looked through the trees to see the cottages and houses of Candara with the tall Spindley Tower rising above. On a hill beyond there was the palace, tall and pinnacled, overlooking the whole town. Suddenly the sun appeared above the horizon, at first just a star-point of light, growing to a glowing red disc. The dawn had arrived. At this moment Joog awoke.

He opened his large golden-yellow eyes and looked around. He wondered why he had slept through the night. Where was the happy dawn chorus that always filled the warm woodland air as the sun rose? Why was it so quiet? What had happened whilst he was sleeping? Had the other nocturnal animals been sleeping too? Had no one been watching? He felt an unusual chill in the air. And then he thought of something that instantly sent a wave of shock washing through him; perhaps a Troubler had entered the Kingdom. He realised that if this had happened he had to report to the King.

He stretched out his strong wings - he had one of the largest wingspans of all the birds in the Kingdom - and left his branch with a jump. He glided at first through the leaves of his oak tree home and then began to flap his wings to gather speed. He now felt the air rushing silently past his soft feathers - oh how he loved flying. He was a

Snowy Owl and he made sure he kept his plumage of white and brown speckled feathers beautifully clean, bathing every day in one of the woodland ponds. But now, as he flew above the trees, his feathers were touched and tinted by the pink of the dawn sun.

Joog was the wisest and the most watchful owl in the whole Kingdom. He was in charge of an elite group of owls, selected for their special qualities of observation and reliability. It was their job to report to the King when they spotted anyone or anything entering the Kingdom at night because occasionally some kind of Troubler with a mind full of evil thoughts would enter the land. These brave and trustworthy owls were the Guardians of the Kingdom of Gems and each owl covered a length of the border. Joog was based in these woods, the Wellspring Woods, where the border zigzagged through and from his high lookout in his oak tree he could see for some miles around. In the past Joog had always spotted any strangers and reported it to the King so that guests could be welcomed and Troublers dealt with.

Joog followed the River Tazer and he flew as fast as he could because he knew that the situation might be very serious indeed. In fact this seemed to bring added strength to his outspread wings, but even though he was flying faster than he had ever flown before he kept watching the land below him - he was looking out for an intruder. He decided that before reporting to the King he would circle above the town and surrounding area to see if he could spot anything. He did not realise that he was passing directly over the Dark Troubler who was still sitting on the log, hidden even from Joog's sharp eyes by the rich green mass of leaves and branches above him.

The Troubler was obviously a wizard of some sort.

This was clear from his long pointed hat and his dark cloak with his coat of arms set on the left. The cloak and

hat of a real wizard are often covered with sparkling stars, but this wizard was different. He had stars on his hat and cloak, but they were black, blacker than the deep black of his cloak, blacker than the blackest black imaginable. They were so black that they looked like holes. His coat of arms was embroidered in gold and black, but it was unusual too; instead of representing light, wisdom and happiness this one was dark and threatening, with gloomy black symbols. There was a raven and a skull, as well as a compass and a crescent moon in the night.

The Dark Wizard Troubler was resting briefly and was eating some food he had taken from his bag that now lay on the withering grass beside him. The Komodo Dragon was lying flat, stretched out, tethered to a tree by the lead and half asleep as it rested after the long journey. Although the dawn air was warm their breath could be seen as on a frosty winter's day, because around them the Troubler's presence chilled the air. Everything near to him had lost its colour and like a black and white photograph showed only shades of grey.

As he ate he was hatching a plan. He clenched his teeth together, grimaced and closed his eyes as he tried to work it out. His hair and beard were black and long which made a strange contrast with his gaunt face of ghostly-grey skin. As he rested on the log he mumbled quietly to himself, his angular features twisting as he agonised over his plans. After a while the expressions on his face eased and relaxed as his plans became clearer. Then he chuckled and opened his eyes wide in glee; they were as black as coal. He nodded slowly as if he had made an important decision.

"Yes, Horrik," he said to the dragon with words as icy as a frozen pond in winter, "I have been working out a plan that will shake this kingdom to its very foundations. And then *I* will be king here."

Horrik stirred, lifted up her great head and spoke, opening her huge mouth to show two rows of serrated razor-sharp teeth, numbering about sixty in all. A long yellow forked tongue flicked out of her mouth dribbling with the poisonous saliva. Her large eyes were also black and her voice came in a deep and slow rumbling, "Will we rule here, Master?" she asked.

"*I* will rule here," the wizard's words hissed out in clouds of breath that momentarily hung in the air and then dispersed. "Through bringing the three gems into my possession... that will do it, but first... well... it is just the simple matter of dealing with the inhabitants who live here. And that..."

The wizard stopped speaking as something distracted him. A black mongrel dog, who had been watching him from under a nearby tree, jumped up and ran towards him. It was Jamaar, a young dog whose lifestyle was obvious from his matted and bedraggled fur and the strong unhealthy smell that accompanied him. He survived by scavenging for food and sleeping in woods at night. From time to time someone in the kingdom would take him in and give him a home, but it always failed and he would be thrown out in disgrace because he was so uncontrollable. He had become a stray not through bad luck but due to his own actions.

As he got close to the Dark Wizard he felt the chill of the air around the Troubler and he could see his breath in the cold air. Then he noticed the bland and colourless surroundings, but he was so hungry that he ignored the signs of danger. With one more step and a fast snap of his teeth he had grabbed the bag in his mouth and turned to run off with it. The wizard looked at him with surprise and suddenly moved extremely quickly, lunged and managed to grasp the strap of the bag. Horrik jumped up onto her short legs and stepped towards the dog, her chain lead tightening and digging into her scaly neck, her head straining forwards. The Dark Wizard and the dog stared at each other and for a moment it was a tug-of-war. Fear gripped Jamaar as he saw the wizard's icy black eyes and heard the rumbling roar of Horrik, still pulling at the end of her lead. Jamaar growled and pulled as hard as he could, but the wizard was strong… too strong.

"What are you doing?" the wizard shouted harshly as he pulled Jamaar along the ground making his front paws skid on the grass. When the poor dog was close enough the Dark Wizard kicked at him. Jamaar dodged and the heavy black boot whistled past his ear, but he clung on even harder. He was very hungry and now he that he was so close to the food that he could smell in the bag he clung on defiantly. But the wizard was much stronger than he expected.

"Get away you smelly creature!" the wizard snapped and he dragged Jamaar closer to him and pulling the strap of the bag upwards he lifted the dog's front paws off the ground. When he saw that the dog was still not letting go he scowled at it and swung his leg again at its head. This time the kick caught Jamaar on his nose and made him yelp and he let go and began to slink away, whimpering and crouching close to the ground.

"Get lost you ugly mongrel!" shouted the Dark Wizard, but then his expression suddenly changed; the angry scowl disappeared and a sly smile curled up the corners of his thin lips. His voice became soft, "Wait a minute! You could be of use to me, a strong young dog like you. Where do you live?" Then he turned to Horrik, "Easy now," he said to her and then pointing a finger at her, he snapped, "Down!" She relaxed and slumped down again until she was flat on the ground.

Jamaar stopped whimpering and stood still, frozen in fear of this stranger and the dragon, and still cowering close to the ground, he twisted his head around to listen.

"Where do you live?" asked the wizard again, his voice hissing with cunning and deceit.

"Anywhere I can," said Jamaar timidly, "I've got no home. I just wander around the kingdom."

"Would you like to move up in the world?" The Dark Wizard Troubler spoke with an inviting voice.

"What do you mean?" whimpered Jamaar still terrified of this black-eyed stranger.

"Well," the wizard began, "Live better. You're obviously hungry. You're thin. I could help you. But you'd have to help me in return. Think of it… food…" Jamaar felt the pain of hunger in his stomach and he licked his lips. "Food… that's what you need, isn't it? Well… no problem, I can give you plenty."

They were both standing still now with the bag between them on the grass and staring at each other. Horrik lay flat and listened.

"Interested?" said the wizard.

"I… I think so," answered Jamaar hesitantly and now pricking up his ears with interest, "But what do I have to do for you?"

"Well, we can do a deal," said the wizard calmly, "Come here." Jamaar approached cautiously and as the wizard reached out his hand Jamaar pulled back blinking and thinking he might be hit again. The wizard slowly stretched further and stroked him gently on the head, "You be my dog, obedient and faithful, and I will be your master and look after you well. Is it a deal?"

"Well, maybe," Jamaar responded, still afraid after being kicked on the nose, but feeling tempted by the offer of food, "Well… why not?" he growled, "Alright then, I'll give it a try… But I'd like to see the food first."

"Good, then come with me," said the Dark Wizard Troubler as he untied Horrik's lead from the tree and pulled at it to get the dragon onto her clawed feet, "Come on then, dog," he said to Jamaar over his shoulder.

Jamaar nodded towards Horrik, "What about that?" he said, "That thing will try to eat me."

"No," said the Dark Wizard, "She does what I say," and he turned to Horrik, "Don't you?" he spat out the words crossly.

The answer grumbled up slowly from the depths of her long body, as her forked tongue darted out of her mouth and back in again, "It smells," she said.

"Look who's talking," the Dark Wizard sneered, "The smelliest beast I've ever met." He looked at her with a malicious smile on his lips. Then he suddenly pulled at the chain with a sharp jerk and snapped crossly, "You do what I say, don't you?"

"Of course, Master," she growled, keeping her eye fixed on Jamaar with a stare that oozed hate.

"There you are!" said the wizard as if it was all settled, "So, for a better life, follow me." He slung the bag over his shoulder and strode away through the trees with Horrik on her lead glaring daggers at Jamaar. She felt consumed by jealousy and disgust for this young scraggy dog, this impostor who was receiving her masters attention. She was her master's pet and assistant and she did not want any competition especially from a youngster like this.

Jamaar hesitated and then decided. He hurried after his new master, passed Horrik, and trotted along beside the Dark Wizard Troubler. He had an extra bounce in his thin legs and the feeling that the good meal he so desperately needed would soon be tasting delicious on his tongue and filling his starving belly. As he followed he felt better and better; yes, at last he had found what he needed - a master to obey and follow - and although he was still afraid he felt that his new master had a special strength about him, a presence which he found terrifying and yet at the same time he was attracted to it. He also felt extremely pleased to have upstaged the malicious dragon; he knew the dragon hated him but already he had taken up a higher position; *he* was at his master's heels, whereas the dragon was behind *and* on a lead. When he thought of this he lifted his nose slightly higher with an air of superiority that made Horrik seethe with envy.

The Dark Wizard Troubler was now walking back onto the path which would take him towards Candara. His black wizard robe flowed out behind him. He stared at the ground as he walked with his breath hissing out in clouds; his thoughts intent upon the plan that was growing clearer in his mind. As he moved the icy atmosphere moved with him and filled the air with stifling heaviness and the flowers close by bowed and died. He glanced up to see Joog circling above the town and scanning the houses and streets below as if he was looking for something.

The Dark Wizard paused and stood still and so did Jamaar beside him and Horrik following. The wizard crouched as they all watched Joog circle once more and then turn and head towards the palace. The wizard's black eyes narrowed as he observed the speedy flight of the owl. Horrik turned her head towards him.

"Was it looking for *us,* master?" she asked.

"I expect so," said the wizard, "But it didn't see us. What's that tower for, dog?"

"People go up," replied Jamaar, "And animals. Birds

land on it."

"But what's it used for?"

"It seems to be just a look-out," said Jamaar, "There's a man who lives in it... in Spindley Tower. He lets everyone in and out."

The wizard turned his head away from the town, "The tower may be useful later, but we won't go into the town now. No need. When the time comes... at the right time... then we will act. I need to think."

"That owl," said Jamaar, "That owl lands on the tower sometimes and watches the town. It works for the King you know."

"And the king lives in that palace?"

"Yes," Jamaar nodded.

The wizard smiled, "He's got a surprise coming."

He stood up, gave the chain a tug to get Horrik moving and started walking back along the path with Jamaar padding along at his heels.

High above the town buildings Joog was enjoying the fresh morning air as he rose towards the palace that was silhouetted against the pink sunrise. From high in the air he could see the kingdom laid out before him like a richly coloured map; across the Flatsage Farmlands with its chequered fields was Blue Lake, reflecting the red sun in its still waters; and beyond that, the Snowpeak Mountains stood in stately stillness in the distance. Candara Palace itself looked beautiful too, dark against the bright rays of the rising sun and sitting proudly on the outskirts of Silvermay Forest.

Joog was always happy even in the most difficult situations. It was as if he was made of happiness; it was in his nature to be happy and he could not be otherwise. When flying he sometimes hooted with joy - it was so delightful to be airborne and this was how he felt today. He had certainly reached speeds today that had surprised him, and as he approached the palace he began to glide and then tilted his outstretched wings to reduce his speed. Most of the other owls, the Guardians, were heading for the palace as well and when they saw Joog they flew towards him. There were about thirty of various different kinds and sizes; there were Barn Owls, a couple of Sooty Owls with their massive eyes, Great Gray Owls, a couple of speckled Short-eared Owls, another Snowy Owl and even one tiny Elf Owl. They glided in gracefully from all directions, floating on the morning air, with their soft feathers making no sound as they headed faithfully for their leader.

Looking up Joog saw the King and Queen's bedroom window open as usual and he landed gracefully on the gold frame and turned to watch the others as they landed on the building wherever they could find a suitable ledge.

"You did the right thing," began Joog looking around at the group perched above and below him, "Mmm... exactly the right thing... to fly here, I mean. But tell me, what happened through the night?"

"I slept!" announced a large tawny owl and all the others nodded their agreement, and some others said, "So did I!"

"All through the night?" asked Joog.

"Yes!" chorused the owls.

"I thought so. So did I. Something very very strange happened last night. It must be a spell for something like this to happen. I think it is best..." he hesitated, considering carefully, "If you return to your areas for now and keep a good lookout for anything unusual. Ask around and see if anyone knows anything about it. Let me or the King know straight away any information that may throw light on this. Apart from that go back to your usual routine and I'll let you know if I need you. Alright?"

The owls hooted their agreement, spread their wings and with a flurry of silently flapping feathers flew off in various directions.

Joog jumped off the window frame and circled around as he watched them go and then pulled his wings in closer to his body as he glided back through the open window. He landed not too gently on the end of the bed and the King awoke with a jerk. He sat up with his deep blue eyes still half-closed. His thinning hair was ruffled but long and tumbled down the back of his neck in silver curls. His face showed the character of a sensitive man who ruled his kingdom with fairness and dignity.

"Ahh!" the alarmed King blurted out, "Who's there?"

"It's me," said Joog calmly.

"Who's that?" the King said, beginning to feel more awake.

"It's me, Joog, it's me, Your Majesty."

"Oh Joog," the King said with affection, who was so surprised by Joog's sudden arrival that he did not know what to say, "Er..." he sat up, pulling his pillow up so that he could lean back against it. He looked puzzled. "What brings you here, Joog? And what time is it?" asked the King, whose eyes were now fully open and beginning to get used to the morning light.

"It's after dawn already. I'm sorry to disturb you like

this, Your Majesty, but it is rather urgent… very urgent," Joog lowered his voice to almost a whisper as he had just noticed the Queen was still sleeping, "You see, there's something very strange happening and I can't say I understand it yet. I fear a Troubler may have entered the Kingdom! I feel it somehow - in the atmosphere. Everyone throughout the Kingdom has been asleep all through the night! And that includes all the Guardians! You yourself are always awake before dawn… and I slept too which has never happened before - never ever. What can it mean, Your Majesty? It must be a spell of some kind."

"Well it certainly is very strange, Joog. Did you see anything on your way here?" asked the King who was now wide-awake. His voice expressed his tender affection for Joog. Joog's eyes glowed a deep golden-yellow as he gazed back at the King.

"Well, it was so quiet… I suppose everyone must have been asleep and I didn't see anyone at all. I did spend some time looking around on my way but no… I didn't see anyone. I… well… I may have missed something. Of course a Troubler could have hidden… that's easy enough. Perhaps I should have looked more carefully but I thought I'd better get up here as quickly as possible to tell you about it all. Could a Troubler have arrived…?" Joog looked out of the window as he wondered about it. His eyes glowed brighter in the growing light.

"I think you'd better go and take another look," said the King, smiling at his friend, "Is that alright?"

"Yes, of course," replied Joog brightly.

"I'll tell you what," the King pushed his arms onto the bed to sit up more, "By the time you're back we'll have breakfast on the table for you. Your favourite cereal,

Joog?"

"That would be great!" declared Joog, giving a hoot, "I'll have a good look from Spindley Tower first and then scout around the area."

"Be careful," said the King, earnestly, as Joog gave his feathers a shake. He raised his great wings, jumped off the end of the bed and flew towards the open window.

The King watched as Joog glided out. He got up and walked to the gold-framed window. The main town of the kingdom, Candara, certainly was still and the King gazed at it with affection as it lay below. At this height and distance it looked like a toy town with the many colours of the houses and cottages pale in the misty morning. It was built in the shape of a unicorn nestled at the foot of the Southern Downs to its south and with the River Tazer running through the centre of it. The tall Spindley Tower was easily the highest building and it stood out against the hazy background of the hills beyond.

He glanced to the east, across Silvermay Forest and towards Whitten. Then looking back he saw Joog glide gracefully through the hazy air and over the houses of Candara and thought how small and vulnerable he looked at this distance. Suddenly he felt deeply fond of Joog and hoped he would return safely. He watched as the owl, now just a tiny dot at that distance, landed on the top of Spindley Tower.

He turned to look affectionately at the Queen who was still in the land of slumber in the warm bed and decided to wake her.

Chapter 2

~ Joog Goes Missing ~

The King and his family always had breakfast in the Round Room at the very top of one of the turrets. There were curved windows set in gold frames all the way around and a window in the spire that was ideal for nighttime stargazing. A round oak table stood in the centre of the room; it was large and heavy and there was space around it for the family and a dozen guests. The table was neatly laid for breakfast and there was a bowl of Joog's favourite cereal on the light blue tablecloth and behind it a branch of an oak tree beautifully smoothed and polished. This morning the atmosphere was happy as usual, but there was a feeling of uncertainty too. The King glanced out of the window in the direction of the town. He had forgotten to brush his silver-white hair and it looked extremely dishevelled.

"Where is he?" he said anxiously, "Where is Joog? He should be back by now... I do hope he's alright. Perhaps I shouldn't have sent him out."

"Oh I expect he's having a good scout around," said the Queen reassuringly, and trying to stay calm. She was looking at her husband's hair and this was putting a smile on her face. Her brown eyes showed her deep affection for him, "You know how thorough he is."

"Yes, and he's so clever," piped up Princess Amalek brightly, but her thoughtful face betrayed her concern for Joog. She had turned thirteen just a few weeks earlier. "Joog always seems to do things in the right way. He must be looking around..." she said, her voice trailing off as she turned away from her mother to look out of the window and gaze searchingly down at the town with her worried eyes. She shook her head slowly and looked uneasy as she stroked back her long wavy fair hair from one of her cheeks.

Prince Seph got up from the table and joined her at the window. "Any sign of him?" he asked.

"None," replied his sister.

The Queen sat down at the table, "Come and have your breakfast, you two," she said kindly, "Staring out of the window won't help."

Seph turned to look at his mother with his large blue eyes. She was unsuccessfully trying to tidy the King's hair by dabbing at it with her hand.

"I'm not hungry," said Seph.

"Neither am I," added Amalek, "Sorry, but with Joog missing..."

"Oh, that's alright," the Queen said, "Breakfast can wait."

Seph was twelve and a natural athlete. He was impulsive, plunging into any action with energy, expecting it to go well. In this way he was the opposite of his sister who was more thoughtful and cautious and yet they were great friends and spent most of their time playing games together and going on adventures in the beautiful lands of the kingdom. He was also fair-haired, like his sister, but his was straight and it hung down past his ears and just above his shoulders. They were the same height so that people meeting them for the first time often thought they were twins. They were very close, so much so that they often discovered on waking up in the morning that they had shared the same dreams whilst asleep, and they would discuss what had happened as they ate their breakfast.

The King was standing behind the two children and he put a hand on each of their shoulders and squeezed gently with affection.

"Well, we won't begin breakfast until he's here," he said, trying to feel more confident. The Queen stood up and joined her husband at the window to watch for Joog. They watched Candara gradually awakening. The mist cleared as the sun rose in the blue sky. The painted houses and cottages looked brighter now with many colours and from the palace it formed a marvellous mosaic, a picture of a multi-coloured unicorn surrounded by the various greens of the trees and grass. Spindley Tower, recently repainted blue, stood like a smart and stately guard looking down protectively on the other buildings.

As they gazed at the beauty spread out beneath them they grew more and more concerned about Joog. Where was he? They could now hear the sounds of the markets opening and began to realise that something must have happened to him. He should surely be back by now and they remembered how fond he was of his cereal. When Princess Amalek and Prince Seph looked at his breakfast bowl waiting for him and his empty branch, their emotions were shaken and they felt close to tears. They loved Joog so much. The Queen wrapped her arms around them both and comforted them.

"That owl seems to have a sixth sense which keeps him safe, and six lives too. I'm sure he'll be back soon," she said kindly.

"Your mother is right," the King agreed, "He is the wisest owl I have ever met, and that's why I appointed him as leader of the Guardians. Any minute now we'll see him gliding over the houses down there."

No one ate a single mouthful of breakfast, or lunch, or tea, because no-one wanted to leave the turret window in case they saw him and by the time evening came the bowl of cereal was still sitting there and the branch was still vacant. The King had sent out groups of men and women to search for him, but the news was always the same - they found no sign of Joog.

The Dark Wizard Troubler, Horrik and Jamaar had walked westwards along Wellspring Walk and then left the path to find a place to hide. They were now south-west of Candara and in another small group of trees, this time at the foot of the Heather Heights, a group of rolling hills partially covered with purple heather. The wizard was sitting on a tree stump with Horrik tied to a tree nearby and Jamaar lying at his feet. The rays of the evening sun sloped through the trees providing bright patches of light and contrasting deep shadows. Around the Dark Wizard the colour had been drained out of everything.

"Jamaar," he growled, "Now that I've dealt with that

owl and stopped it snooping around after us, I have your first job for you and it's a very important one. If you perform it well you will be fed."

"Yes, master," Jamaar replied, and sat up eagerly, gazing wide-eyed at his new master. Horrik had been dozing, but on hearing the conversation she opened one envious eye and watched. Why was this stray dog being given a job to do and not her? Anger stirred, but she kept it to herself and just watched and listened.

"Think of it as a test," continued the wizard, his icy breath hissing out with every word, "A test which has to be passed. I need a base. Somewhere to live for a while... like a... hmmm... a place to perform my business and spread my power. I *have* to have this."

"Spindley Tower, master?" asked Jamaar.

"No. That tower's no good for me, too much in view. I need to take some place over discreetly, quietly, without making a fuss that would draw attention to me. A house somewhere... somewhere secluded. Any ideas, Jamaar?"

Jamaar thought for a moment. An idea did come straight into his mind; the perfect place and probably not difficult to acquire, but he had something he wanted to do, so he kept this idea to himself. He needed just a little free time, "I would have to scout around, master, to find somewhere. I'm sure I could though. But I need some time to look."

"Alright... alright," the wizard said hesitantly, not sure if he could trust Jamaar yet, "You go and sort it out, but get back soon!" his voice lowered to a sinister whisper that made Jamaar cringe with fear as he felt each word bite into him, "If you deceive me I will show no mercy... you will suffer and cry out for mercy, and mercy will not come. Understand?"

Jamaar was not expecting such a cutting warning, "Yes, master, yes, of course."

Horrik was still watching and listening secretly and smiled to hear Jamaar's grovelling words.

"That's good then," the wizard said, "Now go and find the place and report back to me as soon as you've found it."

"Yes, master."

The Dark Wizard watched Jamaar's skinny frame trot off towards the town. Horrik watched too. Her yellow forked tongue flashed out from her mouth sending a droplet of saliva flying through the air and onto the grass where it sizzled for a second or two. A wisp of smoke rose from the burnt blade of grass as she watched Jamaar passing out of sight.

When Jamaar was in Candara he knew he had to work quickly. He headed straight for the home of the elderly Darsan and Harraine Lopery. It was only yesterday that he had been thrown out of their house in disgrace after living there for just four days. It was Harraine, Darsan's wife, now confined to a wheelchair, who had the idea of offering the stray dog a home. She mainly stayed in the house, living on the first floor where she had everything she needed, but it was on a rare trip into the town that she had seen Jamaar wandering through the streets looking thin, bedraggled and lonely. She had fought hard to persuade Darsan to agree to take him in, for he had serious doubts right from the start that it would work. He was generally disliked by everyone in Candara for his irritable complaining character and his morose outlook on life and when Harraine suggested the idea of having a dog living in their home with them he objected angrily. However, Harraine had nagged him so much that in the end he had reluctantly given in to her and Jamaar was invited into their cottage.

Harraine had done everything to try to give him a home, but in the short time that he was there Jamaar had managed to cause chaos. He wolfed down all the food he was given and then shouted loudly for more. When they explained that they did not have endless supplies, or the money to buy it, he proceeded to argue and shout and then chew on the furniture as if attacking a bone. So, with Harraine's agreement, Darsan threw Jamaar out and he now held a bitter grudge against them both and wanted to pay them back for this insult.

The cottage was called 'Relbuort Cottage' at 17 Nathen Avenue, the road that ran along the north of Candara, the back of the unicorn, and the garden lawn at the rear of the house sloped down to the slow-flowing River Tazer. Jamaar followed the river on its southern bank until he could see the Loperys' house on the other side, then he swam across, climbed out and crouching as low as he could, he crept up to the back door. The door was ajar, which meant they were probably in, so he nudged it open with his nose and peeped in. They were not in this room, so deciding to take a chance he stepped through the open door, with river water dripping off his tangled fur and onto the carpet. His plan was to get his own back on them and at the same time gain something for himself. He would steal something of value and so he looked around for something small and precious.

The room was painted a cool green, decorated with

several paintings of local scenes and a new deep green carpet had been laid recently which felt soft and comfortable under his wet paws. The rays of the late evening sun sloped through the window creating a great rectangle of light on the carpet and Jamaar tilted his head on one side and listened, checking that no one was around. He raised a front paw and then paused as his eyes fell upon a small desk that was in the opposite corner and he remembered seeing Darsan sitting and working there.

Still hesitating, and with one paw in the air and poised for action, he wondered what to do. Today the desk chair was empty and a tidy pile of papers rested on the desk surface with a pen beside them. He smiled as he noticed his own tooth marks on one of the legs where he had attacked it in a rage. Then he decided. He moved swiftly and quietly across the carpet, leaving a muddy wet trail and pulled open the lowest drawer by gripping the brass handle with his teeth. He foraged around inside amongst some papers and a couple fell out onto the carpet, but he found nothing. He tried the next drawer up. Again more papers, but then right underneath and pushed to the back of the drawer, was a small object in a velvet bag. He grabbed it in his mouth and lifted it out.

At that moment he heard footsteps coming down the stairs and panicked, knowing how much Darsan hated him. He rushed across the room to the door and as he slipped out Darsan entered just in time to see a flash of Jamaar's black tail disappearing. He looked alarmed and angry as he saw the muddy trail and then the open drawers and the papers on the floor.

"What's this!" he shouted.

"What's happening, dear?" called out Harraine from upstairs.

Darsan ran across the room and towards the back door as he answered, "It's that wretched dog! I told you he's no good!"

"That dog?" called out Harraine, "What... Jamaar?"

Darsan did not pause to answer but by the time he was outside Jamaar had run full pelt across the garden, plunged into the river and was drifting with the flow. He kept tight to the bank and by the time Darsan had reached the river he was a house away and Darsan was left gazing around in vain for the burglar. Realising that Jamaar had escaped he kicked a small bush in temper and turned and walked slowly back up to the house to check if anything was missing.

Jamaar passed two houses before the river flowed under a bridge. Once he had drifted under he climbed out and shook his fur. It was only then that he realised he was still holding the small velvet bag, now sodden, in his mouth. He dropped it onto the grass in disappointment, spitting out some of the muddy water. The venture had virtually been a failure; all he had was a small bag most likely containing something of no value that had probably been lost and forgotten about in the back of the drawer for years. He had wanted something precious, not only to gain for himself but also to hurt them. He opened the bag and pulled out the small object and his disappointment deepened. He decided he would hide it anyway, just in case, in a special place where he hid things of value that he had found or stolen. Then he would return as quickly as he could to the Dark Wizard, make up a story about why he was wet and present his idea of the perfect house for them to live in.

As the day drew in and the sun dipped behind the Snowpeak Mountains everyone in the palace was feeling very concerned about Joog. Then, all of a sudden, as the group watched from the Round Room window with sad and tear-stained eyes, there was Joog just as the King had said, gliding over the rooftops and up to the palace. How the faces of the Prince and Princess lit up.

"Joog!" they both shouted together. Now they cried with happiness. The King and Queen hugged each other with joy as Joog approached the window, gliding on the air but looking slightly lob-sided as one wing hung down slightly more than the other. He sailed through, tucking his wings in as usual, and collapsed exhausted on the table, sending the bowl of cereal tumbling to the floor. The bowl spun on the carpet for a moment whilst everyone stared at Joog lying there near the edge of the table, totally still, and with his beautiful white feathers splattered red with blood. The others gathered around quickly and there were gasps of shock as they saw the blood.

"Joog," exclaimed Seph, looking concerned, "Are you alright?"

"I think…" began Joog, managing a reassuring nod but struggling to speak, "I think I'm alright."

"Oh, my dear Joog," exclaimed the Queen, stroking his

ruffled feathers gently, "What on earth happened to you?"

Joog was too exhausted and too injured to speak any more; he was just content to rest his head on Princess Amalek's hands and his broken wing in Prince Seph's arms and drift off to sleep. He slept for the next hour on some cushions on the floor in the Round Room, whilst the King, Queen, Prince and Princess ate their supper. Princess Amalek had poured out another bowl of cereal for Joog. Prince Seph had placed a fresh glass of milk with a straw in it close to his head and when he woke it was the first thing he saw.

"Oh I'm so thirsty, thank you very much." Joog's voice was no louder than a whisper; he was so weak and battered. The King's eyes sparkled when he heard Joog's voice and he went over to him and crouched down. He twisted the straw until it reached Joog's beak and soon the glass of milk was half empty.

The King smiled, "The best doctor in the Kingdom will be here very soon to sort out your injuries," he said, his words filled with love, "You'd better tell me all about it - was it a fight, Joog?"

"It certainly was," whispered Joog, his round eyes brightening up and glowing with golden and amber light, "Just as we thought, there is a Troubler in the Kingdom. A Troubler with his dog... and a great creature on a lead... a vicious looking thing. I saw him as I was flying around. He was in some trees beyond Candara. He looked weird, he's a wizard but with a black cloak, and his eyes... his eyes are completely black, as black as coal they were, absolutely no colour at all. It was like looking into the darkest night." He paused to swallow and to gather himself together to carry on. Just the memory of the Troubler's eyes was bringing back the fear, "I've never seen eyes like it before! And the feeling, Your Majesty, of dark twisted power... oh!... I could feel it even from such a distance," Joog shivered at the thought, "It chilled me right inside somehow." Joog paused again to gather his strength. He knew he must tell it all to the King. The Prince filled up his glass with milk and held the straw for him to drink.

"Somehow," Joog continued after a few sips of milk, "He knew that I was looking for him, Your Majesty, and at the moment we looked at each other that's when the trouble began. He lifted his arms and pointed them at me, and out of each sleeve flew two black ravens - four altogether - with the same eyes; like black holes of night they were. They came straight for me like arrows! I headed for the woods, Wellspring Woods, and there we had the most tremendous battle. I had the advantage of knowing the woods so well, but there were four of them! I had to dive, twist and turn to avoid their sharp beaks - they fly so fast. Now and again I tried hiding amongst the leaves or in a hollow tree but they soon found me. I fought and scuffled with them. The fight went on all day and it was only because one of them crashed into a beehive and the bees swarmed all around them, stinging them terribly, that I was able to escape. It was almost impossible to fly with one wing hardly working... I could just about hold it out... and covered with cuts... but I knew I had to get back to the palace..." Joog's voice faded. He was too tired to speak any more and he quickly fell asleep again.

The doctor arrived soon and quickly cleaned and stitched Joog's cuts. Then he inspected the broken wing carefully and reset it. It would have to be kept still for at least six weeks to heal and so whilst he was putting it in wooden splints, the King sat still and upright on his throne. It was elaborately carved with scenes from his Kingdom - the town of Candara was there with Spindley Tower, and the wood with Joog's tree, and the lake known as Blue Lake that lay on the other side of the palace, and Candara Palace itself. The whole Kingdom was there in miniature, decorated with sparkling gems and crystals collected from the caves in the Vale of Gems by Amalek and Seph. When the morning sun shone onto it through the window it would glitter and gleam filling the room with rainbow-coloured light that cast kaleidoscope patterns on the walls. The grand arms of the throne were two fine wooden unicorn and when the Prince and Princess were younger they loved to play games feeding them and riding on them.

The King sat completely still and looked peaceful and regal on his throne. After a while he pulled himself up by the spiral alicorns of the unicorns and climbed the winding stairs to see how Joog was feeling.

At this very moment the Dark Wizard Troubler was knocking on Old Howard's door. Petals fell sadly from the flowers, and insects scuttled away or flew off as quickly as they could to get out of the grey presence of the evil wizard and his dog. Old Howard lived in a small dilapidated house that lay apart from Candara, to the west of the town and it was therefore not part of the giant mosaic unicorn pattern made by the houses and cottages. It was situated in a small wood; one isolated house which reflected his own chosen isolation from the people of

Candara. He hated them and they disliked and mistrusted him.

Old Howard was well known in the town as the meanest and most greedy old man in the whole Kingdom, and Jamaar had told the Dark Wizard that after scouting around he thought this would be the best place for them to live.

The light was fading quickly now as the Dark Wizard knocked again, louder this time. Old Howard woke up, got up from his old, tattered and smelly armchair and staggered out of the room. He moved down the hall and opened the door which led into a very small porch. He opened the front door and met a wave of cold air which made him rub his hands together.

"Allo," he said gruffly, peering out through sleepy eyes, "Oo's there?"

"Good evening," said the Dark Wizard Troubler, fixing his black eyes on Old Howard's, "Jamaar and I bring you good news," and he reached down and patted Jamaar on his head, "Jamaar is my dog." Jamaar growled at Old Howard.

"Bah! Only good news oy get is bad news," his voice grew louder and more threatening and yet he gazed at his visitor with interest. He could feel the powerful presence, and felt, that in a strange way, it attracted him, "Tell me wha' yer want, or get yer black oiys off moy land!" Then he noticed, with astonishment the massive creature tied to a tree at the end of his garden, "Wha' is that thing doin' in moy garden?"

"That's only my pet," the Dark Wizard Troubler said dismissively. Then he continued calmly, hissing out the words with his thin but now gently persuasive voice, "Listen, and listen clearly. If you do what I say you will

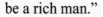

be a rich man."

"Rich? Rich yer say? Bu' oy don't even know oo you are."

The Dark Wizard gazed hypnotically at the old man and tried to make his voice as smooth and inviting as possible, "Who I am doesn't really matter. Not really. It's what I can give you that counts."

"Tell me oo you are then oy'll listen to yer?"

"I am…" The Dark Wizard Troubler hesitated, "I am… I am offering you riches beyond your greatest dreams," Old Howard just stared back and the wizard felt he now had him in his power, "No more work - think of that! You could buy whatever you want... and eat whatever you like... and as much as you can, any time. You could buy a house as big as the palace on the hill, own huge gardens... and be idle all day, every day, all your life...."

Old Howard, now beguiled, was smiling greedily, "Tell me more."

"Good, now you are being sensible," said the wizard who was using each word carefully in order to ensnare Old Howard and just like an animal who is drawn into a trap with the right bait, so was Old Howard following the scent into the evil wizard's plan, "Listen, it's a chance of a lifetime. And I *can* give you these riches, it's just a question of when you would like to be rich, the richest man in the kingdom."

"Stop, stop! Oh, I want it. I want it! I want it!" Old Howard's voice rose to a tremendous crescendo, so loud that the trees shook and the leaves tremored, and like the leaves, Old Howard also tremored, but with excitement. He could hardly believe his luck; here was someone, knocking on his door and offering him exactly what he had always wanted. And yet he felt slightly uneasy.

Would there be a catch? But this feeling was quickly overwhelmed by his rising desire, "But 'ow, tell me 'ow?"

"If you'd be polite enough to invite me in?" the Dark Wizard Troubler asked.

The chill in the air strengthened, making Old Howard shiver, but he was so caught up in his own greediness that he no longer cared. Now he just wanted to be rich. "Tell me 'ow oy can get it," he blurted out, shivering again and rubbing his cold hands together.

The Dark Wizard Troubler stared back and lowered his voice to a hypnotic whisper, "I will explain how it can all be yours for your own delight. You will soon be rich. But you must let me in first."

Old Howard paused for a moment. Then, as darkness descended upon the Kingdom of Gems, he made the biggest mistake of his life. With a beaming toothless grin spreading across his rugged round face he opened his door wide and welcomed the Dark Wizard in.

When dawn arrived the next morning the weather around Candara Palace up on the hill was still and peaceful. It was always calm there. In the rest of the kingdom however, in the village of Whitten and the hamlet of Charin, in the woods, over Blue Lake and up in the Snowpeak Mountains, the weather was unusually fierce. Grey-black clouds filled the sky, racing and chasing in a fierce wind. The branches of the trees whistled as the howling wind passed through them and leaves were ripped from the trees to dance and tumble in the chilly air. The wind was rushing through the streets of Candara picking up anything it could; bits of paper; dust and dirt; cardboard boxes; and here and there a dustbin lid would clatter on the cobbled stones. It was a wild day.

As far as was possible in such a storm, the day was beginning as usual. People were getting up, dressing and eating breakfast. No one was out yet except for one lone figure, bent and round, trudging across the Western Downs in a northern direction. He looked a sad picture of dishevelment with old dirty clothes and trousers which kept slipping down slightly and which he hitched up every so often.

He moved slowly but steadily and leaning into the wind he looked very determined. But what made his walking so difficult, apart from his heavy round body and his battling against the strong wind, was the load he was carrying. In his hand he clutched the end of a branch of wood; the middle rested on his shoulder and on the end was a bundle of his possessions wrapped in a blanket. The bundle clattered and changed shape as it swung to and fro. Then, as he plodded along, something fell out and he stopped, grabbed it quickly off the ground, looked at it briefly and then put it back in the blanket. He was just about to resume his battle against the wind when he stopped again. This time he took something out of his pocket which glinted in the light. He cupped it in his hands as if it was something extremely precious and momentarily studied it with glee. He slipped it back into his pocket, pulled up his trousers that had dropped slightly with the weight of it, and struggled on again. It was Old Howard leaving the Kingdom of Gems.

Eventually he met a path which headed east and he took it. Soon it joined the street that runs steeply down and through the hamlet of Charin.

"Old Howard!" called out a tabby cat, who was sheltering from the wild weather in a children's tree house above Old Howard's head. Large drops of rain were falling now. "Hey there! Old Howard!" Old Howard looked up and nearly dropped his bundle of possessions as a large drop of rain splattered in his eye, "Where are you going?" shouted the cat.

"Bah!" growled Old Howard crossly, hitching up his trousers, "None of yer business. You think oy'd tell you where oy'm goin'? Oy'll be rich soon, you jus' wait an' see! Oy'll show you all! But oy'm not tellin' yer 'ow - nor anyone! Bah!" His growling voice was so loud that if anyone in the town had still been in the Land of Nod they would certainly be awake now. Faces appeared at the windows to see what the noise was and children thinking it was thunder eagerly pinned their noses to the glass to see the lightening.

"Good luck!" shouted the cat, as Old Howard, who was rapidly becoming soaking wet, began plodding heavily on again.

"Good riddance!" thundered Old Howard, as he reached the last of the line of houses and left the partial shelter of the hamlet. At the bottom of the hill he paused to gather his strength, then turned left to continue his journey.

So Old Howard struggled all the way along the road leading north, walking with determination all through the day. He passed the Gem Falls, crossed North Bridge and was leaving Blue Lake behind him when he was spotted again. One of the Guardian Owls, a tiny elf owl called Marli, noticed him with her powerful eyesight. She was perched on her look-out on the top of Point Hill by Lake

Clase-Moy and flew over to investigate. She watched him as he stopped for the night and settled down in some bracken to sleep.

The next day he would head for the great Snowpeak Mountains, then the Northern Borderlands and finally across the border into the next kingdom. Old Howard would return, but not for some time.

Chapter 3

~ Frogs ~

When the next morning arrived the stormy weather had blown itself out leaving the sky cloudless and blue. Over breakfast Joog told the King what Marli had told him about Old Howard's strange journey and they wondered where he was going. The King decided to send out a party of ten men, armed with swords, to Old Howard's house to find out what they could. Why had Old Howard left the Kingdom? Where was the Dark Wizard Troubler? Had the odd weather anything to do with the Dark Wizard Troubler? Joog and the King both felt sure that these mysteries were connected in some way - but how? The King also sent out a dozen men with swords and bows and arrows to look around and ask questions in Candara. A third group of eight men was sent to search the Wellspring Woods. He also sent a further group of eight men to check in Silvermay Forest and enquire among the inhabitants of Whitten.

The air was still and calm and even the tops of the trees were motionless. The sun was resting in the vast blue

ocean of the sky and butterflies of many colours lightly
fluttered around, here and there landing on a plant or a
house and spreading their beautifully patterned wings to
enjoy the warmth of the morning sun. But there were no
butterflies on Old Howard's house.

Inside the house the Dark Wizard Troubler was sitting
in Old Howard's smelly armchair with Jamaar dozing at
his feet. Horrik was outside tied to a tree by her lead and
feeling furious with Jamaar who seemed to be finding
favour with the wizard. She was so angry that she felt
that at the first chance she would attack Jamaar and teach
him a lesson, but she would just have to wait for the right
opportunity. Every now and again a discontented rumble
would vibrate in her throat as she watched the house and
imagined Jamaar inside. Dribbles of saliva would trickle
from her jaws as she thought of eating the exasperating
young dog. The bacterial drops of saliva sizzled as they
made holes in the blades of grass below.

The evil wizard's long thin legs were outstretched, his
long-fingered hands clasped behind his head and his eyes
were closed. In the depths of his wicked mind he was
gathering all his dark powers together so that he could
focus fully on putting his plans into action.

On a shelf sat the four black ravens looking sullen and
swollen from the bee stings and huddled together asleep.
The tattered hole-ridden curtains were drawn and here
and there shafts of brilliant sunlight pierced the holes and
dotted the room with patches of light, their brilliance
tamed by the effect of the wizard's presence. The room
was dirty with layers of dust covering surfaces and
ledges, while swirling particles of dust danced in the rays
of light.

The sun slowly climbed in the sky and as it did some

light fell on the Dark Wizard Troubler's pale forehead. His face wrinkled into a frown.

"No!" he cried sharply as he rose from his chair. Jamaar jumped up as his master cried out and stood there as if waiting for a command. The Dark Wizard Troubler, followed by Jamaar, walked towards the curtains and opened them to look out at the back garden. The light flooded in. The wizard had sensed that Horrik had seen something and his black eyes narrowed as he fixed his sight on a cluster of trees just beyond the overgrown garden. One tree was shaking violently. Horrik was tied to the tree and was pulling hard on her metal lead as she strained after something. As he watched he saw the King's ten men creeping forwards whilst keeping a safe distance from the menacing snapping jaws of Horrik. Then, with swords drawn and gleaming in the sunlight, they walked out of the shadows of the trees and towards the house.

The Dark Wizard Troubler carefully closed the curtains, moved quietly and very quickly across the room and walked calmly up the stairs. Jamaar followed. They entered a back room on the first floor and flung open the window. The wizard leant out and his black eyes widened and deepened as he stared at the men below. They gazed up with surprise at the dark figure leaning out of the window and when they saw the deep black eyes which glared down at them they were held by fear and stood still not knowing what to do.

Gripped by the steely gaze of the Dark Wizard they felt cold inside, as if they had been stabbed by an icy blade and they staggered back a step or two in shock. Jamaar was beside his new master as the Dark Wizard Troubler leant even further out of the window and cried out:

"Black night black, come what may,
I will ne'er give in,
Black night black, on this day,
A Kingdom will I win!
And you will spend all your days
As frogs trapped in my gaze.
Frogs! Frogs! Fro...ogs!"

With his last cry of "Fr...ogs!" every one of the ten men changed into a frog, their fine swords falling onto the grass and their clothes, now far too large for them, fell to the ground like deflated balloons and lay ruffled around them. The frogs clambered out and hopped towards the safety of the trees. They croaked in shock and fear as they retreated. They soon discovered how strong their back legs were and as they became more used to being frogs their hops became bigger and bigger. Horrik roared threateningly as the frogs moved past her, but they kept well clear. One drop of saliva flew out of her gigantic mouth and landed on one of the frogs' feet. It cried out in pain as the foot fell off and began to dissolve. At the window Jamaar barked ferociously at them.

"Let me catch them now, master," he growled.

"No!" hissed the Dark Wizard with a cold authority, "Not now! Don't waste your energy on them. There'll be plenty of time for that later. They can hop back to the palace or wherever they like for all I care. In a couple of days it won't matter where they are… just you wait and see!"

It took some time before the frogs reached Candara and were hopping and jumping all in a row along the stony streets in the direction of the palace. The people of the town wondered what was going on. First there was the strange night when every living creature overslept; followed by the morning with the gale force wind and driving rain; then there was Old Howard leaving the Kingdom; after that, today's sudden change in the weather from storm to calm; and now, well they could hardly believe it, a row of ten hopping frogs, springing and bouncing in a line through the town. But in spite of all their wondering and guessing, no one in the whole town came close to imagining the events that were to follow.

Flying in a northwards direction from Old Howard's house above the Western Downs was a pair of black-eyed ravens. Overhead, in the cloudless sky, the sun reflected in vibrant shades of blue and green on their jet black feathers. To their right lay the chequered landscape of the Flatsage Farmlands a wide flat area where an assortment of crops was grown. Beyond this the ravens could see Candara Palace on a wooded hill and to the north of the palace the bright surface of Blue Lake. Below them the rounded hills of the Western Downs rose and fell. Ahead, and nestled in the hills, was the hamlet of Charin and dotted here and there on the slopes were isolated cottages. The two birds flew side by side.

"I've been wondering, Gerr," said Searle, "Why do you think he picked *us?*"

"It's obvious," Gerr replied quickly, putting on his most knowledgeable voice, "The master wants a good job done. Some of the others don't know the time of day."

"I know what you mean," she said, feeling proud at being selected, "And this is an important job, isn't it?"

Gerr nodded, "Very important. He needs to know, for sure, that they are kept where he thinks they are kept. All his plans depend on it. He needs to know where they are."

"Is that what he told you?" asked Searle

"Yes, and, of course, he told me how to find them."

"How?" asked Searle.

"I'll tell you when we get there," said Gerr, enjoying the feeling of having knowledge that she did not have.

They had passed Charin where they had veered to the right and were now nearing the shimmering waters of Blue Lake. Here the swift waters of the River Gem merged into the lake. The river started high in the mountains where many small streams cut their way through the rocky terrain, joining to create the river which rushed eagerly down to the lake.

"This is it," said Gerr, "Now we find out."

They followed the river upstream to the Gem Falls where water cascaded down a sheer drop of about thirty feet and crashed into the water below with a continuous thunderous roar. The ravens circled above, making sure that they were not being watched and then swooped down to land on the grassy bank at the foot of the waterfall.

"What now?" asked Searle as she looked at the wall of water, and leant her head to one side in puzzlement.

"What?" shouted Gerr, who could not hear her above the deep roar of the waterfall.

"What happens now?" she shouted back.

"We go in," Gerr shouted, "We have to fly through the water."

Searle looked at him quizzically. The cascading water was throwing up a fine mist which was drifting past them on the breeze. "What?!" she shouted, "Is it safe?"

"Completely, as long as we fly through fast enough. Come on."

"Where?" Searle shouted, looking along the thundering sheet of falling water, "How do you know where to fly through?" She lifted her wings slightly and shook her head as if it was an impossible task. Then she pointed with her beak towards the waterfall.

"We try…" shouted Gerr, "We try until we find the place. Let's go!"

"But what's on the other side?"

Gerr was looking impatient now, "A cave. Now… let's do it," he screeched.

He took off with Searle following reluctantly behind and flew along the waterfall just above the water and through the mist. Every so often Gerr would fly into the falling water watched by Searle who refused to go in herself. Each time he flew in he would be whipped downwards by the weight of the descending torrent and forced right under the surface. Then he would bob up in the river a little distance away. After a while he was getting so exhausted that he rested on the grassy bank and Searle flew down beside him.

Searle shouted above the thundering noise, "OK, so we've tried. Can we go now?"

"No!" Gerr shouted, still out of breath, "Think of the Master! He wants to know if there's a cave. We can't give up yet."

Thinking of the Master sent a shiver of fear running down Searle's back and that convinced her that they had to try again.

Gerr stepped towards her and shouted, "You try!"

"No!" exclaimed Searle, jerking her head back in shock, "*You're* the one who was told what to do."

They flew off again and the strange performance began once more. After a few more attempts Gerr did not bob up further down the river and Searle thought he must have been completely washed away by the current, or else he passed right through and into the cave. She circled above the water scanning for him. Then she flew back to the place where he flew in and deciding he must have got through she knew she must follow. She circled around several times to pluck up courage and eventually, somehow abandoning her fear, she closed her eyes and flew at the water.

She found herself above a pool of water with a cave entrance straight in front of her. There in the cave with his back to her was Gerr. She flew in and landed beside him. Together they gazed into the cave. To them it was large and quiet like a great cathedral, although an adult person could have only just about stood. At first it seemed dark after the bright light outside, but soon their eyes adjusted and they could see that the cave had been roughly hewed out of rock with a reasonably flat floor and curved rugged walls rising up to the ceiling above. The far corners of the cave were strewn with rubble and were the darkest parts. It was utterly silent inside the cave, although when they turned around they could see, across the still water of the small pool, the white and grey-green water flashing downwards.

Then they noticed some colours shining at the back of the cave.

"There," said Gerr, "That must be them. First task completed. We can tell the Master that they *are* kept here."

Searle nodded, "He'll be pleased with us. But what do you mean 'first task'?"

"And now…" Gerr began, ignoring her question.

Searle interrupted, "Now we get out of here," and she began to turn.

"Stop!" said Gerr, and then he dropped his voice and whispered with excitement, glancing behind him as if someone might overhear, "Now we steal one."

"That… is not a good idea, is it?" whispered Searle.

"Why not? The Master asked me to."

"Because, you idiot, you can't. I heard the others talking…"

"They are fools, most of them. Look… we've come all this way, we might as well try at least. It's easy. What could happen anyway?"

"I don't know. But I do know that I don't like it. Not at all."

"You tell the Master then," snapped Gerr, glaring at her, "Tell him you were too scared to steal one… that would please him!"

"I… I…" she stammered, "I… well… alright then, seeing we're here…" she felt weak, but somehow found herself giving in to him.

"Good," he whispered quickly and they began walking towards the coloured lights.

Then something made them pause. They felt like trespassers in a private place, like intruders who had no right to be there and that at any moment someone might appear and catch them. The cave was so still and silent. They were not used to such peace and it filled them with apprehension. They stood in the great cave like motionless fish in still water. They hardly dared to make a sound or a movement. They were possessed by fear and felt nervous that the crime they were about to commit might cause some terrible consequence to happen to them. They were on the point of turning, flying out through the curtain of water and fleeing from the cave.

Searle looked at Gerr. Her whisper was barely audible, "I don't like it here," and she shivered, "Let's go."

"No," replied Gerr, "Not now that we're here." He glanced around the cave with frightened eyes, "It's safe... I'm sure it is... there's no one else here."

"You don't sound sure. Look... we can tell the Master that they *are* here. He'll be pleased with that. Come on, let's get out of here."

"No," Gerr whispered, and now he sounded firm and decided, "He'll be even more pleased if we take one back for him. If we don't... well... just think how angry he'll be."

This last statement forced itself upon Searle's mind and she could not ignore it. Her terror of the Dark Wizard rose again. It was even stronger than the powerful fear she was feeling in this place. She decided she would make herself go through with this and in a minute or two they would be out and flying back across the lake.

"OK," she whispered reluctantly.

Cautiously and very slowly they began to walk towards the glowing coloured lights at the back of the cave. As they moved closer they could see that there were three colours; a deep red, a rich blue and a royal purple, which were glowing gently in a small cavity in the back wall. The cavity had a flat floor with the side walls rising to a semi-circular curve at the top. As they approached their clawed feet clicked on the cold rock floor and the cave acted like the sound box of an instrument. The tiny sounds were amplified as they echoed around the walls of rock.

"Shh," said Searle, and they slowed down and moved

more quietly. When they were nearly at the back wall they knew they would have to fly up to the cavity.

"Up," whispered Gerr, lifting his beak up with a jerk to point at the cavity.

They plucked up courage and with a jump they fluttered into the air and landed on the edge of the cavity where a small sill protruded. They gazed in amazement at what they saw.

"It's the red one he wants," whispered Gerr.

There in front of them were three gems resting on the perfectly flat rock of the cavity. All the surfaces inside the cavity, although covered with cracks, had been smoothed and polished, including the curved roof, so that they reflected the light of the gems, enhancing their luminance. The three gems were placed in a triangle with two at the back and the other in front, resting in small holes that had been carved for them in the smooth flat rock. They all shone with extraordinary brilliance, picking up the small amount of light that was in the cave and reflecting it back with astonishing sparkle. Each of the gems was cut in different patterns and placed in a perfect triangle with equal distances between each one. The one in the front was a ruby, glowing deep red, but showing many different shades. At the back on the left was a resplendent blue sapphire and on the right a purple amethyst, lustrous and radiant. It was a sight of splendid beauty.

Behind the gems and carved in the rock forming the back wall of the small cavity was a poem.

"What's that?" asked Searle, nodding at the writing, "It might say something bad."

"It's just words," he replied, "Words can't hurt us."

"Well, let's see what it says."

Searle gazed at the poem and tried in vain to read it.

* THE CANDARA GEMS *

~ * ~

Three precious gems lie here to serve
This plentiful kingdom fair;
Three colours bestow three qualities
For everyone to share.
Clear sky blue and ruby red
Like rich September wine,
And blended purple, deep and full;
Three colours to brightly shine.

*

If the gems stay within this land
To reside where they belong,
Three qualities they will bequeath
And make the kingdom strong.
They will protect the kingdom if
Their legacy is lived,
And then they are protected by
The people to whom they give.

Sapphire stands for honesty
To bring a truthful life,
So faithfulness will grace the life
Of every man and wife.
Purity of word and deed
And strength to speak the truth,
Dwells in this gem as in the heart
Of every growing youth.

✤

Amethyst, ever royal and tranquil,
Brings peace throughout the land,
Her purple light shines far and wide
As calm repose expands.
Friendships bind together in
The aspect of her hue,
When you resign to gaze on her
Then she will gaze on you.

✤

Ruby rests in harmony
To shield the other two,
As proud protection abides in her
To guard the kingdom through.
Just as she sprays out rays of red
To glint in every eye,
This gem will shed her light of love
To heal each heartfelt sigh.

"It's no good. I can't make head nor tail of it," she said after a while, "The odd word, yes, but it's too difficult."

Gerr was staring at the ruby, "I told you, words don't matter. But, look at that ruby."

Searle looked at it. They hesitated, mesmerised by the brilliance of the shining ruby.

"Go on," whispered Gerr, "Take it."

Searle was clearly shocked by the order, "No!" she said, forgetting to be quiet and then realising, she glanced around. She continued whispering, "*You* want to get it. *You* take it."

Gerr looked at the ruby, so close in front of him. All he had to do was lower his head and grasp it in his beak. But still, something held him back. He was afraid.

Searle spotted his hesitation, "Go on… take it and then we can get out of here," she whispered, "Or are you afraid?"

Gerr was still, gazing at the ruby. Then, with a quick movement, he dropped his head over the ruby. The colours bathed his head as he opened his beak. Then he changed his mind, closed his beak and gave it a tentative little peck. There was a flash of bright light.

"Aaaaaah!" he screeched as he jerked his head up and fell backwards off the sill. He landed with a thud on the rock floor and lay there moaning.

"I told you!" said Searle looking down off the sill, and then suddenly feeling concerned for him, "Are you alright?"

"Aahh," he groaned.

"Can you fly?" asked Searle. They had abandoned the whispering now.

Gerr struggled onto his feet, "I think so."

"Let's go then."

Searle took off from the sill and flew out of the cave, over the pool and like an arrow through the curtain of water. Gerr followed quickly behind and they rose in the air as quickly as they could, greatly relieved to leave the cave behind.

"Your beak!" exclaimed Searle.

"I know. It hurts… aahh… it hurts *so* much."

"It looks burnt… singed on the end."

"I know," sighed Gerr with irritation.

"And it's cracked."

"I know... I know," sighed Gerr now feeling cross, "It still feels hot."

"Well, I did warn you." Searle had the last word which made Gerr seethe inside, whereas Searle felt the pleasurable sensation of being right.

They flew out above Blue Lake in silence and did not talk again as they headed back to Old Howard's house to tell the Dark Wizard Troubler what had happened.

In the calm of the afternoon the King looked anxiously, once again, out of the high window in the Round Room. The view of his kingdom was spectacular and he cast his eye in the direction of the town of Candara. The sun was bathing everything in warm rays and glinted brightly off the roof of Spindley Tower. It was a building of unusual character, displaying at once much fine decoration in the form of carvings as well as a slightly comical appearance. It seemed a little too thin for its height and the very top part was somewhat out of line with the rest. It was an excellent look-out position with a balcony running all around it in four places. Joog frequently used it to keep an eye on Candara and make sure all was well.

Joog was beside the King as they watched together for the return of the last group of men. Three groups had returned with nothing to report, and now it was just the group of ten sent to Old Howard's house who were missing.

"Look!" Joog exclaimed suddenly, his golden-yellow eyes wide open and glowing, "Down there in the town!"

"What?" asked the King, who had seen nothing worthy of Joog's loud excited words that had made him jump.

"Down there. Near the baker's. Look! Can't you see them?" asked Joog, completely forgetting that the King had human eyesight and he was an owl with eyes that could see the smallest things at a great distance, "Look! A row of frogs hopping down the street! How about that!" The King still could not see them.

"How many are there, Joog?" asked the King.

"Um…." Joog paused to count, "Ten, Your Majesty."

"Joog," the King said calmly, "You say they're hopping in a row?"

"Well, yes. It's strange isn't it?"

The King scratched his grey beard thoughtfully. There were suggestions of brown hair in amongst the grey still left from his younger days. "*Very* strange," he said frowning, "Frogs just don't do that do they? And the fact that there are ten, and my ten men are missing… well it makes me wonder."

"I see what you mean, Your Majesty."

The King shook his head, "I fear, Joog, that this is extremely serious. I hope I'm wrong, but I think those may be my ten men down there trapped by… well… a spell of some sort perhaps. It would fit wouldn't it? This

Dark Wizard Troubler is extremely dangerous... we know that from when you confronted him... and he's powerful too. It's him, I'm sure it is. But we must end it... stop him somehow. It won't be easy, and it will need great courage, but we must find a way..." he paused for a moment, walked across the room and gazed out in the other direction at the distant mountains which appeared blue in the afternoon haze, "We must find a way to reverse that spell... those poor men... and to get rid of that Troubler altogether."

"Well you know I'm fully with you, Your Majesty, and all my team of Guardians too."

"I know that, Joog," the King said, turning and walking back to Joog, "But it will be five or six weeks before you're flying again. Now your team of Guardian Owls... yes, they could certainly help, and you could give them instructions from here. But we've got to act now before it's too late."

"There's Amalek and Seph, - they're very brave you know." Joog said.

"I know what you mean, Joog," said the King tenderly as he thought of his two bright children, "But they're too young - much too young. How could they fight against such a powerful wizard? No, we must think of some other ways." He crossed the room to look out of another window and down at Candara, the town that he loved so dearly.

"What about the people?" asked Joog, "There is great strength and many talents in them. Not only in Candara, but there's Whitten and Charin as well."

The King turned to face Joog, "I know, but they keep it well hidden, don't they? They are always so reluctant to help... you know, when asked. They have to be persuaded. They're good people, there's no doubt about that, but... well I wish it was different. They say that years ago it was. Many years ago. People were more generous then." He paused to look out of the window again, "What about animals?"

"I'll see what I can do," Joog looked thoughtful, "But what you say about the people applies to them too. Generally they are complacent, just content in their own lives you know. But I could try."

"If you could, Joog."

Joog gazed out of the window and down at the hopping frogs.

"The frogs do seem to be heading for the palace," he said, "I think you're right about the spell."

For a few minutes they watched in silence from the gold-framed window as the frogs continued their journey.

"Your Majesty," asked Joog, "Shall I call a meeting of the Guardian Owls?"

"Yes, definitely," the King said decisively, "The sooner the better. Good idea, Joog."

"I'll send some sparrow-messengers out," said Joog. He twisted his head right around, as only an owl can, to see who was entering the room. It was Princess Amalek and Prince Seph who ran around the table to join Joog and the King at the window.

"Can we draw on your wooden wing?" Amalek asked Joog. She had a silver pen all ready in her hand.

"Yes, can we, please?" said Seph enthusiastically, who was holding a gold pen, "Wizard Elzaphan sent us these pens. They've just arrived!"

They had been delivered by a couple of sparrows, who had made the journey all the way from Wizard Elzaphan's castle in the centre of Summertime Kingdom.

A Guardian Owl, a large Tawny, had spotted the sparrows and allowed them through to make their delivery to the palace.

"Well, you are lucky children," the King laughed, "To receive such a gift from such a great wizard."

"And I'm lucky too," Joog chuckled, "Lucky to have you to decorate me! Draw whatever you wish."

Amalek and Seph soon found out that the pens were magical. The silver and gold that ran out of their pens shimmered like the sun reflecting on the sea, as if the colours were alive. But not only that, for when they thought of other colours which they needed for their pictures, the colours were there, flowing out of their pens and sparkling on Joog's wooden splint. They could hardly believe their eyes. It was not long before the wooden splint on Joog's wing was covered with drawings of every animal that Amalek and Seph could think of.

When all the drawing and colouring had been done, the King, Joog, Amalek and Seph sat together by the window and discussed the problem of the intruder. The evening passed and the rosy red sun sank behind the distant horizon of the hills. Dusk arrived gently and they watched the lights of Candara appearing like stars in a darkening sky. For about half-an-hour it was peaceful, and then a wind began to blow and by the time the night had flooded everywhere with darkness the weather was as stormy as it had been that morning. Dark clouds filled the night sky until all the stars were gone, extinguished like candle flames in a wind. The temperature dropped rapidly making people light fires in their hearths. A chilly wind rose from the east until it whistled through the trees, sweeping cold rain across the land in heavy sheets.

The men trapped as frogs felt miserable as they hopped

along in the falling rain. At last they finished their long climb up the hill and arrived at the wrought-iron gates at the entrance to the palace grounds. On top of each of the huge gateposts sat a unicorn, one made of silver and one of gold. They looked as if they were guarding the palace. An ancient legend told of a time long ago when they sprang to life to fight and protect the Kingdom from a terrible invasion of evil Troublers but that was only a legend and no one really believed it. After all, nobody had ever seen either of them move at all - not even a twitch of a tail or a nose. But the legend continued to be a favourite story with the children of the Kingdom and the Prince and Princess used to sit for hours looking at the unicorns and imagining that they were moving.

The row of frogs finally arrived at the palace grounds. They hopped up the path to the great front door. At first they sat down and croaked as loudly as they could in the hope that someone would hear them. Then they tried bumping into the door and jumping up at it. The noises they made were just not loud enough and the door stayed firmly closed. In the end they gave up and hopped around the palace looking for a way in. Luckily they found a slightly open window that was left open for the palace cats, Tilly and Flop and one by one the frogs jumped in.

Joog sent out the sparrow messengers to all the Guardian Owls telling them to report to him at the palace immediately after their night watch. He often used sparrows who were always willing to take or fetch messages and they flew off in pairs chirping happily.

The night now engulfed the whole Kingdom. The storm was the most fierce that the King had ever known and with the events that had happened over the past few days he was extremely concerned. He knew that he needed to work out a plan to rid the Kingdom of the Dark Wizard Troubler, but he felt strangely lethargic. He could not decide with any clarity what the right course of action would be. One minute he thought he should venture out straight away and then he thought it would be a foolhardy thing to do on such a wild stormy night.

For some time he dithered, pacing up and down and hesitating. In the end he decided to go to bed and rise early the next morning to sit on his throne and he felt confident that the answer would then come to him. Had he known the wicked plans that were in the mind of the Dark Wizard Troubler at this very moment he would not have delayed it until the morning.

Chapter 4

~ The Spell ~

T he Dark Wizard Troubler was making plans. He sat in the old dirty chair and concentrated his powers, whilst the ravens, still swollen and miserable, sat on the shelf looking down at him. Jamaar lay drowsily in a corner of the room. The wooden boarded floor and sparse furnishings made the slightest sounds echo in the eerie quietness; the room itself had adopted the dingy mood of neglect. Upon a small table beside the chair were the remnants of several meals, an untidy clutter of plates, mugs and leftover scraps of rotting food that were beginning to reek of mould.

The Dark Wizard Troubler, who was leaning back in the chair with his legs outstretched and crossed at the ankles, was completely still except for his slow breathing. His head was tilted back and his eyes were closed. The gentle light of two black candles glimmered with pale yellow in the gloomy room. One was on the mantelpiece and the other on the floor and as the flames wavered in the draughty room they cast ghostly dancing shadows on the plain walls.

He was pleased that the two ravens had confirmed the location of the Candara Gems and that would be invaluable later on. He had got the information about the whereabouts of the gems from Old Howard who said he had heard a rumour about where they were hidden. Like most of the inhabitants of the Kingdom of Gems, Old Howard did not believe they existed at all. The Dark Wizard Troubler was unsure whether to trust the rumour that this old man said he had heard and so he decided to send out the two ravens in the hope that they would bring him certain knowledge of where they were. Now he knew and this delighted him.

The disappointment of the raven's failure to steal the ruby, the gem which had the special strength of protection, was not too bad. He was expecting this because the double protection was working; the gems protected the kingdom as long as the people were living under the influence of the gems. It worked like a mirror; the gems received back from the people the qualities they were giving out and thus they protected each other. They were each others strength and safety.

Before he could fully control the kingdom he would have to obtain the gems and take them out beyond the kingdom boundaries. Then their effect would instantly disappear, the Kingdom of Gems would fall and he could rule. Stealing them from the cave would be easy but this could not be done until he had dealt with all the creatures living here. This would leave the gems unprotected and this was the difficult part. He believed that the dark plan he had thought of would work.

There was a collection of things lying on the floor in the dingy room and amongst them was a cage about the size of a large dolls house. The sides and the top were made of a fine metal mesh which held captive a mass of over a hundred butterflies, some of which were fluttering to and fro whilst others were resting wherever they could find a place to land.

The Dark Wizard pulled himself up from the chair, roughly grabbed the cage by the handle on the top and strode out of the room with it. His boots echoed loudly on the floorboards. He carried it up the stairs and dropped it in one of the rooms with a bump, which caused all the butterflies to take to the air and flutter chaotically about. Stooping down he opened the cage door and immediately some of the butterflies flew out. He stood up and brushed a butterfly off his shoulder. Then he left the room, closing the door behind him and descended the stairs.

Once back in the chair he surveyed the strange variety of things that lay on the floor in front of him. There was a large silver dish filled with hot steaming water; a black pepper pot; a rat in a cage; and the black wax candle with flickering flame. The steam from the silver dish was swirling up to the top of the room and gathering there in misty clouds. The cage rattled as the rat tried to escape in vain, for the door was tightly fastened.

Also on the floor, placed to one side near the wall, was a block of gold about the size of six bricks. It was perfectly square except where one small bar had been cut out of it. It reflected brightly in the flickering light of the two candles.

The Dark Wizard Troubler just sat there in deep concentration. Outside the gale howled. It was the coldest, stormiest night ever to visit the Kingdom. The driving rain turned to hail and then to snow which very soon began to fill up the streets of the town and weigh down the branches of the trees. The blizzard drove snowflakes into every small corner, every crack, every nook and cranny it could find and drifted snow up against Old Howard's house.

It was not until midnight that the Dark Wizard Troubler moved. Suddenly, and quickly, as if he knew exactly what he was going to do, he pulled himself up from his chair and crouched down beside the collection of things on the floor. On his face a heavy frown faded as the hint of a smile touched the corners of his mouth.

"At last," he whispered, "At last! Now I have the power! I have the spell! Tomorrow I will have the Kingdom!"

Glancing up at the ceiling where the clouds of steam were still gathering he hissed, almost whispering, "Good. That's perfect."

With a jerk of his head he spat at the candle on the floor and the flame went out with a hiss, leaving the room lit only by the candle on the mantelpiece. In the semi-darkness he grabbed the black candle with his bony hand and using it like a piece of chalk he swiftly drew a unicorn on the wooden floor with the black wax. Then he began to stare at the water. Within a minute the water was solid ice.

Slowly he began to whisper,

"Black night black, this spell I cast,
and I shall win again.
Black night black, all good is past,
a kingdom I shall gain.
This spell will bring me that which pleases
for every time a creature sneezes
it will freeze throughout all time,
this Kingdom will be mine!"

His words resounded in the dim room. For a moment they seemed to hang there and then the power of the spell went deeper, seeping into everything, possessing everything, permeating the substance of the walls and then spreading further still, throughout the land, invisibly causing changes everywhere in the kingdom. Jamaar stirred and growled.

The Dark Wizard nodded and then smiled with the effect that he could feel was happening. Then he picked up the pepper pot, stood up, and shook it into the clouds, which by now were swirling slowly in the top half of the room, and soon they were filled with grains of pepper. He crouched down and shook the pepper pot above the rat's cage. The rat sniffed, scratched its nose with a paw and then sneezed. Immediately the rat froze and the Dark Wizard Troubler looked on gleefully to see the rat so utterly still. He picked up a stick and, through the bars, poked the rat hard to make sure the spell had worked. The rat could not be moved.

"Good, good!" he cried, his harsh voice resounding around the room, "I knew it would work. Dog!" and he glared into the dark corner of the room, "What's your name? Oh, yes… Jamaar. Look at that rat!"

Jamaar, who had been watching from the corner of the room got up and walked towards his master. He had undergone an extraordinary change; he had grown bigger, more muscular and very clearly broader across the chest and back. He was even slightly taller. He was no longer the underfed young stray, but powerfully built, with strong jowls and legs with bulging muscles. His fur was still scraggy and untidy. Dribbles of saliva dripped from his massive jaws as he fixed his black eyes on his master. He looked mean and angry as if he was ready to devour any living thing that came close.

"Yes, master," he growled as he sat at his master's feet and stared up at him, "Where is the food you promised me? I'm starving!"

"Well," the wizard said with a wry smile, his voice echoing in the cold room, "Look at you! It's worked even better than I expected. I wanted a *real* dog with a bit of fight in him... but, well... I like the transformation! And you're starving are you? I'm not surprised with that great hulk of a body to feed!"

The evil wizard picked up a chair and smashed it into the cage with all his might. The cage disintegrated.

"So..., starving did you say?" he said looking down at the eager dog, "Would you like rat for supper?"

Jamaar leapt upon the frozen rat with his front paws but the rat remained unmoved as if it was made out of the hardest and heaviest rock. Jamaar stepped back and jumped at it again. This time he gripped it in his massive jaws and with a tremendous effort lifted it high in the air. There was the crack of breaking teeth and Jamaar yelped in pain, letting go and two pieces of white blood-stained teeth fell together with the rat which thudded onto the floor without bouncing at all, like a lead weight. The bits of teeth rattled across the floor.

"Good, good, good!" said the Dark Wizard, rubbing his hands together with glee and with a hideous smile spreading over his face. Then he dropped his voice, "Thank you, Jamaar!" he was speaking softly now, slowly, with a sinister clarity, "That was a good test. Now, let me tell you, instruct you, on your duties. Your primary role is to guard this house with your life, like a good guard dog would. But I may take you here and there, or send you on tasks. Understand?"

"Yes," Jamaar growled, blood dripping from his mouth, "But where's my food?"

"Patience," snapped the Dark Wizard, "You will work for your food."

"But, our agreement?" growled Jamaar, "The deal, remember? You said…"

"The agreement stands," the wizard was raising his voice, "But *I* am master and I tell *you* what to do." He swung his leg viciously at Jamaar's side and landed a kick so powerful that he skidded across the room and back into the corner, "Who's the master?" he snapped.

"You are," snarled Jamaar reluctantly, and then adding, "Master."

"That's right, and don't you ever forget it. You will get food in due course. When *I* say, and, don't fear, there will be plenty. Plenty! But you cannot demand. No, no, no, you will earn it." He turned his attention back to the rat, which now had touches of white frost on it, like powdery icing sugar. The wizard smiled, "Good!" he exclaimed again.

With this excited cry he left the room with Jamaar following on his heels. He climbed the wooden stairs and walked into one of the bedrooms, the one without the butterflies. He sat down in a chair by the window and looked out. A quiet evil laugh hissed out of his twisted mouth as he thought about what he had achieved. He gazed at the view from the window and began to mutter to himself.

"This… all this… this kingdom here… is falling to me. I claim it for…" his words turned into a menacing sneer as his thin lips spread again into a smile, "I claim it for me."

The icy weather that had struck the Kingdom so suddenly took everyone, people and animals, by surprise, for it was mid-summer. The bitter driving blizzard lasted all through the night and the woodland animals and insects were not prepared for the extreme cold. The animals who made their homes underground, the rabbits, foxes, otters, moles and badgers, huddled together; birds pulled their nests around them; insects found cracks in trees and buildings to shelter in; the grazers - sheep, horses, cows and donkeys, - struggled against the blizzard into Candara, Whitten and Charin, where they knocked on doors with their hoofs. People gladly let them in to shelter. But in spite of all their efforts to keep warm everyone, people and animals, whether inside or outside, was shivering, and most inhabitants of the Kingdom caught colds. This, of course, was exactly what the Dark Wizard Troubler wanted to happen.

At dawn the wind dropped away and the air became still and crisp. The snow continued to fall steadily and

heavily, and the Kingdom had been transformed into a beautiful whiteness. The snow lay as smooth as the icing on a wedding cake. The grazer's hoof-mark tracks had been covered, and, as yet, no one had ventured out.

The falling snow fluttered and flurried down in large fluffy flakes and as it grew lighter it could be seen that something else was falling from the clouds too. Swirling around and in between the dancing snowflakes were tiny grains of pepper. The Dark Wizard Troubler's spell, which he created in miniature in Old Howard's house, was now happening to his greedy delight throughout the Kingdom.

Inside their homes people were eager to get up and light a fire to warm their shivering bodies and cold feet. John Chardley, who lived by the River Tazer in Candara in a house that joined onto Spindley Tower, was the first to get up. He had two jobs; he looked after the tower and was also the town beekeeper. He provided the people of the Kingdom with honey. Most of his bees were kept in the woods, but he also kept a few hives in his house and their gentle happy buzz could be heard this morning.

John Chardley quickly dressed, and still shivering, he began to descend the stairs. Half way down he sneezed.

"Ah... ah... ah... choooo!"

On the instant, just as he was stepping from one step down to the next, he froze and although he looked completely off balance as if he was bound to topple forwards and tumble down the stairs, he was absolutely still.

The sneeze woke a horse in the hall downstairs, who looked up to see John Chardley there, his eyes closed and his face wrinkled from the sneeze, apparently standing half way up the stairs.

"Well, people are funny!" thought the horse, who like all horses usually slept standing up, *"Sleeping half way up the stairs, and sneezing in his sleep! These are strange times."*

He clattered a hoof on the floor, shook his head and flicked at a passing bee with his tail. Then he closed his large brown eyes to dose a little more, for he was very tired from the long walk through the blizzard. Just then some pepper blew under the door and into the hall. It formed a little cloud and rose and swirled through the air. It seemed as if it knew where to go as it moved from one beehive to another, passing inside each and after a chorus of tiny bee sneezes moving on to the next. Some bees that were flying and buzzing around the room were also chased by the pepper cloud, surrounded by it and forced to sneeze. Very soon John Chardley's house was dotted with bees frozen in mid-air all as still as stars resting in a night sky.

By this time the horse was fast asleep. The pepper cloud found it's way to the horse's head and hovered there. The horse, still with his eyes closed, lifted his head back, shook his long brown matted main, and sneezed.

Immediately the horse was frozen as still and cold as if it had been carved out of rock.

In Relbuort Cottage, 17 Nathen Avenue, the spell had also struck, lulling the house and its inhabitants into its iron-hard lifeless grip. Darsan had sneezed through cold during his morning wash whilst a determined cloud of pepper had ambushed Harraine and tickled her nose into submission as she sat in her wheelchair. The house was consumed by a deathly hush, which had descended as surely as night follows day and had taken complete possession of this household.

The whole Kingdom of Gems was in the grip of the freezing arctic weather and gradually all the living creatures were sneezing and falling into the grip of the Dark Wizard Troubler's spell. Everyone in Candara, Whitten and Charin, as well as others living in the houses dotted on the Western Downs, was frozen and in all sorts of positions too. Some were half out of bed; some were cleaning their teeth; some were eating their breakfast; some were staring out of the window, destined, it seemed, to stare out forever; some were dressing, with jumpers being just pulled over their heads; others were just getting into the bath, or in the bath with shampoo covered hair, or just getting out; some were peeping out of the door and now the snow was settling on their faces and hands. One lady tripped over her dressing gown at the top of the stairs, tumbled down, sneezed just before she hit the floor and froze, suspended in mid-air.

Dotted around in the air were a few insects and birds in mid-flight, completely still, as if time had never existed. Snow settled on their bodies and outspread wings. Spiders on half-made webs could not move even one of their eight legs; for they were caught in the spell as surely as the flies they had trapped and tangled in their webs. All the creatures in the Kingdom from the largest bear that lumbered in the woods to the tiniest baby red spider that had not yet left the spider nest and with the tiniest softest sneeze you can imagine, came under the curse of the Dark Wizard Troubler's spell.

There were only a few people who had not caught colds in the icy chill of the night, but even they could not escape the spell. The pepper clouds slipped through keyholes and under doors, quickly found their victims, tickled their noses and created a sneeze. And so, by eight o'clock, all creatures had become motionless frozen statues, dusted with white smudges of frost.

The Dark Wizard Troubler was still sitting at the window upstairs in Old Howard's house. As he looked through the falling snow in the direction of the town he could see some birds and some of the townsfolk at their windows or peeping out through their doors, but most important of all, he could see that they were absolutely stock-still. This delighted him, bringing a smile of enjoyment to his thin lips. Jamaar had been sent out to check in the town, to make sure that everyone was frozen, on the promise that he would be fed on his return and he was fighting through the ever-deepening snow as he moved from house to house.

Through the thick whiteness of the descending snow, however, the Dark Wizard Troubler could not see the palace on the hill. He would dearly have liked to know what was happening there, although he was hoping, of course, that everyone was too frozen for anything at all to be happening.

Throughout the kingdom; in the Wellspring Woods and

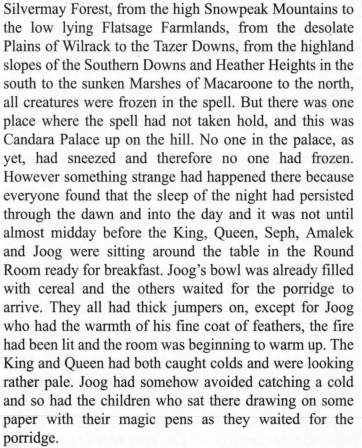

Silvermay Forest, from the high Snowpeak Mountains to the low lying Flatsage Farmlands, from the desolate Plains of Wilrack to the Tazer Downs, from the highland slopes of the Southern Downs and Heather Heights in the south to the sunken Marshes of Macaroone to the north, all creatures were frozen in the spell. But there was one place where the spell had not taken hold, and this was Candara Palace up on the hill. No one in the palace, as yet, had sneezed and therefore no one had frozen. However something strange had happened there because everyone found that the sleep of the night had persisted through the dawn and into the day and it was not until almost midday before the King, Queen, Seph, Amalek and Joog were sitting around the table in the Round Room ready for breakfast. Joog's bowl was already filled with cereal and the others waited for the porridge to arrive. They all had thick jumpers on, except for Joog who had the warmth of his fine coat of feathers, the fire had been lit and the room was beginning to warm up. The King and Queen had both caught colds and were looking rather pale. Joog had somehow avoided catching a cold and so had the children who sat there drawing on some paper with their magic pens as they waited for the porridge.

Seph glanced out of the window. "Look!" he exclaimed, "What's that falling with the snow?"

"Dust?" asked Amalek.

"Looks like dust," Seph looked puzzled, "But… why? Why is dust falling with the snow?"

The Queen shook her head. "It is very weird," she said, "We've had sand falling once in the rain and it turned out that it blew over from that creeping desert in the east. People out walking were getting sand in their eyes. But, dust… in the snow!" She turned to her husband, "What do you think, dear?"

"I've never heard of it, or seen it. It's worrying… very worrying, especially with this Troubler around."

The snow was still falling so thickly in large fluffy flakes that they could not see the town below and had no idea what had happened there. This made the King feel even more worried about the people of his Kingdom and he realised that he would have to venture out to make sure that they were alright. But he would wait until after breakfast, by which time the Guardian Owls would have arrived. Due to his oversleeping he had missed sitting on his throne as he had planned.

"Oh, why am I delaying everything and oversleeping, Joog?" asked the King as a frown furrowed his brow. He was absent-minded at the best of times, but now he felt even more forgetful than ever, "I feel all out of step with things."

Joog was sitting on his branch by the table with his broken wing hanging down with the weight of the wooden splint. He was watching everything with his round yellow eyes and looking calm and wise. When he spoke his voice carried the same qualities.

"Yes, it certainly is not like you, Your Majesty," said Joog, ruffling up his feathers to keep him warm, "The very presence of this Troubler in the Kingdom is affecting your thoughts and actions. You mustn't let it, Your Majesty, you mustn't. The safety of your people is at risk. There is danger amongst us."

"You're right, Joog. Thank you," said the King, already feeling stronger and more confident. "You are a good friend. One of the very best, Joog."

"I'm wondering where the Guardian Owls are," Joog

looked concerned, "They should be here by now."

"Well," said the King, "We've all overslept... *they* must have as well."

The door opened and in came the palace cook carrying the porridge in a large bowl and handed it to the Queen to serve. The cook left the room, closed the door and then sneezed.

"Bless you!" called out Prince Seph.

But there was no reply from the cook. She was as still as Sleeping Beauty sleeping for a hundred years.

"I'm afraid I caught a terrible cold in the night," said the Queen, "Wasn't it freezing!" And she took out a handkerchief to blow her nose, and then began to serve the porridge.

"I caught a cold too," said the King, sniffing, "Do you think its something to do with that Dark Wizard Troubler? It never snows at this time of year. As soon as I've eaten breakfast I'll spend some time on the throne and decide what to do. Or perhaps I ought to go out now and... well... look around. Yes, I'll to go now... with some of my men. Would you come with me, Joog?"

"Of course," Joog began and then he turned to Seph, "Would you meet the Guardian Owls when they arrive, and tell them..."

"Ah... Ah... Ah... Aaah Chooooo!" The Queen's head jerked forwards as her sneezing nose met with a large spoon-full of porridge that she was about to put in the Princess's bowl. This caused the porridge to fly in all directions and with the sound of the sneeze it was like a firework exploding. The porridge splattered them all and when they looked at the Queen they were amazed at what they saw. The Queen, their darling Queen, who they all loved so dearly, was a frozen statue with her nose in the serving spoon.

"Oh no!" the King exclaimed.

"Oh no!" cried the Prince and Princess together, as they ran to hold their mother's hand and tried to move her fingers. But they very soon discovered that she was icy cold to the touch and they could not bend a frozen finger even a fraction. Amalek burst into tears. Just at this moment something else happened - the King sneezed.

"Ah... Aaaah... Chooooo!"

Joog and the children stared at the King who stood there, gazing with glazed eyes at the Queen with her nose in the spoon. The King was now frozen too. The Dark Wizard Troubler's spell had arrived at the palace in spite of the protecting atmosphere of peace that dwelt there. Now the King and Queen had joined the other creatures of the Kingdom who were held firm in the frozen grip of the spell. The evil magic had descended like a shroud upon the whole land. Joog looked at the two children with tears brimming up in their eyes and knew he loved them with all his heart.

"We mustn't sneeze," Joog said firmly, "Even if you feel you have to."

Amalek and Seph nodded. He spread his healthy wing and put it around Amalek's shoulders and a few of her tears ran down his feathers and pattered onto the deep blue carpet.

The children felt heartbroken and frightened. They could hardly believe what had happened and every now and again one of them looked at the King and Queen to check that they were still frozen. Joog was calm. He realised that the Dark Wizard Troubler must be very powerful to cast a spell strong enough to reach the palace and he knew they would have to fight him with all their strength and intelligence. When he had seen the Dark Wizard he had felt he was meeting a special power; a power that felt overwhelming, like when a small group of soldiers is sent to fight a great army. He looked at the two children.

"This spell is indeed bad," he said quietly. His voice sounded earnest but untroubled, as if he was describing an event that could not be avoided and now had to be dealt with, "I fear the Guardian Owls have fallen to it, else they would be here. With this spell he is trapping everyone. He is trying to take over the kingdom. I bet he's after the Candara Gems, that's if he knows about them."

Amalek was looking at Joog, with panic in her eyes, "What can we do, Joog?" she asked.

"It's important to remember that spells can be overcome. Spells can be reversed. There are ways of making spells disappear." As he spoke the Prince and Princess felt comforted. "It will not be easy but we will overcome this evil wizard somehow. The first thing to do is..."

"Joog!" exclaimed Seph suddenly, interrupting him, "Your wing! You're moving it!"

"My goodness, Seph, you're right! I hadn't noticed that myself. How extraordinary! It shouldn't be healed for a few weeks yet. But how…?"

Joog lifted the wooden splint which covered his wing right above his head.

"Well," Joog said slowly, still perched on his branch, "That's mysterious. That's very strange," and he brought his wing down, holding it out to the side, "It feels perfectly alright now. Somehow it's healed! When I broke my leg a couple of years ago it took six weeks, and even then I was hobbling for a while. I'll take the splint off and try flying around the room." He looked at the two children, "Can you help me please?"

Amalek and Seph had just started removing the binds from the wooden splint when they heard a sound at the door which had been left just slightly ajar. They all stared in the direction of the noise. Immediately a terrifying thought flashed into their minds: was this the Dark Wizard Troubler? Or was it one of his vicious fighting ravens?

"Hide," whispered Joog urgently.

They glanced around for a place to hide but it was too late. Amalek and Seph found themselves crouching to the floor where at least they were partly hidden by the table. Joog thought of flying up to the top of a tall cupboard, the tallest piece of furniture in the room, but then remembered the wooden splint still on his wing. Amalek and Seph were gripped with fear as they heard a creak. Very slowly the door was being pushed open... All their eyes were fixed on the opening gap when they saw something black appear. It looked like the end of a boot. They held their breath and tensed, ready for something to happen. Suddenly Seph stood up.

"No," whispered Amalek, grasping her brother's arm to hold him back protectively.

"It's alright," said Seph, "It's a cat's paw."

Amalek looked back at the door. She realised with great relief that Seph was right, and then the door swung open and in walked Flop.

"Flop!" cried Amalek, as Flop trotted towards them. He was a fluffy black and white cat with an attractive tinge of ginger here and there and a tail as bushy as the tail of a fox. He looked frightened and out of breath as

Amalek picked him up, enveloped him in her loving arms and stroked his fur tenderly. He wore a collar which the children had coloured with their magic pens so that it glittered with stripes of silver, gold, green and blue.

"Oh, Flop," she said.

"Hang on," said Seph, suddenly looking anxious again, and turning to Flop and whispering, "Were you being chased?"

"No," said Flop, now calming down, but still looking on edge, "What's going on?" he asked, looking from face to face, "Everyone is frozen. Everyone, except for us. Just outside there the cook is frozen," and they looked through the open door. There was the cook, utterly still as if made of rock, with her head slightly lowered after the sneeze. A touch of white frost coated her face. Joog jumped off his branch and landed on the table, his wooden splint bumping and then scraping on the wood as he moved closer to the others.

"What about the rest of the palace," he asked Flop.

"All frozen," Flop said, as Amalek put him down on the table next to Joog, "First it was Tilly. She sneezed - now what's unusual about that? But she was frozen on the instant. Then all of our five kittens, one by one. Lila was the first and then the others. I tried to stop them but it happened so quickly. Then I ran from room to room - everyone is frozen you know. Everyone! My poor Tilly... My poor kittens... Thank goodness I found you." He looked around from face to face, "What can we do?"

"It's a Troubler, Flop," explained Seph, "We think he's cast a spell and this is what it's doing. He must be trying to take over..." As he was speaking he felt strength growing in him, welling up from somewhere deep inside. He felt ready to fight for Tilly and their kittens; for his mother and father. Somehow they had to be released. He would take on his father's duty to look after the kingdom, and he would fight this dark intruder.

"We'll fight him and win," he said with determination and a touch of anger in his voice.

"Do you really think so?" asked Amalek, looking at her brother with her blue-grey eyes wide and full of hope. As she asked the question she began to feel the same sense of strength rising in her.

"Yes I do," he replied decisively.

"Well let's start by making a plan then," said Amalek, whose practical mind had already begun working out the possibilities, "Firstly, Joog must test out his wing."

"Well, you are fine young people," said Joog, his yellow eyes looking with love at the two children, "Can you help me get this thing off, please."

He looked at the splint on his wing, covered with the sparkling coloured drawings of the Prince and Princess, and began once more, with the help of the children, to remove it from his miraculously healed wing.

Chapter 5

~ Aram and Halo ~

ithout the usual sounds of living creatures moving about and talking, the kingdom was unusually quiet, but it was an uneasy and unnatural quietness. It weighed upon the land like a heavy burden. The hushed air was loaded with a sinister flavour of doom. The silence was so complete that the snow could be heard as it fell on the windows of the Round Room like the gentle tapping of fingers on the glass. The snow was building up, layer upon layer and many plants and small bushes were completely covered now. Where it had been swept into wave-like drifts even some small trees had disappeared. If there were any foxes, or rabbits, or badgers out they would have had to tunnel through the snow to get anywhere at all, but of course they were all frozen in their underground homes - every single one of them.

The wooden splint was nearly off now and Joog was all ready with a calm eagerness to try his wing out in flight.

"Stop!" shouted Amalek suddenly, making the others jump with surprise. They were not used to her shouting. She had been sitting on the floor, leaning against the wall and trying to work something out. Suddenly she had got the answer, "Stop! Listen, I've got it. It makes sense now. The magic pens, that's what it is - don't you see?"

They all stopped still and stared at the Princess, who realised that they did not see and that she would have to explain it further.

"The ink from the magic pens healed Joog's wing. And what's more, why do you think we're the only ones in the Palace... and maybe in the whole Kingdom who haven't sneezed... and who haven't been frozen? It's obvious now. Joog has magic ink on his splint, Flop has it on his collar and we have been either holding our pens, or we've had them in our pockets since we got up this morning! And you've got some on your cheek somehow, Seph. The magic pens are protecting us!"

"Yes, of course, it must be!" said Joog, "After all the pens were sent by Wizard Elzaphan. You're right. Well, thank goodness that he sent them when he did? Do you think he somehow knew of our danger?"

"Well," answered Amalek, who felt happier as she remembered Wizard Elzaphan, "He does seem to know what's happening without seeing it... and even when it happens miles away too."

"That's true," said Joog, "I don't know how he does it. He is the most extraordinary wizard I've ever met... and I've met a good few in my time." Joog paused, and looked earnestly at the two children, "Now, you two," he continued, "Don't let go of those pens whatever you do. One sneeze and that's it - you'll be frozen like the rest. And I mustn't take off this splint."

They sat there on the soft carpet for a few moments not knowing what to do next. Amalek was looking down and fiddling with a shoe-lace. Then suddenly she looked up.

"We'll have to draw with magic ink on ourselves," she said, "Seph, where would you like to be drawn on?" She smiled at her brother. Although for the moment the fear of only a few minutes ago had slightly loosened its grip on them, still the sense of danger lingered. It felt like a cloud obscuring the sun and casting a threatening shadow into their lives.

"Oh, I think an ankle would be best," replied Seph, and he stooped to roll down a sock.

Amalek dabbed the pen on Seph's ankle and then did the same to one of her ankles. When it was Joog's turn the Princess carefully removed the bandages and plasters that covered the wise owl's wounds and bruises, and gently ran her pen along Joog's cuts. They healed instantly. Meanwhile Seph was busy using his pen on Joog's feathered legs, dabbing some gold ink on.

"Thank you," said Joog, as he slipped his wing out of the wooden splint, "I think I'll try a spin around the room."

He flew quickly and with ease, completing three laps of the Round Room with a hoot of delight. He found that his wing was as strong and supple as it used to be, so he carried on doing circuits of the room and they all smiled with wonder. This brought them some relief, if only for a moment, from the terrible seriousness of the situation. The power of the Dark Wizard Troubler was only too clear now and they had only escaped it themselves through what seemed like a miraculous stroke of good fortune.

Joog landed on the table next to Flop whose fluffy

black and white tail hung down over the edge. Amalek and Seph sat cross-legged on the carpet and on the other side of the table were the King and Queen, captured and held rigid by the spell, their faces and hands coated with frost. The four friends realised that they would have to get some help and this meant leaving the Kingdom. They all felt strong now in the love of each other's company and determined too, but they were not sure what to do next. Things seemed to be happening so quickly and they needed a little time to get ready for the next step and to decide what that would be. Joog was the first to speak.

"You know who we need," he said, stretching out his feathered wings as he spoke, "Wizard Elzaphan. Now *he* could help us. I'm sure he could, there's no doubt about that. This Dark Wizard Troubler is certainly very powerful, but so is Wizard Elzaphan." He paused thoughtfully, and then continued, "Yes, that is who we need."

The others nodded.

"Wizard Elzaphan is the one to beat this Troubler if anyone is," said Seph.

Amalek stood up, "But… how can we ask him to help? All the sparrow-messengers are frozen."

"This is the difficulty…" Joog shook his head, "Getting there to tell him about it all. I could go, but I don't want to leave you here."

"Then we all travel there together," announced Seph.

Flop shivered, "Travelling in this sort of cold weather is not for cats like me!" Flop shivered at the thought, "It's out of the question. The cold and snow is definitely not for cats, so I would have to stay here whilst you go for help."

"Oh Flop," said Amalek as she stroked him on his

back, "You can't stay here alone. That awful Dark Wizard might come up to the palace."

This thought produced another shiver down Flop's spine and his magnificent fluffy tail flicked to and fro.

"Well, perhaps," he said slowly, "If I'm all dressed up and carried I might consider it."

"I'll carry you, Flop," Seph offered.

"Thanks," said Flop gratefully, relieved to have sorted out his dilemma.

"But, travelling in this weather!" said Amalek, who was over by the window and looking out at the wintry scene. The snow was still falling heavily and gusting here and there in the gathering wind. It was already knee deep. "Look at it! It would take us ages and ages to go just a few steps down the road… especially the way it's falling so heavily and getting thicker all the time. Let's face it… we're trapped here by the snow."

This fact put an end to the conversation and the other three joined Amalek at the window to look out. It was clearly the case that trying to walk anywhere at all in such deep snow would be extremely difficult and possibly dangerous. The only one who could make the journey quickly to Wizard Elzaphan was Joog of course, but he was reluctant to leave the others there. He knew that at some time the Dark Wizard Troubler would come to the palace to check that his spell had captured the King and Queen. The evil Wizard would find the Prince, Princess and Flop and what would happen then? Joog shuddered at the thought. But if he did not fly off by himself to find Wizard Elzaphan then the Dark Wizard Troubler would find them all. Perhaps together they could try to fight him, but they would have to work out a plan that gave them an advantage.

As Joog wondered over his difficult choice they all moved over to the fire which was beginning to die down. The Prince and Princess put some more logs on. The fire crackled and started spluttering back to life and soon it was ablaze with yellow and orange flames. After a while Joog had decided what to do.

"My dear friends," Joog began calmly, "We have a problem here. A serious problem. I have been wondering whether or not to fly off to find Wizard Elzaphan by myself. Well, I have decided. I think it is best if..."

Joog stopped abruptly and turned to face the window.

"What is it?" asked Amalek.

"Shhh," said Joog, "Listen."

They all kept still and listened. Then they heard it.

"Someone's out there," said Joog softly, "Walking through the snow."

They all listened. Joog was right. There was the distinctive sound of feet crunching in the snow.

"It must be him," whispered Seph, "It must be the Dark Wizard Troubler because he's frozen everyone, hasn't he?"

Flop jumped down off the table, "I'll take a look," he said and trotted over to the window, jumping up onto the sill.

Amalek and Seph followed him slowly and quietly and then Joog glided across, landing on Seph's shoulder. They looked anxiously out through the gold-framed window and the falling whiteness of snow. It was hard to see very far, but they could all clearly hear the footsteps and so they stared in the direction of the sound. Everything was heaped with snow. Through the haze of snow flurries they saw ghostly outlines; just visible were the great gates where Palace Path entered the palace grounds, the stiff metal softened to candyfloss; white trees still and heavy-laden with snow; bushes like white clouds. As they strained their eyes to see they felt the fear rising. The sound was certainly someone walking up the hill from the direction of the town. It must be the Dark Wizard Troubler. It must be him now walking up the snow-covered Palace Path which led to the front door, intent on his plan to take over the kingdom. Suddenly Joog, with his excellent owl's eyes, saw a form, a movement in the wintry scene.

"Look," he whispered, "Over there! Look!"

They all looked but saw nothing. Then they saw it. Their eyes opened wide in amazement. There, walking up the path through the deep snow, lifting legs high with each sturdy step was a golden unicorn. They welcomed the sight and their fear melted away into a joy that lit up all their faces with surprise and happiness.

"It's Aram!" cried Amalek with amazement, "Oh, look at that - the legend *is* true. He's alive! I knew it! I knew it somehow! Look!"

"And there's Halo!" called out Seph, "Look, just behind Aram. There she is! It is!"

It was an extraordinary moment. The two unicorns grew closer and closer as they moved gracefully, in spite of the deep snow, towards the palace. As they approached they appeared to shine and light up the snow that was fluttering around them. Aram shone with gold light from his strong golden body and Halo shimmered silver light all around her. It was a beautiful and magical sight and the four friends gazed from the high tower window with amazed faces. At the sight of the two beautiful unicorns the feeling of relief was indescribable.

As they watched, Aram and Halo lifted their heads and

looked up at the window.

"Hello!" they called out together.

"Hello!" called back the four friends.

Aram and Halo began to trot, and then to gallop up to the palace. As they did they lowered their heads and pointed their spiral horns, called alicorns, in front of them and the snow cleared a path for them to pass through, blowing up into swirling white clouds and then slowly settling again behind them leaving the snow as deep as before.

"You'd better let them in," said Joog quickly to Flop, "You're the fastest down the winding stairs, Flop."

But before Flop had time to move a whisker they saw, to their utter amazement, Aram and Halo continue their gallop straight up the palace wall.

"Open the window!" cried Flop.

Amalek and Seph quickly lifted the handles and flung open the gold-framed window just before Aram and Halo came leaping through. Snow whipped into the room on the wind and Amalek's wavy fair hair was swept back. The two unicorns hurtled past them, together with a swirling mass of snowflakes which were lit up by their golden and silver light and landed on the carpet by the round table. Slowly the snow fell onto the blue carpet, melting into droplets of water that looked like jewels as they reflected the gold and silver glow of the unicorns. Aram shook his long mane and sparks of golden light flew off it in all directions. Amalek and Seph quickly closed the window to keep out the icy wind and the snow. Suddenly it was calm again.

"Hello," said Aram, turning his great head to look at the Prince and Princess who were standing by the window and had just managed to get out of the way of the unicorns' sudden and dramatic arrival. His voice was deep and strong and as they listened they felt deeply comforted by the sound, "It is good to meet you properly after all this time."

Then Halo spoke with a voice that sounded as beautiful and pure as the sweet trickling of fresh spring water, "We feel as though we know you all so well after watching you for so many years. We know your names, you know."

The four friends just stood there, mouths open with utter surprise and delight and glowing with a refreshing feeling of calm. For a moment no one said a word.

Joog broke the silence, "Well, we are very glad to see you too," he said. He was perched high up on a shelf above the windows and looking down on everyone, "We were sure it would be the Dark Wizard Troubler."

"Dark Wizard Troubler?" Halo queried.

"We've started calling him that," replied Joog, "He's definitely a wizard of some sort."

"Wizard?" asked Halo.

Seph replied, "Yes. He's cast a spell and it's freezing everyone."

"Well, you know we only awaken when the Kingdom is in grave danger. The last time was over six hundred years ago. Since then we've been watching and waiting. This must be very serious indeed."

"You'd better tell us all about it," said Aram, shining brightly, "We are at your service, you know, so tell us as quickly as you can and then we'll decide what to do."

So the four friends sat around the two magnificent unicorns and between them they told the story. Aram and Halo looked down at the others, nodding now and again and asking questions.

"Now I see," began Aram earnestly, when they had

heard the whole story, "I see why we have awoken. You'll find that the spell has affected the whole kingdom. But thank goodness for the magic pens." He looked closely at Joog's legs, "So that's the ink that is protecting you, Joog. But what about you two?" he asked, turning to Amalek and Seph.

Seph pulled down his sock and showed the ink to Aram, and Amalek did the same.

He nodded and then turned to look at the King and Queen who were still exactly as they had been when they sneezed, "It sounds like a fallen Wizard. It's very sad but it occasionally happens. A good wizard turns away from his true way and decides to use his powers, which are a gift of course, to get things for himself. He forgets that his powers are to serve the good of everybody. It could be, I think, that he is one of these. But this Dark Wizard Troubler is clearly very powerful and we'll have to get help, as you say, from Wizard Elzaphan to fight him."

"We ought to go now then," said Amalek, who was afraid that the Dark Wizard Troubler might walk in through the door any minute now, "Can we ride on your backs?"

"Of course, of course," said Halo immediately, "We can carry you and help you."

Aram's deep voice joined in, "But the real responsibility lies with you I'm afraid. Yes, we can help. Also Wizard Elzaphan can help too... he can help a great deal... but as it's your kingdom that is being attacked then you must fight to save it. But you need to talk to Wizard Elzaphan about these things."

"Right," said Seph, "Let's go then before that evil wizard decides to visit the palace."

"Listen!" exclaimed Joog, who was now perched by

the window, "I can hear footsteps in the snow!"

They all moved over to the window and again heard the distinctive rhythmic sound of someone crunching through the thick snow. The snow was falling even more thickly now and the wind was turning into a gale. At first they could not see who it was. This time, surely, it must be the Dark Wizard Troubler. The crunching footsteps grew louder. They gazed through the descending snow at the great gates, the entrance to the palace gardens. They saw some snow fall from the metal as one of the gates was pulled open. Then they saw just two black dots. A black shape emerged, and a moment later they could see it was him, the Dark Wizard Troubler, in full view, with the deep black stars on his cloak and pointed hat looking like holes in the night as he trudged through the ever-deepening snow. They could feel his terrifying presence reaching out to them, aimed at them through his eyes which were staring straight at them, piercing into them with icy coldness. Fear gripped them as they felt trapped by the unseen power of his freezing gaze. Beside him was Jamaar also staring, black-eyed, straight at them. Aram and Halo quickly moved away from the window before he saw them.

"I've got you now!" he cried out, staring at the four friends.

As he shouted these words with his harsh voice he lifted his arms and pointed them at the window. His cloak flapped in the blizzard as two black ravens appeared, one from each sleeve and clung to his hands.

"Go!" the wizard shouted, shaking his arms to release the ravens, "Go and get them!"

The six friends saw the two ravens jump off his hands and a chill of fear ran through them as they watched the ravens flying swiftly and directly towards them.

"Turn away," Aram commanded, "Turn away now! You must fight his power! Quick! Now! Turn away!"

They felt they were being pulled into his dark mind, grasped and drawn by invisible hands, by a power that was hard to resist. The world began to swirl uncontrollably. They heard Aram's words echoing in them and with a tremendous inner effort forced themselves to turn away from the pull of the Dark Wizard. They moved back from the window and felt his hold over them weakening. The ravens were closing fast now, almost at the window, and screeching with glee and keen anticipation.

"Get them!" screamed one of them eagerly.

"Quick!" called out Aram, "Out of the room you four. Run! Quick! Down the stairs."

There was a crash as the raven smashed through the window sending splinters of glass exploding into the room. At the same time the door slammed shut with a thud and the four friends dodged past the poor frozen cook and started descending the stairs. The second raven shot into the room and straight at Halo's head, cutting her on the forehead with its sharp beak. Silver blood trickled down her face as she staggered backwards. The first raven circled the room once and then attacked, diving at Aram.

He swung round and aimed his alicorn at the raven.

"Feathers!" shouted Aram.

Immediately the raven's feathers disappeared and unable to fly it fell heavily to the floor like an apple falling from a tree. It lay there motionless, knocked unconscious by the fall and looking smaller, skinny, rather scrawny and black. Even its wrinkled skin was black. Halo had recovered although the cut was still bleeding. The raven had turned quickly in the air and was swooping skilfully to attack her again with its beak outstretched.

"Feathers!" shouted Aram again, aiming his golden alicorn at it. As it fell featherless, Halo caught it with her silver alicorn and with a flick of her head threw it out of the broken window where it tumbled through the falling snow to the white ground far below.

"Let's go," said Halo urgently.

They left the Round Room and began to clatter down the winding stairs with the sound of their hooves echoing around the stone walls.

Whilst this was happening the four friends had reached the bottom of the stairs and were making their way through various rooms and halls towards the back door. Here and there people were standing and sitting, frozen mid-task, caught like flies in a web by the dark spell and whitened with sparkling frost like a sugar coating on a cake. They entered the large kitchen that was used to prepare food for all the people living in the palace - about fifty in all. It had two doors, as did most of the palace rooms, ten cookers, three tables and rows of shelves with a multitude of pots and containers, some containing food and some for cooking. As they were passing through the kitchen they heard a little voice.

"Amalek! Seph! It's me - Miriam. Up here."

They all looked and on a kitchen working surface, peeping out from behind a large shiny saucepan, was a tiny harvest mouse.

"Well how amazing," said Joog, clearly surprised, "Why aren't you frozen?"

"I don't know," replied Miriam with her high squeaky voice, "I've no idea. Everyone else is!"

"I know how," Amalek piped up, "You ran across Joog's wing when he was asleep. We found little scratchings on our drawings! The magic ink on your claws protected you."

Flop had quietly climbed onto the working surface, his fur was standing on end and his claws were ready to pounce as he stared at Miriam. She suddenly noticed him and darted back to the safety of the saucepan.

"Flop," said Miriam, her tiny voice suddenly loud and muffled as it echoed round the saucepan, "This is one of those times when we must stop fighting - surely. All of my family are frozen, and yours are too - we're in the same boat. We have a common enemy. We must work together and forget our differences. See - Joog has. Follow his wise example."

Flop had not heard because all his attention was focused on the saucepan with his body crouched low. Then Miriam poked her head out again, and with his eyes fixed intently on her, he moved; his back legs propelling him forwards. He was almost upon Miriam, who again disappeared quickly back behind the saucepan.

"Stop!" shouted Seph and he snatched Flop up in his arms. Seph stroked him on the head and spoke gently but firmly to him, "We mustn't fight each other. We have an enemy to overcome together, don't we?"

Flop wrestled inside himself with his instinct which seemed so strong. Then he decided.

"You're right," said Flop smiling at his own foolishness. He relaxed and his fur lay flat on his back once again and he withdrew his sharp claws, "Yes, you're right."

Miriam heard this and her whiskered nose poked out from behind the saucepan. Seph put Flop down on the working surface and he landed silently on his padded feet. He now showed no signs of hunting, moved towards Miriam, stretched his head forwards and they sniffed noses.

"Get on my back, Miriam," he said softly, "If you'd like a ride, that is."

Miriam cleverly climbed up Flops leg, up onto his back and nestled in his fur between his shoulder blades. The clomping of Aram and Halo's hoofed feet had been growing louder and they all looked up as the unicorns entered the kitchen. Amalek saw Halo's cut and took her pen out of her pocket.

"Shall I try this?" she asked, holding up the magic pen.

"Yes, please," said Halo, "It will work on us too."

And indeed it did. One touch with the magic ink and the cut vanished without leaving even a trace of a scar.

"Let's go," said Seph, "Before the Dark Wizard Troubler arrives."

"Wait," said Joog, "Is the front door locked? It would be best to keep him out as long as possible."

"We don't usually lock it," said Amalek.

Seph stepped towards the kitchen door, "I'll go," he announced.

At that very moment they heard the front door being opened. They all stopped moving and listened. All was utterly silent. They felt a wave of cold entering the kitchen and chilling their faces. It was the draught of air that sweeps though a building when a door is opened during winter. But it seemed more than that; a sinister numbing presence was seeping through the whole palace and it terrified them. The Dark Wizard Troubler had arrived.

"He won't know where we are, but still we'll have to move very quickly and very quietly," whispered Joog, as he glided over to a washing basket in the corner of the room and gripped a bundle of clothes in his powerful talons, "Here you are," he whispered to Aram and Halo, dropping the clothes beside them.

Amalek and Seph hastily tied a piece of clothing around each of their hoofs to stop their noisy clip clopping on the hard kitchen floor. Then the children very quickly pulled on some more clothes and dressed up Flop ready for the cold weather outside. The others did not need extra clothing: Miriam was cosy in Flop's fur and under his clothes; Joog had his thick plumage; and Aram and Halo were unaffected however cold or hot it might be. Within a few seconds they were ready. Then they heard a noise in the hall.

"Quick!" whispered Joog, "We'll go out of the back door... but be careful and as quiet as possible." Then he quickly looked around, "Where's Amalek?"

"In here," she replied. She was in the larder and busily grabbing some food and stuffing it into a bag.

"He's coming!" said Joog, flying into the larder and circling above her head, "Come now!"

The bag was only half full but she stopped immediately, slipped her arms through the straps and followed Joog back into the kitchen.

They crept quietly over to the far door which led into a long hall. This hall led to the back door and to escape. Joog led the way, at times hovering absolutely still in the air. Then came Halo, Amalek, Flop and Miriam, Seph and Aram. As they left the kitchen they heard the unmistakable noise of the other kitchen door being opened. This spurred them on down the hall. They moved quickly and quietly, with the clothes around the unicorn's hooves working well to muffle their clattering sound.

"When we're outside," whispered Aram, "Seph jump onto Halo's back. Amalek and Flop, with Miriam of course, can ride on my back. Then we'll gallop away as fast as we can."

They reached the massive wooden back door. Seph glanced back down the hall. There was no one there, but he knew the Dark Wizard Troubler must be coming because he was so close behind. The Princess turned the door handle.

"Oh no!" she whispered, "It's locked!"

Aram and Halo immediately swung around and pointed their magic alicorns down the hall, expecting the Dark Wizard Troubler to appear any second and a battle to begin. Seph looked at the large keyhole trying to think of a way to open it. He knew where the great key was kept; it was hanging up in a cupboard under the stairs and that was back down the hall, past the kitchen door and around a corner. He could run it in a few seconds.

"I'll get the key," he said turning and taking a step.

"No," said Amalek.

"It's alright…"

"No," Amalek insisted, "I know a better way," and she looked down at little Miriam who was peeping out from under Flop's clothes, "Miriam, do you think you could fit in the keyhole."

"I've opened a locked door before," said Miriam in her high squeaky voice and she pushed her way out from under Flop's clothes and stood up on her hind legs looking up at Amalek.

"Sshh," whispered Joog, "We don't want to be heard."

"Sorry," Miriam whispered, "Put me in the keyhole."

So whilst Aram and Halo stood protecting the others and ready for battle, Miriam squeezed her little body into the keyhole.

Clunk! Miriam's head appeared again. She squeezed out and jumped onto Flop's back.

"Well," whispered Flop, as Seph turned the door handle, "I'm glad you came along! You're so little too, but you've saved us all!"

Amalek glanced behind. There was still no sign of the Dark Wizard Troubler down the hall.

"Where is he?" she asked.

Seph replied quickly, "He must be searching other rooms in the palace. Perhaps he's gone up to the Round Room. Let's get out of here."

Together they pulled on the great door. It opened with a creak and snow tumbled in around their feet. An icy blast of freezing air and swirling snow met the seven friends as they moved outside into the blizzard. In front of them the deep snow seemed like a great white ocean stretching away into the storm. Without the unicorns to carry them travelling would be impossible.

At this moment they heard a noise behind them, back in the palace, of someone moving down the hall to the back door.

"Close the door!" shouted Seph. Amalek pulled with him and managed to half close it before it jammed on the snow that had tumbled in.

Amalek picked up Flop and hauled herself onto Aram's back. Seph mounted Halo and the two unicorns lowered their beautiful spiral alicorns. Just then two black ravens appeared out of the snowstorm that surrounded them and dived for attack. They went for the Prince and Princess.

Chapter 6

~ A Deep Snowdrift ~

"Look out!" shouted Flop, whose eyes were always quick to spot anything moving and had caught a glimpse of the two ravens through the thick descending snow. They were falling upon the Amalek and Seph like two black arrows.

But it was too late. The ravens swooped down, adjusted their flight with stunning skill as the blizzard tried to sweep them away and struck both children on their cheeks with sharp beaks, cutting them badly. Seph's cut crossed the smudge of magic ink on his face and it healed instantly, but Amalek's cut was painful. She clung on tightly to Aram's golden mane and the pain eased.

The ravens attacked again. One dived at Flop, but he was alert and ready, with eyes intent he tracked the raven as it sped towards him. It closed fast and Flop dodged his head to one side to avoid the raven's beak. Then, with lightening speed, his legs propelled him into the air, like the release of a spring. He caught the raven by the back of its neck in his mouth. Locked together they tumbled into the deep snow. Flop gripped on as he scrambled to his feet and shook his head from side to side, trying to shake the life out of the raven. Flop's teeth sunk in, through the black feathers and then through the skin. The raven cried out in pain. It stopped struggling and Flop dropped it in the snow. It lay there whimpering.

"Well done!" squeaked Miriam, who had clung onto Flop's neck.

The other raven attacked Aram, who could not turn his alicorn quickly enough to protect himself. It dived for his neck with its beak. Golden blood trickled from the cut. Joog was hovering and watching, waiting for an opportunity to attack. Just as the raven rose above Aram and turned for a second strike he fell upon it like a stone. He locked his powerful talons around it, gripping a wing and its angular head at the same time. It struggled violently and cried out. The pair of birds tumbled out of the air, swept sideways by the blast of the blizzard, crashing into a snow covered hedge. Snow tumbled all around them as the raven screeched in pain. Joog's claws held it trapped and it flapped its wings in panic to escape. Suddenly it broke free and was rising, dodging and weaving in the air with Joog in pursuit. Joog followed it, matching every twist and turn perfectly and was closing. A burst of speed and Joog recaptured his foe, closing his talons around it again, this time holding its wings to its sides. Joog gripped with all his might and his sharp talons pierced into the raven's body. A second later and its body went limp. The fight was over and Joog dropped it in the snow where it lay unmoving.

"Everybody ready?" called out Joog. He had to shout to be heard in the howling wind. The back door opened behind them.

"Yes… No!" shouted Seph looking around to check.

"Where's Flop?" cried Amalek, looking for him through the driving snow.

"Here!" replied Flop from below in the snow.

Amalek slipped off Aram's back and swept him up in her arms. She put him on Aram's back. Then with Aram's help who lifted up his front leg to make a step for her, she was up on his back again.

"Ready now?" called out Joog.

"Yes!" they chorused.

Snow was swirling in the wind and settling on their heads and clothes.

"Let's go!" cried Joog urgently. Glancing behind he had seen the intimidating frame of Jamaar in the doorway glaring at them with black eyes.

Aram and Halo lowered their alicorns again, and a pathway appeared in the snow. At the end of the pathway stood the Dark Wizard Troubler. Behind them Jamaar emerged from the palace and barked ferociously at them, slavering at the mouth and showing his sharp teeth. They were trapped. The Dark Wizard stared at them with his black threatening eyes. He looked sinister and menacing with his arms stretched above his head in victory. Then he laughed with selfish glee.

"Now," he shouted, "Let's sort this out once and for all!"

The Dark Wizard Troubler was still laughing with selfish glee, with his head tilted upward and squinting into the driving snow, when Aram shouted.

"Go, Halo, go!"

The two magnificent unicorns began trotting, then accelerating into a gallop along the pathway through the

snow that was piled up high on either side. The wind and
the falling snow whistled past the ears of the seven
friends and the clothes still tied around the unicorn's
hoofs fluttered vigorously like excited flags on a stormy
day. Jamaar was at their heels, chasing and snapping
frantically at them. The two unicorns were galloping side
by side and as fast as they could, unleashing all their
energy to accelerate towards the evil wizard. Clouds of
snow blew up into the cold air and surrounded them. The
Prince, Princess and Flop held on tightly to the gold and
silver manes and Joog flew skilfully above watching
everything below.

The Dark Wizard Troubler was taken completely by
surprise by Aram and Halo's sudden burst of speed. His
wicked laughter ceased and he lowered his head to look
at the cloud of snow rapidly approaching him. Just at that
moment a strong gust of wind blew the snow in his face,
making him blink. Looking through blurry eyes he did
not know what it was that was approaching him. He had
seen the two unicorns, but this was something different.
The unicorns had gone and here was something else
bearing down on him fast.

He tried to think of a spell, but what spell? As he
watched he saw a big white shape looming larger and
larger. He saw the two alicorns at the front and thought
they were eyes. He heard the flapping clothes and
thought it was the roar of some fierce creature. Was it a
monster attacking him? In his panic he began to call out.

"Black night black..."

That was as far as he got. The snow-cloud was upon
him. Aram caught him with his alicorn, lifted him off the
ground and carried him there for a few seconds. For a
split second their eyes met and the Dark Wizard lifted his

arm and began to swing a punch at Aram's head. Just before the punch landed Aram acted; with a tremendous fling upwards of his golden head he sent the Dark Wizard Troubler spinning upwards into the air. The evil wizard almost hit Joog, who gave him a fierce peck as he flew by. He tumbled on the wind through the thick falling snow back towards the palace. He landed near the palace wall in a deep snowdrift, which cushioned his fall like landing on a bed of feathers. As he lay there on his back, stunned and surrounded by deep snow he felt the pain where Joog had pecked him, the owl's sharp beak ripping through the sleeve of his robe and into his arm. He glanced at the wound and clenched his teeth in anger. It was a nasty jagged cut and a patch of blood was blooming in the snow like a bright red rose.

"That wretched owl!" he muttered to himself clutching his arm, "I'll get him - and the others. I'll get them all."

Meanwhile Jamaar was still chasing the unicorns with all his might as they dropped down the hill from the back of the palace. The change he had undergone had given him such strength that his legs were incredibly fast and strong and he was still right up behind Aram and Halo as they galloped side by side. It was like a whirlwind of snow clouds as they sped along. Jamaar was closing, but then some of the clothes flew off the two unicorn's hooves and a towel landed on Jamaar's face. Momentarily he could not see. He slowed and shook his head and the towel flew off. He quickly caught up again and when he felt he was within reach he summoned all his energy and leapt at Halo's heels with his great heavy jaws open. His sharp teeth flashed as his jaws snapped closed to bring down his prey. He missed by a whisker and he prepared for a second attempt. He released a burst of speed as a surge of energy rippled through his body. His jaws opened. Then Halo, who was aware of his first attempt, suddenly slowed down surprising the frantic dog on her heels. Jamaar tried to slow, skidded on the snow. His head hit Halo's legs, his jaw meeting her rising hoof with a thud, jerking his head back, knocking him off balance and sending him spinning and tumbling sideways into the snow. The chase was over.

For a moment he lay there, exhausted and angry. Then he scrambled to his feet, with his chest heaving as his lungs gulped in the cold air. His legs were shaky from the sprint and worst of all bright red blood was dripping from his battered jaw into the white snow. His jaw was numb from the blow and the cold. He glanced at the unicorns who were already a distance away and he knew he had failed. He felt despondent and miserable in his failure as he turned and started walking back up the hill to his master.

The Dark Wizard Troubler was now hauling himself onto his feet in deep frustration. One part of his plan had failed and this made him furious.

"They will pay for this," he whispered to himself, his eyes narrowing with determination, "I will get them, and then they will pay."

As he hissed out these words he looked up and around, with the dim hope that he would be able to see them and then to follow, but all he saw was white. He had plunged into a deep snowdrift. He was surrounded on all sides by snow which towered up above his head. The snow that he had caused and that was meant to harm others and win him the kingdom was now hemming him in. This increased his anger even more and he let out thunderous scream of frustration and collapsed onto his knees shaking with fury. He realised that to try to pursue them was now impossible; they would be far away already. They had escaped.

Chapter 7

~ The Great Crack to the
Centre of Ruddha ~

A ram and Halo sped down the hill amidst the whirling snow cloud and headed towards Blue Lake. The falling snow had eased now and the ferocity of the fierce wind was slightly less intense. At the foot of the hill where the slope levelled off Aram and Halo slowed down a little as they knew they were well clear of the Dark Wizard Troubler and Jamaar. However, they wanted to put as much distance as possible between them and the evil intruder and therefore felt reluctant to stop for a rest yet. He could possibly dispatch some more of his ravens after them so it was best to keep going. By slowing down it made the ride much easier for the passengers who had been clinging on tightly when the magnificent unicorns were at full speed so that they were not swept off and left behind.

Ever since Amalek and Seph were very young they had often sat on the backs of the unicorn statues and imagined themselves galloping at great speeds, escaping from imaginary foes or going into battle. Now it was actually happening and the ride was thrilling. They had never travelled so fast before and felt invigorated by the excitement. Inside the snow cloud it was warm and comfortable, even though the wind blew through their hair and their clothes flapped as they sped along. Looking ahead they could see the unicorn's alicorns which were gently glowing. They were beautifully carved with intricate patterns along their spiralling surface as they thinned to a fine point at the end.

Amalek began to feel the pain on her cheek where the raven had attacked her. She touched it with her hand and then grabbed Halo's mane again. She had felt the damp warmth of blood and a jagged cut. She knew she had to cling on and so the cut could not be treated until they stopped. The most important thing was to get away as far as possible so she did her best to ignore it.

The two unicorns were galloping side by side. Amalek and Seph looked across at each other and exchanged a smile which said, "This is amazing." Then Amalek glanced at Flop. He was not at all at ease travelling so fast and with the rising and falling motion of the back of this great unicorn. At first his eyes were wide and frightened as he watched the scene flashing by through the snow cloud. He much preferred to control his travelling and the speed himself. But with great effort he had begun to get more used to it now, although his eyes still betrayed a feeling of apprehension and the end of his tail twitched. Miriam's eyes and nose peeped out from under Flop's clothes.

"Are we nearly there?" she squeaked, "Are we nearly there?"

"Patience," came the deep-voiced reply from Aram, breathing heavily after all the exertion, "We're well on the way. Now just sit back and relax, little Miriam."

Aram and Halo kept a steady pace and soon they reached Blue Lake which was a vast flat area of whiteness with clouds of powdered snow blowing across the surface. The entire Lake had frozen over and the snow had settled layer upon layer. Today it was 'White Lake'. The unicorns decided to go straight across as they knew that the surface would be frozen. This would be much quicker than going around the edge and as they moved onto it the sound of their pounding hooves changed.

They passed between Sratt Island and the tiny Isle of Ig. They were close enough to see them through the snow cloud. The Isle of Ig was low and flat, whereas Sratt Island rose in a smooth white gradient away from them and then fell away abruptly at the towering cliffs on its western shore. The sound of the hooves changed again as they passed from the lake to skirt the edge of the frozen Marshes of Macaroone. They crossed a river, a solid channel of snow-covered ice and then Lake Clase-Moy, much smaller than Blue Lake, which rested at the foot of the Great Mountain. This monumental mass of rock was the largest mountain in a range which ran east to west across the north of the Kingdom of Gems. These were the Snowpeak Mountains and soon they were climbing up and into a wonderful forest where all the trees were laden with snow. As they sped past some of the branches sprung upwards freed from their burden as the snow was dislodged by the turbulent air their speed created. Patches would slide off like mini avalanches and crash into the snow below.

As they rose higher into the mountains the snow became a fierce driving blizzard. Here it was deeper which made galloping impossible for the unicorns and they were forced to slow down. Where the snow was deepest it reached their chests and they could only move at walking speed. For most travellers it would have been virtually impossible to proceed but by pointing their magic alicorns the unicorns could plough a pathway through. Then the snow would be less deep again and they could speed up, only to be slowed by another drift.

The mountains were completely robed in white and every jagged rocky crag was transformed to smooth curves. Layers of snow coated everything as the racing snow whipped through the air in front of them like a mad rush of a million white bees.

They stopped high up on a mountain side when they found a sheltered spot under some trees. Here they were protected from the wild wind and the driving snow. It was like a peaceful haven after the blast of the blizzard, and only the occasional flake found its way into their shelter.

Joog landed in the tree just above their heads and Aram and Halo turned to look back towards the palace. They could just about see Lake Clase-Moy, but then the scene faded into the grey curtain of the blizzard so they could see no further. The riders stayed on the unicorns' warm backs and looked around too. Amalek stroked Flop who was pleased that the galloping had stopped and started purring happily. Then suddenly he felt a wave of sadness wash through him. He felt homesick as he remembered Tilly and their five kittens and in his mind's eye he could see them there in the cellar, completely unmoving and icy cold to touch. He felt his eyes dampen with tears and blinked sending a couple falling through the chilly air and pattering onto the soft snow.

"What's the matter, Flop?" asked Amalek's kind voice. This jolted him out of his sad thoughts.

"Oh, it's just my family..."

"I know, but we have to leave them to help them... and everyone trapped in the spell. It's the best thing we can do for them," and she stroked him again.

Amalek's words lifted Flop out of his sadness as he realised that this journey was for the sake of his family and all the inhabitants of the Kingdom of Gems. It had to be done. It was the right thing to do and meant there was hope for the kingdom and for his family. So he decided to put all his energies into helping their quest.

"Are we there? Are we there?" squeaked little Miriam.

"Soon," answered Aram with a sense of looking after his tiny companion with care, "Just beyond these mountains we will reach the border."

"Now," piped up Seph, "Who's got a cut that needs healing?" He took the top off his magic pen and looked at Amalek. Blood had trickled down her cheek and dried, but the cut looked deep.

"Good idea," Amalek replied and Halo stepped closer so that Seph could reach across. He ran the pen along the cut and the effect was a miraculous instant healing. She felt the pain ease and then fade completely. With some snow she washed the blood off her face.

Then Seph reached down and began to draw it along the wound on Aram's neck.

"Thank you," said Aram, "But hold on a moment. Can you find any drops of golden blood there?"

"Yes," said Seph, wondering why, "There are two."

"Perfect," Aram nodded, "That's one for you and one for Amalek."

The two drops had run out of the cut and dried on his

golden skin. Seph carefully eased them off and held them in the palm of his hand.

"But why?" asked Seph.

"Well, you see, they're magic. Take them with you."

"Thank you," said Amalek and Seph together. Then Amalek added, "But how do they work?"

Aram dipped his stately golden head closer to the two children, "I'll explain later how you can use them... when we get to the border."

"Thank you," said Seph again, stroking the unicorn's soft golden mane as he put one golden drop into a pocket with a flap that buttoned down. Then he reached across to pass the other one to Amalek. She also put it into a safe pocket and buttoned the flap. Then she slipped the bag off her back and let it fall onto the snow.

"Anyone hungry?" she announced.

"What've you got?" asked Seph.

"There's some bread, but I'm not sure what else because I was just grabbing the closest things."

She took out the food carefully and spread it on the snow. There were three loaves of bread and two pots of honey, one half full and the other about a third. Then she drew out two other jars and a small packet. She held them up in turn.

"Tunroot... ghicky nuts... flour..."

"Flour?" exclaimed Seph smiling, "And ghicky nuts...yuk!"

Amalek smiled back, "Well, I just grabbed... but, hang on..." She reached into the bottom of the bag and lifted out three spoons and a squashed packet and held it up triumphantly, "And... cheese."

"Now, that's more like it!" said Flop, standing up and sniffing the cheese.

Together, they rested in their sheltered spot under the trees and ate. They tried to quench their thirst with mouthfuls of snow as they gazed in silence into the white scene. They found that the melted snow only created a tiny amount of water, but it was still refreshing.

Under normal circumstances the scene would have been beautiful, but today the shadow of the evil wizard was with them. They felt the burden of his terrible power and the doubt in their hearts that they could stand against him and win. They were on edge; he might be following, or watching them and waiting to strike. Throughout the kingdom the land had changed with the casting of the spell which had spread its dark influence everywhere. Just as the nighttime falls upon the land like a blanket covering everything, where nothing can avoid it, so had the spell spread a sinister heaviness through the kingdom right out to the borders. They all felt this, of course, but now, as they sheltered and ate in silence, something arose in them to defy and stand up against it. It was a strong sense of determination to fight and not allow this evil wizard to just walk in and take over. They would fight him whatever the cost. The seven friends were bound together in this difficult mission and they were bound together in love for each other and for their loved ones trapped by the spell in the Kingdom of Gems.

The light was fading quickly now, turning the white scene into grey and then black. Around them the mountains seemed threatening, like huge giants looking down on them.

"We'd better go," announced Joog from the tree above, "That's if you're rested enough." They all nodded, "Good..." he continued, "Because he may be following... he and that dog of his, and maybe ravens too. He could have more ravens. *And* there's his komodo dragon. We've travelled fast, overall, but... well... we don't want to risk him catching up, do we?" Again they all nodded their agreement, "Also, there's this snow... we don't want to be snowed in, do we?"

"Definitely not," said Amalek as she quickly put the uneaten food back into her bag.

Halo turned her head towards Aram, and her voice rang with gentleness and beauty, like sweet warm rain on a spring day, "Side by side, Aram?" she asked.

"Yes," he replied, "Let's go."

They walked out from their sheltered place under the trees and into the driving snow. The icy wind blew the unicorns' flowing manes and caught the children's clothes making them flap and shake. Aram and Halo began to trot in perfect unison, but then they hit a snowdrift and had to slow. They powered through and then gradually accelerated away. Joog watched from the branch in the tree and let them build up speed before jumping off. At first he glided and with a few strong flaps he was catching them up and then flying directly above. Seph looked up and waved and Joog dipped a wing in reply. Once again the seven friends were speeding along through the wintry mountain scene. The four riders were surrounded by the snow cloud and within that they enjoyed the warm glow of the unicorns' gold and silver light.

Aram and Halo were strong, forcing their way skilfully through the rugged terrain, from valley to mountain slope and then down again. It was not until dawn was beginning to spread a gentle light across the smooth snow-covered slopes that they stopped to briefly to rest in a sheltered spot. Amalek and Seph were so tired that they nodded off to sleep on the unicorns backs. Flop dozed too, as well as Miriam, who was still snuggled in Flop's long fur.

After half and hour Joog announced loudly, "Time to go!"

Once again the thought that the Dark Wizard Troubler might be pursuing them stirred them into action and soon they were on their way again. They travelled through the day, stopping only twice and by evening the land began to level off. They were moving onto a flat region called the Northern Borderlands.

Aram and Halo slowed and the snow cloud surrounding them thinned. They could now see further, and up ahead they noticed how the snow suddenly stopped, both the deep snow on the ground and the falling snow. They knew this was the border which divided the Kingdom of Gems from the next kingdom. Aram and Halo slowed to a halt and in a second the snow cloud had been whipped away by the wind. Joog landed on Seph's shoulder and the travellers looked around.

"Are we there? Are we there?" asked Miriam with her shrill squeak.

Aram answered, having to shout above the whistling wind, his deep voice contrasting with Miriam's, "We've reached the border, little Miriam."

"That's amazing!" exclaimed Seph, "Just across the border it's as hot as summer. Look!"

They were all staring across and even in the twilight as the sun set they could all see the extraordinary change that happened only a few feet away. Flowers were in bloom, the grass was a rich summer green and there were flies and bees buzzing in the air. At the border itself, where the snow stopped abruptly piled up as if against an invisible wall not even one tiny star-shaped flake fell into the next kingdom. It was a strange contrast; they were standing in a snow storm with a strong wind driving into their faces and deep snow all around, whilst a few feet away calm summer weather filled the air.

"It's called Summertime Kingdom," shouted Joog, "It's always summer there."

"Well," Halo began. Even though she was shouting to be heard her voice was still soft and kind, "You still have a long and important journey ahead of you."

"And you too?" yelled Amalek. She thought that Aram and Halo would take them all the way and there was disappointment in her question.

"We are not of that kingdom," replied Halo nodding across the border, "We belong here and our duty is here. Our magic would disappear immediately if we stepped across the border. In fact we can't... we'd be statues again."

"But... but..." began Amalek, shouting through the blizzard, "How do you know? Are you sure?"

"It's clearly laid down in The Ancient Laws of the Kingdoms," replied Halo, "And they cannot be broken. We can never cross the border."

"I see," shouted Amalek, "But be careful, won't you? I mean with that wizard around."

"We will," shouted Halo, shaking her silver mane and releasing tiny silver sparkles.

Joog was still perched on Seph's shoulder. He stepped off and flapped his wings to help him climb up Aram's mane and onto his head. Turning towards Halo he shouted, "Yes, you must remember how cunning he is. For all we know... he may be almost upon us now."

"Don't worry about us," Aram joined in, "We'll be

alright. Now… where are those golden drops, you two?"

The Prince and Princess took them carefully out of their pockets and clutched them tightly. They did not want them to be blown away or fall into the deep snow.

Amalek and Seph stepped across, out of the deep snow and howling wind and onto the grass where the air was warm and comfortable. Immediately they smelt the sweet scent of flowers that hung in the air and felt the gentle warmth on their skin. Aram was standing right next to the border now with snow whipping past his face.

"Now," he shouted, "Hold them towards me in the palms of your hands." Halo moved next to Aram and they both pointed their spiralled alicorns at the golden drops. The two children watched with excitement as they saw them glow in the fading light. Then they felt them tingle and tickle the skin on their hands.

"All done," shouted Halo, "If you need a little magic just rub them in your fingers. They'll know what to do. But you can only use them once so save them for real emergencies, like a matter of life or death, alright?" They both nodded, "Hopefully you won't need to use them, but you never know."

"Thank you," chorused the children together. They slipped them back into their pockets and buttoned the flaps for safety.

Joog flew over next and landed on Amalek's shoulder. The snow which had settled on his white feathers immediately melted and turned into droplets of water, which sprayed off as he shook his body. Next was Flop, with Miriam clinging to his fur. He jumped off Halo's strong back, across the border and onto the grass, landing gently on his padded feet. Flop was very interested in the constant summer weather as he loved comfort and warmth. It was like a hot summer's evening and the sunset stained everything red as it cast its last rays of the day across the land. They began to feel hot and started taking some layers of clothes off.

Flop was relieved to be out of the snow and if the horror of the Dark Wizard Troubler and his spell had not been on his mind he would have been purring with contentment. "This is amazing," he said, lying down and stretching on the grass.

"Amalek?" asked Halo, "We finished all the Tunroot, didn't we?"

"Yes," Amalek replied.

"Good. You should fill the jar with snow. Wash the jar with snow first… you know how strong tunroot is… and then pack it full of snow. It'll melt quickly over there and then you'll have at least a little water to drink."

Amalek looked in her bag, pulled out the empty jar and did as Halo suggested. She placed the jar of snow back in her bag. Then she took out the two honey jars. With a spoon she scraped the remaining honey from one jar into the other and filled the empty jar with snow as well.

"Good-bye and good luck," called out Aram across the border, "Catch!" and he jerked his head towards them and something small flew from his alicorn. At first the wind caught it but as soon as it crossed it flew toward Seph who caught it in one hand. He opened his hand and saw a tiny silver unicorn. "It's a whistle," explained Aram, "Blow the alicorn and we will hear. Use it when you return and we'll come to meet you. Now go!"

"Good-bye!" they called back. Then Amalek found tears bubbling up in her eyes and she suddenly jumped back into the snow and the howling wind and gave Halo an affectionate hug around her neck. A moment later and the five friends were all back over the border and hugging Aram and Halo.

"You must go now," shouted Aram, and they jumped back into the warmth.

Aram and Halo turned and galloped away, with a shout of "Tally-Ho!" and a white cloud of snow. They watched the snow cloud disappear into the haze of the driving snow.

"They've gone," said Seph, "Aren't they wonderful?"

"Yes, and we'll be meeting them again, do not fear," said Joog, now perched on Seph's shoulder, "But we must press on... and keep our wits about us. I would guess that the Dark Wizard Troubler knows where we are heading and may be following. He must know who lives here, therefore he must know that we are trying to get help from him."

Together they turned away and started walking down a path into Summertime Kingdom.

"Would he be frightened of Wizard Elzaphan?" asked Seph.

Joog considered this for a moment, "I would have thought he would be... yes," he answered, "He *should* be. He will do his best to stop us reaching him, no doubt about that."

"But…" said Amalek thoughtfully, "He can't leave the Kingdom of Gems without his spell going with him, can he? The spell would end. So we are safe."

"*He* can't leave, you are right," Joog's round eyes were fixed on Amalek, "But we are not safe. He will be planning ways of stopping us... probably right now. And his ravens, those evil slaves of his, *can* cross the border, so we are definitely not safe. He could send that dog too. And there's that other great creature I saw, the komodo dragon." He paused, thinking it through, "He needs to get rid of us for two reasons. Firstly he knows that as long as we're alive we will try to stop him. And secondly, if he knows about the gems and I bet he does, he cannot steal them if we *are* alive. Our lives protect the gems. I'm sure he's after those gems."

Amalek and Seph looked at each other and wondered what the future might hold for them and although it frightened them to think about it they felt ready to do their best. So the little party, now reduced from seven to five and all weary from lack of sleep, began their journey to the heart of Summertime Kingdom. This was their destination, for to the north of the kingdom, on Keill Island, lived the great Wizard Elzaphan. Their pace was much slower now without the speedy unicorns to ride on and as they travelled the night closed in. Gradually the sky dimmed as the darkness dampened the colours of the day into greys and they began to think about settling somewhere for the night. Soon they picked up a rough path which Joog knew headed in the right direction, and as they walked they looked out for a sheltered spot where they could stop.

Suddenly the twilight stillness was shaken by a distant roar.

"What was that?" exclaimed Amalek as she looked towards the direction of the sound. It came from their right, the east, and they all gazed that way but it was too dark to see. There were more sounds of roaring and then howling as well which echoed around them in the warm air. Although the sounds were distant they carried a frightful sense of aggression. Amalek shivered.

"What is it?" she asked again, looking up at Joog.

"Oh that," said Joog, sounding completely

unperturbed, "That's the bears and wolves fighting. There's a forest over there, called Juran Forest. See it?" he asked.

They nodded.

"Well, "Joog continued, "That's where they live, the bears and wolves. And they've been at war for as long as I know. The bears are massive creatures and no one goes in the forest for fear of them and the wolves."

"Why do they fight?" asked Seph.

"I've been told," Joog replied, "That they're fighting for the land. Both groups want the whole forest for themselves."

Just then there was another huge roar from deep within the forest, followed by a screech... and then silence.

Joog saw the alarm on their faces, "Don't worry, they never leave the forest. Now, come on you land creatures, you need to walk faster."

They increased their pace along the path. It was not until they had been walking for over an hour that they saw through the darkness the ideal spot to spend the night. Fairly close to the path there was a large outcrop of granite rock. It sloped back underneath itself to form an overhang and there was just enough room for all of them. A thick mass of bushes grew all around the rock that meant they would be hidden as well as sheltered. They were all tired after the journey and so they quickly clambered in and huddled together feeling enclosed and safe in their hideout. Amalek opened her bag and passed the food around as well as the jars with just a little water in them from the melted snow.

The memory of the Dark Wizard Troubler was still with them. It was like a shadow that could not be left behind. It haunted them. When they looked out towards the bushes they kept imagining him in the dark shapes of the leaves and when they closed their eyes to sleep his frightening image would appear even more clearly. As Amalek and Seph began to drift off to sleep the same scene flashed into both their minds. The Dark Wizard Troubler was staring up at them through the falling snow and they heard him scream at them, "I've got you now!" The fear gripped them like a vice. The evil wizard released the two black ravens from his sleeves which flew like arrows towards them with their beaks ready for attack. Then, to their relief, the image disappeared as they heard Joog's gentle voice.

"We need sleep," said Joog, "But we need to keep watch as well. We must keep watch just in case. I have nighttime eyes and so does Flop, as well as the ears for listening, so we will take turns." He looked at Flop.

"That's fine with me," said Flop, "Shall I start? I often stay awake at night, and you haven't slept at all yet."

"Thank you, Flop, but I feel wide awake. I'm happy to start."

"Alright," answered Flop, "Just wake me up when it's my turn," and he settled comfortably down between Amalek and Seph.

After the escape of the Prince and Princess the Dark Wizard Troubler had spent the night in Candara Palace. He had been so angry with Jamaar for failing to catch the unicorns that he had kicked him down the cellar steps and locked the door and it was not until the middle of the next day that he had let him out. He ignored Jamaar's sporadic barking and shouting through the morning as he wandered around the palace and wondered what to do. When he came across the room with the King's throne he smiled. He entered and sat on the throne for about half an hour enjoying the feeling that he was now king. Then he climbed the winding stairs to the Round Room where the blizzard was blowing through the window that had been smashed by the ravens. He broke up a chair and used the wood to board it up, throwing the rest on the dying embers of the fire. Then he sat and stared at the frozen King and Queen for a while. Suddenly he stood up and bowed low to the King.

"Your Majesty," he said in mock respect, "You are relieved of your duties. You have been... er... succeeded by a stronger man."

He stepped closer to the King until their faces were only a few inches apart. He looked at the King's frozen sightless eyes with an expression of disgust, "You have filled this palace with sentimental love, but *I* will rule with real power."

He turned away and grabbed another chair and swung it at the King with all his might. It smashed into the solid figure and broke up spraying bits of wood and splinters all around, leaving the King rocking very slightly for a moment. He turned to the Queen, stepped forwards and bowed to her.

"Your Royal Majesty," he said, "You look... pale. Are you a little under the weather today? Is the weather too cold for you?" He reached out and touched her on the face, running his fingers down her cheek and collecting some frost on the tips, "You *are* cold, Your Most Royal Majesty. You should take more care of yourself... because sneezing can be fraught with dangerous implications.

Didn't you know?"

He rubbed the tips of his fingers and his thumb together until the frost had dissolved.

"I'll deal with you two later," he snapped, and then turned and marched out of the room and down the winding stairs.

He went to the cellar door, unlocked it and then called down into the darkness.

"We're going back to Old Howard's house, dog. I can't stand it here any longer. Come on."

Jamaar ran up the stairs and followed his master. The Dark Wizard opened the great front door to a blast of icy wind and driving snow.

"Come on, dog."

Jamaar was terrified of the Dark Wizard so he quickly trotted out and into the wintry scene and they began battling their way through the deep snow. They did not talk at all as they travelled because the blizzard was strong which made communication impossible without shouting. They were both sulking in the misery of their failure.

They walked down the snow covered Palace Path, but instead of entering Candara they cut across the southern edge of the Flatsage Farmlands in a direct line towards Old Howard's house. Two hours later the Dark Wizard entered the house and shook the snow off his cloak. Jamaar padded in close behind, then stopped and glanced upwards on hearing the commotion of the sounds of cackling birds from a room above.

"What's that?" he whispered to the Dark Wizard.

"Ravens," he replied coldly, "Now come in here."

They were both extremely tired because the journey back from the palace had been an exhausting fight through the deep snow. They both walked wearily into the room where the spell had been cast and collapsed, the wizard into Old Howard's smelly old chair and Jamaar onto an old rug which was now his bed in the corner of the room. Almost straight away they fell asleep and neither woke until night had descended. The Dark Wizard Troubler was the first to stir and then to wake.

"Jamaar," he said, looking into the dark corner, "Are you there?"

This woke Jamaar whose sleep was light and he jumped up immediately, "Yes, master," he said stepping out of the dark corner and waiting for a command.

The wizard lit the two black candles, one on the floor and the other on the mantelpiece. He pulled up his sleeve and unwound a bandage from his wounded arm, letting it drop onto the floor. The blood had dried and was forming a scab.

"That attempt to stop the enemy escaping didn't go too well," he commented, his sharp icy voice echoing slightly in the shadowy room, "Not as expected, shall we say. I'm disappointed... bitterly disappointed. As for you," he gave Jamaar a chilling glare, "As for you... next time you get the chance don't just let them get away. Fight!"

"But, master, I almost got them," snarled Jamaar, "Almost... another centimetre and I'd have caught that unicorn."

"But you missed," hissed the wizard with venom, "And they escaped. Now we have to deal with that. Horrik could've done better than you, even with her short legs," he stared hatefully at Jamaar, "Disappointing!" he snapped, "I was sure you'd catch them. You reckon they're heading for... who did you say... a wizard called

Elzaphan?"

"Yes, master."

"Are you sure," the wizard stared at Jamaar intently, "Are you sure that's his name?"

"Yes, master. He lives in the next kingdom, north of here, in the direction they headed. He's visited here, so... well... it makes sense that they'd go to him for help."

The Dark Wizard shook his head and narrowed his eyes in hate. A frown furrowed his pale-skinned forehead, "I've heard of him. He's powerful, but I have more power. If they are going to him then we will meet resistance, and that is better avoided. Therefore we must get them before they reach this Wizard Elzaphan."

"I can hardly wait, master," growled Jamaar, with loathing in his tone.

"That's better. Revenge is a good motivator. And we *will* get them," the Dark Wizard was thinking it out, "They think they've got away. Well, they'll have a surprise that will teach them not to mess with me."

He left the room and returned a few minutes later with a large bowl of food for Jamaar.

"You'd better have this," he said sharply, and he placed it on the wooden floor with a clatter, "You need your strength."

Jamaar's saliva started running when he smelt the food and he dropped his head close to the bowl and took a large bite. He immediately yelped with pain, letting the food drop out and onto the floor as he opened his mouth and jerked his head up.

"Oh, my jaw!" he cried, "That unicorn! That stupid unicorn!"

As the pain faded down he looked at the food again. The smell filled his nostrils, exciting his hunger even more and so he dropped his head and sniffed. He started eating again, but this time he was cautious, moving his jaw slowly whilst taking small bites. When he had finished and was licking the bowl clean the Dark Wizard picked a large bone out of a box on the shelf and threw it onto Jamaar's rug. He was still hungry and he jumped at it as if he was hunting a live creature. In his excitement forgot all about his jaw and bit hard into the bone. He yelped again as he felt a sharp stabbing pain, dropped the bone and growled. Then, slowly and carefully, he began chewing, his face wincing with pain at each movement.

Directly underneath where the Dark Wizard Troubler was sitting, Horrik was lying down and dozing in a dank cellar. She was tethered, as always, by the metal lead which was looped around a water pipe and securely fixed. The cellar was dirty, thick with dust, and very dilapidated. As well as the entrance from inside the house, where a door opened to some steps which descended into the cellar, there was a second entrance. This was a door which opened to some outdoor steps which climbed up to ground level. This door let in a little light from a glass window in the daytime, but now that it was night it was very dark. The walls were damp and so were the wooden floorboards. Many of these boards were so rotten that they had crumbled away leaving large gaps in the floor where directly underneath a rubble of stones and rocks could be seen.

Horrik lay in the dark beside a wall where her movement was restricted by the chain. She hated being shackled like a prisoner but it was not always like this. In the beginning, some time ago, when the evil wizard had captured her and forced her into his service he spoke to her explaining how it would work.

"You are lucky," he had snarled at her, "Very fortunate; honoured, in fact, to be selected to work for me. But there are certain... mmm... shall we say important rules you need to know. One... you obey me completely. You do *exactly* what I say. Two... if I am not with you for some reason to tell you what to do, then you do what you know I would want you to do. Three you never, *never* try to escape. Follow these and all will be well with you. Break any rule and I will inflict pain upon you that will make all your scales shudder right down your body. If you escape I will hunt you and then strike you down.... you will be extinguished, just like a candle flame can be snuffed out. It is that easy for me I promise you. Understand?"

Horrik had said she understood and for while all had been well. She had enjoyed working for him in his evil doings and she had been rewarded with many sizable meals. She had been allowed to run free and had followed the rules exactly, until one day something unfortunate happened. She had taken the initiative, following the second rule and had pursued an enemy who then managed to slip away and hide. Her master, the Dark Wizard, had thought she was trying to escape. Try as she did she could not prove anything to him and he would not believe her story despite her pleadings of innocence. He had inflicted terrible pain upon her by using a rope to hang her up by her tail for three days in the hot sun until she fell unconscious and was on the very verge of death. When he got her down she fell to the ground and on waking she found herself tethered by the black metal chain.

After this he no longer trusted her, and her dark mind flooded with frustration and anger when she thought of how misunderstood she was and how, as a consequence,

she had lost her freedom.

This was all bad enough, but the final straw was this dog, this Jamaar, stepping into her shoes and taking over her rightful place. As she lay tethered in the damp cellar she mulled over these things and tried to work out some way of getting revenge. Her mind kept returning to the dog and all her malice and pent up fury focused upon him. But there was nothing she could do at the moment, unfortunately, so she would have to rest in her anger for now and wait for the right chance. Then she would strike.

In the room above her master was thinking about what to do next.

"Right," the evil wizard said decisively, "I have a plan…"

Jamaar jumped up and padded over.

"I don't need you," the wizard began, "Not at the moment. Not yet. Soon, yes. So get back in your corner and wait."

Jamaar turned and walked back to his corner, slumpng down on his rug.

"We can help!" a voice from the shelf announced. It was one of the ravens. Their swellings had gone down and they looked rested and full of energy.

"Yes, I know," said the wizard cunningly. A plan was already forming in his evil mind, "I hadn't forgotten you. Come with me and join the others," and then his voice grew cold and menacing, "I'll send you on a mission which will deal with the enemy once and for all."

He released the buckle on a bag that was lying on the floor and reached in with his hand. He lifted out a black metal chain. Hanging below, on the chain, was a compass, which looked just like a pocket watch, except it was a made of the same black metal. On the hinged lid that covered the glass face was a delicately engraved coat of arms which was his coat of arms. He stuffed the compass into his pocket and opened the door. The ravens jumped off the shelf and with a single flap of their jet-black wings swooped skilfully though into the hall and up the stairs to join the others.

Joog's night watch passed and with a few hours of darkness still left he nudged Flop with his beak to wake him.

"Your turn, Flop," Joog whispered. Flop looked comfortable and warm snuggled in between the two children with his head resting on Amalek's leg. He opened his eyes sleepily. Seph moved in his sleep and then settled again.

"Just give me a moment to wake up," Flop whispered, as he stood up and stretched, first his back legs and then the front.

"I'm ready," he whispered to Joog.

Joog slipped in between the children and closed his eyes and Flop sat just in front of them and looked out at the bushes. The bushes were very close and blocked his view but he found a small gap to look through and out into the depths of the night. In the darkness his pupils dilated fully and his ears flicked this way and that, his sharp sense of hearing picking up the slightest of noises. Every so often he heard a wolf howling in Juran Forest behind them. Then the roar of a bear was followed by other animal noises in the distance. Flop shivered as the sounds echoed in the stillness of Summertime Kingdom's warm air and he began to feel an uncomfortable edge to the calmness of the night. A sinister presence, faint at first, was tainting the atmosphere as it loomed and settled around them, heavy and unfriendly. Flop fidgeted uneasily. The time seemed to drag, like pulling a spoon through thick treacle and he wished the night away and the bright dawn to arrive, but this just seemed to make it pass slower than ever.

Flop was alert picking up every slightest noise with his sensitive hearing and then he heard something that made his ears flick in its direction. He instantly tensed and became utterly still, statuesque like an Egyptian sphinx and staring toward the sound. It sounded like footsteps moving along the path. Someone was walking from the direction of the Kingdom of Gems. The steps became louder and then stopped. There was a long pause before something happened that made Flop's heartbeat accelerate and thump in his throat. The steps started again, but this time quieter, on soft grass now. He wished he could see, but the bushes blocked his view. The steps seemed to be moving towards them.

He listened.

The steps slowed and now there were noises in the bushes in front of him. Flop listened and stared. The sound stopped and then began again, moving closer. When they had chosen this place it had seemed good to be concealed behind these bushes. Now he wished the bushes were not there and then at least he would be able to see what it was. The sound moved closer still. Were they being hunted? Flop quietly nudged the others to wake them.

Amalek opened her eyes, "What is it, Flop?" she said sleepily and immediately the sound in the bushes stopped.

"Sshh, be quiet," whispered Flop "There's something over there," and he gave his head a tiny nod toward the bushes in front.

They were all awake now, huddled together and keeping still. Amalek and Seph stared blindly into the dark bushes. Then the sound happened again, the quiet rustling of leaves as someone brushed past, closer still and getting closer with every second.

Miriam's tiny head peeped out from Flop's fluffy fur on his neck, "What is it?" she whispered into his ear, "What is it?" Again the sounds stopped.

Silence.

Then, again, they heard sounds, rustling and they all stared, straining to see. It was so close now. Then they recoiled together as there was the crack of a twig snapping underfoot right in front of them. They all looked down together and saw the end of a boot underneath the leaves of the bushes. They braced themselves for something to happen and the Prince and Princess unbuttoned the flaps on their pockets and reached in for the magic drops. It was so close now that they could hear breathing and they held their breath so as not to be heard. Fear gripped them. Exactly together, Amalek and Seph closed their hands around the magic drops. For a moment, which seemed like an eternity, nothing moved.

Then there was a step... and another. The bushes shook as they heard the footsteps move away, across the grass and onto the path. Then two steps on the path and another pause. Amalek closed her eyes, gripped her hand tightly around the magic drop and wished that the steps would start again, walking away and leaving them alone. The steps began and gradually grew fainter, moving into

Summertime Kingdom. They began to breath freely again, but stayed still until the sounds had completely faded into the night and the chilling feeling of danger was less intense.

Joog was the first to speak. He spread his wings and turned to look at them, "I'll take a look," he whispered.

"Be careful," whispered Amalek.

"I will."

Silently, on his soft-feathered wings, he took off and disappeared into the night. In a few seconds he was back, dropping down between the rock and the bushes where the others were huddled in the dark. The evil presence had almost faded completely.

"There's nothing there now. He's gone. But there's something I don't understand about it," Joog said, looking concerned.

"It was the Dark Wizard, wasn't it?" asked Seph.

"Yes, I think so, but it's strange because… well… he won't leave the Kingdom of Gems… I was *sure* of that, but now I don't know," Joog replied, looking very serious.

Amalek shivered at the thought of the evil wizard, "But it must have been him."

"Yes, but we know that if he does leave the kingdom he takes the spell too and then everyone is free again, so surely he wouldn't do that! Now that he's cast the spell he's tied to the kingdom. Unless he's found a way…" He shook his head, "It did feel like him, you know, that… feeling that we met before… but…"

Amalek shivered again, "It was him, I'm sure. And he was so close."

"But," began Miriam, "Why did he just go like that?"

"That's strange too," said Joog, "He must be desperate

to get us… and he must have known we were here because he came straight to us. It's weird… he gets right next to us… and then," and he held his wings out like two hands in a gesture of surprised disbelief, "He just leaves us and goes!"

Amalek looked up, "Perhaps he found us by instinct or something. He didn't *really* know we were here. Like guessing, but more than that."

Seph nodded, "And he left just after I held the magic drop in my hand. Perhaps that helped us."

"And I held mine too," said Amalek.

Joog looked thoughtful, "Well, we'll probably find out in due course. But for now, thank goodness he's gone."

"What happens now?" asked Miriam.

"We sleep," replied Joog, "We sleep… and watch. Flop and I will watch together this time. Alright Flop?"

"Yes," said Flop.

Amalek, Seph and Miriam all found it difficult to sleep after what had happened. They slipped in and out of restless light sleep as the rest of the night crept by uneventfully. The dawn sky gradually brightened to herald the rising of the sun and by the time the first direct rays of sunlight touched the top of the granite rock most of their fear, but not all, had melted away like frost in the morning sun.

Breakfast was sparse but delicious because they were so hungry. They finished the bread, half a small loaf, eating it with the last of the honey which they scraped out of the jar. Then they ate the few remaining ghicky nuts. They shared the last drops of the water in the jars and then got ready to leave. The night had been warm and they could already feel the temperature beginning to rise as the new day was born.

"Well;" said Amalek, "That's the last of the food."

She put the empty jars in her bag and then they set out. As they walked they had plenty of time to look around and see what this Summertime Kingdom was like. Joog had often glided above and over the border and in fact he was the only one who had journeyed into this kingdom. This was several years before when the King had sent him to collect a magic birthday cake for the Queen from Wizard Elzaphan. So, luckily, Joog knew the way. For the others it was a completely new kingdom.

It was a land of green fields, woods and forests. Juran Forest was quiet now and looked ghostly with a mist hanging amongst its trees. It was an ancient forest composed mainly of massive redwood trees, the oldest of which were over 2,000 years old.

To the north-east they could see the bright water of Lake Burney which caught the morning sunlight on its glass-like surface. Also reflected on the lake were the snow-capped peaks of the Becci Mountains looking still and majestic in the hazy distance. Today the lake was as still and smooth as a shiny mirror and reflecting the world above perfectly in every detail of colour and shape. The heat grew, the sky was completely clear of clouds and they wondered when it rained here in Summertime Kingdom.

They asked Joog about the weather and he explained that rain was an occasional event. The rain came only once every week or two, but then it would be short-lived and torrential, dousing everything with such a downpour of fresh water that all the trees, plants and creatures would have sufficient until the next rains came.

They all felt relaxed as they walked along in this beautiful country, although lying in the back of their minds, haunting them like a persistent ghost, was the frightening threat of Dark Wizard Troubler. The Princess shuddered when she thought of him and then looked up at the clear sky, wide and blue above her head, a vast open space and there was Joog, his wings outspread and his feathers fluttering as he effortlessly glided along. Joog swooped down and up again lightly touching the Princess with the tip of his wing under her chin and tickling her for fun as though he knew her fears.

They were walking along a stony track through some trees. The two children moved steadily along, but Flop, with little Miriam on his back, would be behind one minute and ahead the next. He was easily distracted by interesting things.

"I'm hungry," he said, "Shall we have lunch?"

As soon as he had spoken they all realized how hungry they were.

"The food is all finished," said Amalek, "Remember? We finished it this morning."

"I'm thirsty as well," Seph added, "It's this hot weather."

"We'll have to use the magic golden drops," said Flop, without any doubt in his voice, looking up at Amalek and Seph with appealing eyes.

"Don't be silly, Flop," said Seph, "Remember what Halo said? She said 'You can only use them once,' so we save them for real emergencies. And being hungry and thirsty is not an emergency! Not yet, anyway."

Flop accepted this, although he did not really agree. This felt like an emergency to him. Food and warmth were his two favourite things. He ran on ahead a little way, turned to watch the others catching up slowly and sat down to think about how he could get some food. It even crossed his mind that Miriam would make a very tasty morsel for a hungry cat, but he let go of the thought immediately and laughed. He was surprised how fond he had become of his little companion.

"I would never be that desperate!" he thought.

He stood up again and wandered on. The trees thinned out as the little wood ended and long grass covered the ground ahead beside the stony path. Then he saw something that made him stop and gaze. It was a huge crevice in the ground in front of him. Joog had described it to them earlier as they walked along, but to see it was stunning. It was deep and dark, a crack that extended downwards for a great distance. This was the Great Crack to the Centre of Ruddha which was said to drop deep beneath the surface to the underground dwelling of hoards of barbaric fire-creatures. Flop ran up to the edge and looked over and he could feel the heat rising from the molten rock below. Smoke curled up from the depths and he stepped back and looked around for the others who were now catching up.

Just along the great chasm and spanning the Great Crack was an old wooden bridge that was singed black underneath by the continuous heat. There was an old wooden sign hanging at a strange angle by one rusty nail which named the bridge: Marrin Bridge. The bridge had clearly been patched up many times with new planks of wood being hammered on and Flop wondered how safe it was. The others now arrived and they all stood on the edge together and for a few minutes they surveyed the amazing crack with its rising heat and smoke.

Joog hovered just above their heads.

"We'd better cross," he said after a while, "Come on... we need to keep moving. The sooner we get there the better."

"Is it safe?" asked Amalek, "It looks so rickety and burnt. Is there a way of testing it first?"

Seph put one foot cautiously onto the bridge.

"Be careful," warned Amalek.

Then he stamped on it and it shook but held firm.

"It is completely safe," answered Joog, "Wizard Elzaphan always has it repaired when necessary."

Wizard Elzaphan was held in such high respect that the mention of his name was enough to reassure them and they began to cross. Flop could feel the bridge hot under his paws and the smoke snaked into the air around them and through the gaps in the wooden planks. The bridge creaked with each step as they moved in a line; firstly came Seph, then Amalek, then Flop and Miriam, whilst Joog hovered above their heads. When they were half way across they felt the bridge swaying and this spurred them on and they moved faster. Suddenly Seph noticed something.

"Look!" he exclaimed, "What's that rope for?" The rope lay along the bridge in front of them, running along the side and then continued onto the path where it turned and disappeared from sight into the long grass. Joog swooped down and followed the rope. After a moment they heard his alarmed voice calling to them.

"Run!" he cried, "Run for your lives!" They ran, but a

second later someone or something pulled the rope making it jerk suddenly. There was loud 'clunk' from the centre of the bridge and they felt it jolt under their feet. The whole bridge juddered and they glanced around to see an incredible, alarming sight. The bridge snapped in the middle.

For a moment the two ends of the bridge held and it seemed that the brave travellers would make it to the other side. But their weight was too much and with a loud creaking wrenching sound it began, slowly, to slope towards the middle as if it was hinged at the place where it joined the other side. Flop, who had run faster than anyone up the sloping half of the bridge gripping the wood with his claws, leapt to safety, followed by Seph. Amalek tried to jump but lost her footing and started slipping down along the sloping bridge towards the great chasm. A second later and the bridge was hanging straight down into the crack. Amalek fought to find a grip as she slipped faster and faster towards her doom. It seemed that she would fall but then, miraculously, she was able to grab onto the end, the very last plank of wood.

"Hold on!" cried Seph. Without a thought of the danger he started climbing down as fast as he could on what was left of the bridge. It creaked and shuddered. Soon he was within reach.

"Quick!" cried Amalek, "I can't hold on much longer!" Seph stretched out his hand, gripping the bridge with the other.

"I can't reach any further," he cried, "*You'll* have to reach *me!*" She let go with one hand and stretched it towards him; six inches…three inches…two inches…one inch. The gap closed. Then their hands touched. At that moment the bridge juddered, Amalek's grip slipped and suddenly she fell.

"Aaahhh!" screamed Amalek as she plummeted into the smoke filled crack and disappeared.

Chapter 8

~ A Long Stripy Scarf ~

Seph felt as if he was frozen to the bridge. Tears of despair steamed down his face.

"No!" he cried as all the love he had for his sister focused in one agonised scream of anguish.

"Move… now! Climb!" shouted Joog from above with such authority that Seph found himself moving up the hanging bridge like climbing a ladder whilst the tears still flowed. He hardly knew what he was doing, but what he did know was that Amalek, his dear sister had gone, had fallen to certain death into the fires of the Great Crack. The heat was so great that survival was impossible. The bridge was still creaking and moaning as it only just hung on. Then there was a huge cracking sound and it snapped. Seph lunged upwards and off the falling bridge and grasped a multi-coloured stripy scarf that was hanging over the edge. The scarf was pulled up as he clung on tightly and then he was up and over the edge and lying on the grass. At the other end of the scarf was a huge white bird that looked like a seagull but much bigger.

Seph buried his face in the scarf and sobbed. Joog landed beside him and put a comforting wing around him. Then Flop and Miriam joined them too. In the shock of what had happened no one spoke and deep sadness completely took over their hearts.

"Seph!" came a weak frightened voice from behind them. They all looked around and there, rising up from the Great Crack, first her head, then shoulders, body and legs, was Amalek.

"Amalek!" shouted Seph with amazement and joy, "But how? What's happening?"

Amalek hovered towards them and then fell to the ground and lay there. Her hair and clothes were singed and her face was red with the heat. They all rushed to her as she strained to lift her head and speak, "I rubbed the magic drop!" she gasped, "It worked! I was lifted up on a current of warm air and... well... here I am!" She gasped again, and she began to sob. The shock had left her drained and upset, "It's hard to breathe... down there in the... heat." She took the drop out of her pocket and looked at it. It had lost its magical glow.

Then, whilst she was still sobbing, she began to laugh with relief, "That was close!" she exclaimed shaking her head, "That was so close."

Joog flew swiftly to the trees and scouted around and then returned to the others. They were all hugging each other and he watched from above and sighed with relief that they had all survived. When they had finished celebrating they turned their attention to the great bird with the scarf which they had realised was an albatross. It stretched out its great wings and then folded them carefully and they could see the wingspan was massive. It was all white, except for the black tips of its wings and it stood on two huge webbed feet.

"Now," said the albatross opening it's long, hooked, yellowish-pink bill, "I can see you're wondering who I am, where I came from and how I got here, are you not? Well, by way of explanation, I came when Amalek rubbed the magic drop in her fingers. Wizard Elzaphan sent me and I am called Neville. I am here to help you, to serve you. I am at your service."

"You've served us already!" said Seph feeling such overwhelming joy and thankfulness that he was now beaming, "Your scarf saved me."

"True," said Neville, "It's probably seems to you too hot in this kingdom to wear a scarf, but no," and he leant his head forward and lowered his voice as if telling them a secret, "It's a magic scarf. It has sorted out many a tricky situation." He shook his head as he spoke making the scarf ripple all the way down its full length.

"Wizard Elzaphan sent you?" asked Joog.

"Yes, of course," replied Neville, "He told me that you would be coming and he sent me out to find you. He said you might need help. It's my first job for him. But finding you was easy. I was gliding above those trees over there," and he waved one of his huge wings to point, "And my scarf tingled all the way down! I knew someone was using magic close by... and it was you," he looked at Amalek, "Rubbing the magic drop. So, here I am."

Joog noticed that Seph was looking up at something with an anxious expression growing on his face.

"What is it?" asked Joog looking up as well, "Ah! I see. That looks like… yes it is! Ravens! Three of them. Get down! Quick!"

They crouched and stayed completely still as the three ravens flew directly overhead.

"Where are they going?" asked Amalek softly when they had flown past.

"I don't know," Joog replied quietly, keeping his eyes

fixed on them, "But they'll be up to no good that's for sure. Hang on... they're turning back. Under that tree. Quick!"

They moved quickly and quietly under the tree and looked up through the mottled cover of leaves and branches above their heads. The ravens circled, scanning the land below with their beady black eyes, hideous angular shapes, dark against the clear blue of the sky. They cackled harshly to each other as they searched and then they began to descend. Amalek grabbed Seph's hand and gripped it.

"Just keep still," he whispered to her, "Keep completely still."

The ravens suddenly dropped into a tree that was fairly close by. The party of travellers were wrapped in fear. They knew they were fierce and ruthless and they did not have the help of Aram and Halo to fight them. The ravens carried the strength of the Dark Wizard with them and even at this distance they could feel that the warmth of the air was being smothered by the chill of evil. They stayed completely still and listened. Then one raven spoke.

"... the master wants us to search as we go... and..."

"I'm in charge of this... he put me in charge..., so we press on. We'll go now... OK?"

"But..."

"No! We must press on. Let's go."

"But what about the search then, Jeg?" the third one snapped.

"We *are* searching, fathead! We search as we go..." and then he dropped his voice and the other two stretched out their necks towards him and tilted their heads on one side to listen.

Down below, the travellers listened, but now the ravens were talking too softly. Amalek moved slightly as she strained to hear. The branch of a bush shook. Jeg jerked his head down and stared below.

"I thought I heard something," he said, "Down there… over there," and he nodded his beak in the direction.

The other two immediately looked down. After a moment one of them spoke.

"What shall we do?"

"Go down and look?" asked Jeg.

"No… not that. That's probably just a stupid mouse or something."

"Well… you know what I think we should do," Jeg snapped, "And I'm ordering you to do it. We go now. We must get on."

"OK!" announced the other with a rasping voice. "You win. But if it goes wrong then you're to blame, not me."

"It won't go wrong. Come on. Let's go."

The brave group below heard the flapping of wings and after a second they saw the three ravens rising into the air again. They watched with relief as they flew northwards and soon they were out of sight.

"Stupid mouse, indeed!" said Miriam, and they all laughed.

"Well, at least they've gone," said Seph, "And without seeing us."

"Yes," Joog nodded, "It sounds as though they have a job to do. We must be alert for ravens at all times."

They all nodded their agreement and then Amalek turned to Neville to continue the conversation.

"Where do you usually travel then?" asked Amalek, picking up the conversation with the albatross again. Her face was cooling down now.

"I just go wherever I am needed," replied Neville, "Or whenever I am called to help. And then that is where I go. And I never know where that will be until it happens. So I never know the plan for the day, and I often wonder which way will call! But when there's something that requires sorting out then I know the way and go there to help. I'm called a Wandering Albatross; I wander on the wing, sometimes for days and days, until I'm called. It's very exciting really. I have visited many, many kingdoms in this way. Never planning but just drawn to places when needed. Just floating on the beautiful currents of air. But it's slightly different now." He paused, lifted his bill higher in the air and said proudly, "Last week, Wizard Elzaphan asked me to work for him. He called me! And that's an honour that is. I couldn't refuse."

"Have you been to the Kingdom of Gems?" asked Joog now perched on the Amalek's shoulder.

"No, not yet, that is one I haven't seen... but you never know. You come from there don't you? And I've heard about the sad state of affairs going on… the spell and all that. Perhaps as we journey on you can tell me all about it."

"We will," said Amalek, "But who did this to the bridge?"

"Well," began Joog, "I went to search in the trees over there... and before I got there I saw a figure, a person, but it was so grey and ghostly in the shadows. Someone was definitely there, but I couldn't see who it was. It moved and that's when I shouted, 'Run' to you. When you were safe, Amalek, I took another look but there's no one there now."

"Was it the Dark Wizard Troubler, Joog?" asked Seph.

Joog looked thoughtful, "I don't know. It's his work,

I'm sure."

"Whether it's him or not," said Amalek, "He's behind it! He wanted us dead and he's failed."

"But he'll try again," Joog fluttered into the air, "Keep alert! We should have spotted that before it happened," then he turned to the albatross, "You're travelling with us then, Neville?"

"At your service!" and he open his gigantic wings and tried to take off. He started running along on the grass in a most ungainly way, with his head and body wobbling from side to side. He looked clumsy and cumbersome as he waddled as fast as he could.

"Eh up!" he cried, "I think I'm lifting off!" He jumped awkwardly but just fell back again. "I need a slope!"

"Keep running!" shouted Amalek, "And you'll come to a slope."

Neville followed her instruction and soon the grass began to fall away and all of a sudden he was floating just above the grass. With a skilful tilt of his wings he was airborne. The transformation was extraordinary. In flight he was graceful and smooth as he effortlessly rose with hardly a flap, his great white wings bright in the summer sunlight. On the ground he looked lost and out of place, like a fish out of water, but now, as the fresh air rushed by, he was perfectly at home.

He circled with superb control above their heads, using small movements to adjust his massive wings as he rode the warm breeze. He looked down at the others below.

"I'm at your service," he yelled, "For as long as you need me! And as we travel here's a riddle-song for you to work out."

He swooped over them and sang the first line as he

glided above their heads. There was a pause as he rose, turned, swooped back and opened his hooked bill to sing the next line. And so it proceeded until the riddle-song was finished.

> "My body is extremely long,
> but very, very thin,
> and many eyes watch in surprise
> as I wriggle in.
>
> "Only once I zigger-zag
> to find my place of rest,
> and then again some extra strain -
> I'm pulled and tugged and stretched!
>
> "Two times a day at least, we meet,
> or maybe three or more.
> and many a way throughout the day
> I'm in and out the door.
>
> "I am important in my place,
> lose me and you're forlorn.
> but cats are pleased when I am freed,
> and across the floor I'm drawn!"

When Neville had finished the young travellers looked at each other in puzzlement.

"Well," said Amalek, enjoying the challenge, "What is it?"

"I don't know," Seph was equally mystified. Joog was on his shoulder, "Extremely long, but very thin? Flop? You should know because it mentions cats at the end."

"Well, I think I know," said Flop, "At least I've got an

idea. But I need to hear it again."

Joog jumped off Seph's shoulder and circled silently in the air. "Sing it again, Neville, but we'll listen as we go. We need to keep moving."

So Neville sang it again and again until everyone knew the answer. He flew just above their heads as they walked along a stony path and Joog glided above Neville keeping watch with his excellent eyesight for the slightest movement. The incident at the bridge had frightened them all and although Neville's riddle-song had lifted their spirits they found themselves continually looking around to check they were not being followed.

They moved steadily and after several hours they found they had made good progress. Their thirst was growing and they were feeling they needed a rest when they were delighted to find some apple trees growing by the side of the path. The trees provided some shade from the hot sun and they all enjoyed the sweet crunchy apples with soothed their thirst as well as their hunger.

Once they had eaten and felt sufficiently rested they started travelling again with extra spring in their legs. They knew that they would have to find something to properly quench their thirst soon, or send Joog or Neville off to fetch some. Just when they were becoming desperate they came across a little stream which ran alongside the path for a short distance. It was almost completely hidden by long grass and it was the babbling sound that told them it was there. The water was fresh and cool in their mouths as they gulped it down thirstily. Amalek filled up the jars with water and they were on their way again.

In the high land of the Becci Mountains, right up on the peaks and a little below that too, the snow always lay thickly. Whereas elsewhere in Summertime Kingdom rain was occasional but heavy, up here snow was almost a daily treat. That is how the Mountain Hares of the Becci Mountains felt about it because the snow was their home. With their thick white fur they could stay warm by huddling together in the snow, digging underneath and making cosy snow burrows sheltered from the icy winds.

In the community of hares news was passed from burrow to burrow by word of mouth. Each snow-burrow was linked by a tunnel and so it never took long before every hare was up to date with the latest story, and today there was some unusual news in the air.

"Did you hear what's happening in the Kingdom of Gems?" Jack asked his wife Jymette.

"No," she said.

"It's snowing!"

"Well, that's not so amazing is it?"

"No, except it's not like the normal snow they get, you know, just patchy and for a few days. No, this is really thick snow! Layer upon layer. Real snow. Our sort of snow. *And* it's summer there!"

"How strange," said Jymette, "Do they like it?"

"Well, that's the other thing. I've heard they're all frozen!" he continued, "As frozen as icicles! All of them."

"I'm not surprised!" laughed Jymette, "They can't handle the snow and cold like we can. To us it's normal, but to them...."

"No!" exclaimed Jack, "You're not following me. They are *actually* frozen... you know... completely still without moving at all... with cold *and* a spell. That's what folks are saying. It's a dark and evil spell cast across the whole land!"

And so the strange news went on spreading until early the next morning it reached the ears of one young hare called Tally.

"We must help," he said enthusiastically, "Some of us, the younger ones, must go and help."

"Don't be silly!" said one of the older hares, "We never leave the Becci Mountains... and there could be terrible danger there."

"It would be plain silly," said another, scoffing at the idea, "We have enough problems of our own to deal with."

"He's right!" announced another joining in, "How could hares like us make a difference? We don't fight like warriors, do we? We can only hop around!"

"Well," Tally piped up, "I'm going to help. I don't know how, but I am. Who's coming with me?" This was met with silence, and then laughter.

"Tally's gonna fight an evil spell!" one said and laughed again as if the idea was utterly ridiculous.

"You're cowards, you are!" said Tally looking around the group one by one as he spoke, "All of you! And why can't I fight?"

"When you're older and more sensible you'll realise why," one explained, with a superior attitude, "Then you'll give up your crack-pot ideas."

Over the next few hours Tally threaded his way through the burrows and told others of his plan to help. He invited them to join him, but the answer was always "No," and they thought the whole idea was a big joke. Then they gave reasons why they could not go. Tally, however, would not be weakened in his resolve to help, even though they tried to persuade him not to go.

Tally decided to call on his grandfather who had brought him up from when he was just a few weeks old. He would talk to him about it. He loved his grandfather and spent a lot of time with him. It seemed to Tally that he was old and wise. He remembered when he was very little and the old hare would tell him bedtime stories: he was amazed at his Grandfathers skill at making up so many exciting tales. There would be wonderful stories of great adventures and battles, wizards and spells. Sometimes he would show him an old chest in which he kept things he had collected from his journeys. There were candles, pens and other trinkets which Tally imagined had magic powers, as well as maps and strange diagrams.

"Tally!" said Hawkeye, as he saw Tally entering his burrow. He was called Hawkeye due to his amazing eyesight which enabled him to spot a hawk or other predators hovering above and send a warning to all the hares, "Come in and sit down."

Tally hopped across the burrow. Upon the floor of flattened snow lay an old patterned blanket which was fixed at the four corners with a nail hammered into the snow. The room was warm and simple an Tally sat down in his usual spot next to the small chest. This is where his grandfather kept his collection of maps and other things, and Tally called it Hawkeye's Chest.

"Gramps," said Tally, "I want to go on an adventure. You know, like those stories you used to tell me."

"Good," said Hawkeye with a twinkle in his eye. Tally sat up, wide-eyed with surprise as a wave of excitement flowed through him, "And I know what this is about. It's the news about the Kingdom of Gems, isn't it, Tally?" Tally nodded, "Yes, you ought to go. You *must* go!"

"But all the others say I mustn't go."

"Don't listen to the others," said Hawkeye, "Someone's got to help, eh? Those others... well they've lost all sense of a challenge. They've forgotten what a hare can do! I tell you, help is needed... badly. You must go as soon as possible. With things of this importance any delay can mean it's too late." Tally was staring at his grandfather in wonder and listening to every word. He could hardly believe his ears and he remembered all those wonderful bedtime stories.

"Gramps," he said, looking thoughtful, "You know all those stories you used to tell me?"

"Yes?"

"They *were* about you, weren't they?" asked Tally, hoping that the answer would be 'yes'.

"Yes, they were," said Hawkeye, "So now you know. You wouldn't think it now, would you? That I travelled so far and fought for what I knew was right. Now I'm too old and weak, but you... you are young and, as far as I can see, have all the qualities needed for this difficult task. You must offer your help and, you never know, you may have an important part to play. The essential thing is to do what is needed, Tally. Just follow your instinct and then act in any way you are able... but make sure that what you do is...well... the right thing at the right time."

"How will I know, Gramps?"

"As I said, Tally, follow your instinct. And stay awake, and by that I mean keep all your senses open... Look, listen, smell, feel. A hare has good senses... very good... you should value your senses. They can tell you what's going on. If you really listen it's amazing what you can hear. Smell properly and you'll pick up all sorts of scent. But if you go around in a dream and thinking too much... or worrying... well you're not in touch. You'll miss things. If you're alert in this way you'll find you'll know what's right. Do you understand, Tally."

"I think so, Gramps," Tally said perkily.

Hawkeye thought for a moment, then he spoke with extra gravity in his voice, "KYWAY," he said, "The key is KYWAY. It stands for Keep Your Wits About You. You can remember what you need to know all in one word."

"I see," said Tally, "KYWAY."

They talked for more than an hour, and when Hawkeye felt he had given him all the advice he could, as well as a good meal, Tally was ready to set out on his adventure.

"Before I go, Gramps," said Tally, "Could I hear that poem about the bell?"

Hawkeye looked kindly at his grandson. He could see a lot of his own youthful enthusiasm in him and felt proud, "Of course. Does it thrill you, Tally?"

"Yes," said Tally nodding, "It always has. And it's about you, isn't it?"

"It is... yes..." said Hawkeye, smiling as he remembered the events spoken about in the poem.

"I'll get it, Gramps," said Tally eagerly.

He reached over to the chest beside him and lifted the lid with a paw. He loved looking inside at all the interesting things. He recognised the rolled up piece of paper immediately and reached in, grasped it with two paws and lifted it out.

"Thank you, Tally," said Hawkeye as Tally rolled it over to him. The old hare unrolled the paper carefully with his paws, placing a stone on the top and tucking the other end under the tips of his back feet to stop it rolling up again. When it was reasonably flat on the carpet he cleared his throat and began to read.

The BELL

In days before sweet peace did calmly dwell
Upon our cherished Kingdom's summertime,
There came a Troubler bearing an evil spell
Who made a bell of misery to chime.

*

The massive bell was caste in Gugeol,
And dragged from Glyifild's deepest iron mine,
Then rung from hilltop casting a spell so cruel
Whilst watching, as the sun forgot to shine.

*

The doleful land was steeped in shadow deep,
The Troubler slayed the King and stole the throne,
A kingdom trapped where all did groan and weep,
And heavy air pressed down 'till earth did moan.

*

And misery filled each cosy dwelling place
Of every hare and human, bird and beast,
As evil showed to all its icy face,
To numb the lovely life when freedom ceased.

*

Until new courage rose on snowy slopes,
Led by a one so true and brave and strong,
And like spring blossom heralds summer hopes,
he gladdened the land where peace had once belonged.

*

This leader followed every righteous turn
As brave as any famous knight of yore,
And led them to the freedom they would earn
When light would dawn and night would rule no more.

*

When darkness dimmed to light the Troubler fell,
The shuddering earth restored to previous grace,
The leader's strength proved stronger than the spell,
The kingdom again became a peaceful place.

★

Tally had always felt a spark of excitement in his young heart when he heard this, even when he was tiny and he would drift off to sleep with Hawkeye's wise voice gently speaking the poem. This time the spark leapt in his heart again and he felt a wave of inspiration. He felt strong enough to conquer the worst Troubler.

"Gramps," he asked, plucking up courage to ask about something which had always been shrouded in mystery, "Is that how my parents died? Did that Troubler kill them?"

Hawkeye sighed, "Yes. They were brave... very brave... but yes, the Troubler killed them. He brought a darkness that was *so* heavy," he shook his head as if he could hardly believe it had happened, and Tally could see a great tear welling up in his eye until it burst and ran across his fur and down a whisker, "Wizard Elzaphan came to help, thank goodness. But when he arrived there was no King ruling because they had killed him during the attack... so Wizard Elzaphan took over."

"What about Wizard Candara?" asked Tally, "Was he alive then?"

"No, Tally, no. He was *long* before... hundreds of years before," said Hawkeye smiling affectionately at his grandson, "You need some history lessons, you young scamp! When we have time I'll tell you more, with dates and everything. When your parents died... well... it was a bad time. And without Wizard Elzaphan many more would have perished under the power of Gugeol and the terrible sound of that bell... it seemed to vibrate through everything. But you must not be sad. No, be glad that you are young and strong thanks to the part your parents played in freeing the kingdom. *They* would want you to do this."

Tally was feeling sad when thinking about his parents, but Hawkeye's words soothed and encouraged him.

"Don't be sad, Tally," Hawkeye added, "Let your love for your parents spur you on."

"I will," Tally responded, perking up and doing his best to drop all his sadness, "And I'm ready to go."

"Excellent. You'd best be off then."

Tally hesitated by the hole which led out of the burrow, suddenly feeling the enormity of the journey he was embarking upon. He looked out of the burrow and sniffed the fresh air. Falling snow gently touched his thick fur.

Hawkeye put his paw on Tally's neck, pulled the youngster back in and hugged him, "I am so proud of you, you know." Then he paused and when he spoke his voice was earnest and solemn, "Just trust your heart, Tally. That's what I always did. What you feel in your heart… this pull to go and help, to help others and fight for what is good and right… this is true. This is right. You *must* trust it."

"Yes I will," said Tally positively as he jumped out of the snow-burrow. Then he turned and called back into the burrow, "Bye, Gramps. And thank you!"

"Bye, Tally. And good luck!"

With inspiration in his young heart he began hopping away. Hawkeye clambered out of the burrow into the soft snow outside. He stood up on his back legs to get the best view.

"Don't forget," called out Hawkeye, "KYWAY!"

"Yes, Gramps, I'll remember. KYWAY! And thank you!" Tally called over his shoulder as he scampered away spraying snow up behind him with each spring of his large hind feet. Hawkeye felt content that he had offered young Tally all the advice he could and had tried to pass on the lessons he had learnt through his own experience.

It was mid-morning as Tally hopped away through the snow carrying inspiration in his heart from his grandfather. Hawkeye was watching from above as Tally moved down the mountain and suddenly felt anxious for this brave young hare; he was proud of his grandson and for a moment closed his eyes and he wished with all his strength that he would see Tally again. He was old and he knew his days were numbered and he also knew that every step Tally took would move him closer to danger.

He opened his eyes and looked for Tally. He had gone. He took a deep breath and looked up and into the falling snow. He turned and hopped into his burrow.

As Tally moved down the mountain side he heard familiar voices calling to him. It was a few hares who had seen him go and had dashed out after him.

"Stop!"

"Come back! Don't be a fool!"

"If you get into trouble we can't help you!"

"Come back!"

But Tally ignored these and carried on until they had faded into the distance behind him. The snow felt wonderful under his feet and in the air it swirled around him, gusting here and there on the wind. It was not long before the snow became less deep and he could see ahead where the snow ended altogether.

When he descended below the snow line the snow stopped falling and he was travelling under a bright summer sun. He was now in territory that was totally unknown to him and he found this exciting. All he carried with him was a small pouch containing some folded paper fixed to the fur on his belly. Hawkeye had recommended that he travelled as lightly as possible and told him that there would be plenty of food that he could find as he travelled. His heart was filled with a wonderful sense of freedom and adventure, for he had no idea what would happen. He was launching into the unknown.

The Dark Wizard Troubler was slumped in Old Howard's chair with his long thin legs stretched out on the floor, crossing at the ankles and his lean sinewy hands clasped behind his head. One of the black metal chains was around his neck with a black compass hanging on it and resting on his chest. He was feeling pleased with himself.

"Yes," he thought, *"My plan, my spell, was…mmm…clever, even ingenious. And it has worked. I was sure it would. How wonderful to see all those people and creatures frozen by me. In my control."* He closed his eyes in delight and sat there for a while, half dozing and half thinking. He was content in the knowledge that he had obtained a kingdom; in fact he really felt this was now his kingdom and a smile of glee flicked across his lips. But his greed was like a hot furnace burning in his selfish heart and he felt he wanted more. A few days ago the thought of gaining one kingdom was his great aim and he thought he would feel fulfilled if he could only achieve it. But now, as he sat in the chair contemplating the things that had happened, it seemed like a good start and that now he could begin to build an empire. If only he could conquer another kingdom then this would be twice as good as one and then he could go on from there. But first there was the matter of those who had somehow

escaped his spell and left the kingdom. This concerned him and had to be dealt with. It was like a nagging problem in the back of his mind that frustrated him and he knew he could not really relax until he had completely destroyed the determined opposition of the Prince and Princess. How had they escaped his spell? He could not work it out. His desire was for the Candara Gems and the children and the others were the only thing standing in the way. They had to be dealt with.

He had already put certain plans into motion that he was sure would dispose of the Prince and Princess once and for all, but he suddenly thought of something else that he could do; something extra. Although it would be a major drain on his power he thought it would be worth it. He pulled himself out of the chair and stood up. Jamaar jumped up from his rug in the corner and trotted to his master's side.

"Yes, master?" he said eagerly, "Is there anything I can do for my next meal?"

"Not at the moment, dog," the Dark Wizard replied gruffly, "Get back in your corner."

Jamaar reluctantly did as he was told; his eager enthusiasm deflated as he walked slowly and miserably back to the corner and flopped down on his rug. Down below, in the cellar, Horrik heard the sounds of Jamaar padding around freely. Hearing his freedom sent a wave of hate through her and she shifted uncomfortably shaking the chain that tied her by her neck to the pipe. The frustration and jealousy she was feeling was almost unbearable and she suddenly opened her great mouth sending drops of bacteria-filled saliva spraying across the dusty floor. A few wisps of smoke rose from the fizzing dust. Then, from the depths of her massive scaly body, like a volcano erupting from the centre of the earth, she let out an almighty heart-felt roar of pent up fury that shook the walls of the house.

In the room above the roar made Jamaar jump up, eager to impress his master in his role as guard-dog.

"It's alright, Jamaar," said the wizard, "It's only Horrik. That stupid animal becomes more of a nuisance every day. And somehow, I trust her less each day. You know, Jamaar, she tried to escape from me once."

"I wonder why?" said Jamaar in mock surprise.

The wizard picked up the sarcasm, "I hope you're not mocking."

"Of course not," said Jamaar, wishing he had not spoken with such sarcasm. He cringed inside, "I meant it. It was foolish of Horrik. A foolish foolish thing to do, master... foolish... so foolish... I mean trying to escape... she's a fool... I like being in your service. I enjoy it!"

"Of course you do," the Dark Wizard said suspiciously, "But remember those rules I told you about?"

"Yes, master."

"Let me remind you, just in case you get any ideas of escape. Horrik tried, you know, and look what's happened to her. The third rule... never *never* try to escape."

"Yes, master. I remember," growled Jamaar.

"But, Horrik," continued the wizard, "She's a vicious beast and has her uses. And she's powerful. I've seen her rip other creatures apart with ease. She's down there now, tied up, but when the time comes I'll bring her out and use all that strength and anger on the enemy."

Jamaar sat down and then curled around to settle on his old rug. The wizard left the room and climbed the stairs. A draught blowing down caught his cloak fanning it out slightly behind him like washing on a line blowing in a gentle breeze. He went into the bathroom and, after a great crashing sound, came out carrying a mirrored cabinet which he had ripped off the wall. He took it to the room downstairs, placed it on a table and then sat down in front of it. With his elbows on the table and his head resting on his hands, he stared into the mirror.

An hour passed and then another and still he sat there, with his black eyes fixed, staring; glaring without a flinch, at the mirror. Suddenly, as he stared, he chuckled. Then he laughed. He had started to see what he wanted to see, what he had been thinking of began to appear in the mirror, very dimly at first, but growing clearer.

"Jamaar," he hissed. Jamaar jumped up as eagerly as before, "Come and look at this!" Jamaar trotted over, lifted his front paws onto the edge of the table, and looked into the mirror.

"Oh, master!" he said with praise in his voice, "Master, this is clever!"

"Yes, I know. Do my powers surprise you?"

"Yes, master, I am lucky to be in the service of such a great wizard!"

"Well then, don't forget it!" the wizard snapped, "Now, don't distract me. When I am at this mirror, and working it, you must never distract me. Understand?"

"Yes, master," he growled.

"Now, I must begin," the Dark Wizard Troubler sounded menacing and cruel, "Go away, dog."

Jamaar again looked upset and miserable as he dropped his front paws down from the table and walked dejectedly back to his corner.

Chapter 9

~ The General ~

The group of six travellers had kept moving into the night and then slept on the grass beside the path. It had been warm and fairly comfortable and they felt safer sleeping out in the open where Joog and Flop could keep watch with their nighttime vision. The night passed peacefully and they woke with the rising sun stretching its first warm rays across the land. There was no food left for breakfast, but at least they had the fresh water that Amalek had collected from the stream. They shared the water and then resumed their journey.

The walkers, the Prince, Princess, and Flop with Miriam on his back, moved along the stony path and by midday they were ready to rest. With the hot sunny weather which made travelling hard work they were becoming hungry and extremely thirsty. Joog and Neville glided above keeping a close watch on their friends below and chatting as they flew.

"We'd better take a rest," said Seph, "We'll shelter under there."

They moved off the path and into the shade of a wood.

They sat down to rest beside a small clearing surrounded by beautiful copper beech trees, their delicate leaves trembling in the warm summer breeze.

"We'll have to use that magic golden drop now," said Flop, "Or soon. This is becoming real emergency!"

"Well," Joog said from a branch in one of the trees, "I don't know. I know we're thirsty, but we can still travel on. I could go on ahead and look for a lake or a stream whilst you rest up here."

"I'll join you on the wing," said Neville from above where he was skilfully circling with his colourful scarf trailing slightly behind. It seemed much shorter now than before. "Lake Beautiful is still a distance away though... but we might find a stream."

"It sounds like the best plan to me," said Amalek hopefully.

Joog spread his mighty wings and soured up to Neville and then together they rose above the trees, disappearing from view as the others watched. No sooner had they left than they heard the sound of footsteps back along the path in the direction from which they had come. Someone or something was approaching, walking quickly and hidden from their view by the trees. For a moment they watched and waited.

"What if it's the Dark Wizard Troubler?" whispered Seph, his heart beating faster at the thought, "He might have decided to follow us."

"You could be right," whispered Flop, whose fur was standing up on his neck in fear, "Let's hide. Quick, in those bushes."

They all moved quietly, but as quickly as they could, over to the prickly gooseberry bushes. The thought of the sinister Dark Wizard Troubler with his penetrating black eyes and terrifying presence made them panic and they scrabbled frantically to hide, ignoring the pricks and scratches as the thorns caught their skin. After only a few seconds four pairs of eyes peeped out and watched anxiously along the path. They hardly dared move as they huddled together in the gooseberry bushes and listened to the sound of the footsteps growing louder. As they stared along the path something in the sky caught Flop's eye; it was a jet black raven flying above the path and towards them.

"Look!" he whispered, pointing above with his black and white paw.

They looked up and saw the raven too. The footsteps were closer now. A dark figure appeared. The path was overhung with trees, almost hiding the figure in the shadows. Then as it stepped out of the shadows and into the bright sunlight there was no doubt; it was not the Dark Wizard Troubler but Old Howard. He was staring straight at the gooseberry bush. As they looked at him and their eyes became used to the shadows they saw something shocking; Old Howard had black eyes.

"I know you're in there!" he shouted, "Come out, you cowards! You fools! I 'ave news for yer!"

The four friends huddled closer together. Old Howard kept walking quickly towards them, his short legs almost running. They felt caught by fear; intense fear of danger, as if they were being sucked into a bottomless pit and were helpless to stop it happening. Then Old Howard stopped.

"My Master 'as caught them meddlesome unicorns," he shouted still louder, "They're 'anging up by their 'orns in the old elm tree by the palace. Come back an' save 'em. Come on, if yer dare to! They won't live much longer, but if yer try yer might save their loives. Ha! Come on, or are yer just too cowardly to troy! Ha!"

Suddenly Seph jumped out of the bush. Without a thought of the danger he felt he had to confront Old Howard.

"Stop!" shouted Amalek, alarmed and afraid for her brother's safety, "Stop!"

Seph picked up a large stick and ran at Old Howard. He lifted the stick above his head, ready to strike. Old Howard was clearly surprised by the sudden unexpected attack and stepped back. Perhaps he thought the stick was a sword and certainly Seph wished it was. Old Howard stepped back further, back into the shadows of the trees behind him and Seph stopped running and searched for him with his eyes.

"You're the coward," shouted Seph, "And you're a traitor to the kingdom. Show yourself and fight!" Amalek, Flop and Miriam observed all this in utter amazement. They had never seen Seph be so brave, but Amalek was tense with apprehension at her brother's foolhardy move. They all looked for Old Howard, scanning the dark shadows beneath the trees. As they gazed intently they thought they saw his stout figure move... dart quickly back. And then even the shadow was gone and he was out of sight, but still that dreadful sense of danger remained.

From the sky above the raven dropped upon Seph. His sharp pointed beak was ready for attack as his black eyes fixed on the Prince. Amalek spotted it.

"Look out!" she shouted.

Suddenly Joog and Neville appeared as if from nowhere and sandwiched the surprised raven between them. Joog gripped one of the raven's wings firmly in his talons, whilst Neville held the other in his huge hooked beak. The poor raven squealed and squawked, struggling in vain to escape.

"Let me go!" it screeched, "Caaaah!"

"We need to talk to you," snapped Joog, "We need answers to some questions. Neville, we'll land down there in the woods."

As they carried it off to interrogate it in the woods all the energy drained out of it and it went limp. The shock of being captured had killed it. They dropped it as they flew above the trees and it fell lifelessly through the branches and thudded onto the ground below.

Amalek, Flop and Miriam, who was nestled in Flop's fur, were still huddled in the gooseberry bushes and looking out for Old Howard. Suddenly they heard a sound close behind them. They spun around to see the old man with his black eyes staring coldly at them. He was right upon them and was gripping a large sack in both hands which he swung through the air towards Amalek. She dodged and Old Howard lost balance and slipped on the grass. As he fell the sack landed over Flop. He scooped up the sack with Flop wriggling and hissing inside and before Amalek had time to do anything he turned and ran into the trees. Amalek jumped up and ran after him. She thought she saw him, a shadowy figure against the tangled background of trees and bushes, but once again, as she looked, he was gone. She was left standing there gazing at the trees, bewildered by the speed at which things had happened and upset at the loss of Flop and Miriam. Seph ran frantically towards them as fast as he could.

"What's happening?" he called. He knew it was something serious, so he slipped his hand into his pocket and his fingers closed around the magic drop, but instictively he knew that he was too late.

At this moment Joog and Neville returned and swooped down to the Prince and Princess, Joog landing on a branch and Neville staying airborne. Seph had joined Amalek now beside the gooseberry bush.

"He took Flop and Miriam!" cried Amalek.

"Who?" asked Joog.

"Old Howard! He's here *and* he's got black eyes. He took them in a sack and then disappeared!" Her eyes were wide with concern and wet with the tears that were welling up.

"Disappeared?" Joog looked concerned.

"Well he seemed to," said Amalek, anxiety filling her voice, "It was all so quick. He tried to get me but I dodged him... and now they've gone. I didn't even have time to do anything. Oh Joog! What can we do?"

Neville was circling in the air above their heads, "I'll have a good look around," he said, "And see if he's hiding somewhere," and he gently flapped his huge white wings and glided gracefully off.

"So the Dark Wizard Troubler," began Joog earnestly, "Has got Old Howard working for him. I'm not surprised. That old man always had bad tendencies. We saw him leave and this is where he was sent."

"But," began Seph, looking thoughtful and concerned as he sat down on a log, "Why did he send him here? Old Howard left before the spell and everything. Maybe the Dark Wizard was planning ahead... in case someone escaped from the spell."

"Yes, probably," Joog fluffed up his feathers as he fidgeted uncomfortably, "Who knows what he thinks or plans in that selfish mind of his?" and he spread his wings using them like arms in a questioning gesture. Then, seeing Seph's face suddenly dropping with gloom and fear, he added, "But we must stay strong against him."

Amalek frowned and looked cross as she glared at her brother, "You shouldn't have jumped out at him," she snapped, "Why can't you think before you do things like that."

Seph stared back at her. An intense feeling of anger rose in him, the feeling that always came when his older sister told him off, "How could I know what would happen?" he pleaded.

"That's why…" Amalek spoke firmly but with an edge of superiority in her voice, like a school teacher talking to a naughty boy, "That's why you should think. Got it?"

Seph jumped up in anger from the log. His face was hard with rage as he gave Amalek a furious look. Taking a step towards her, he paused with his fists clenched and their faces a few inches apart.

"Why do you always say things like that?" he shouted.

"Because it's true!" she retorted.

"Well *you* think *too* much," he shouted back.

They both felt they had been stabbed inside as they glared at each other. Joog just watched from above, looking down from the tree he was perched in. A deep frown of anger furrowed Seph's brow and tears bubbled up in Amalek's eyes. Her mouth quivered with hurt.

"If you thought more," she shouted, "Flop and Miriam would still be free!"

Seph was lost for what to say or do next, so he turned away and swung his leg at the log, his foot hitting it with a thud. "Ah!" he cried out in pain and ran off, limping, into some trees. Amalek's tears flooded out now and she slumped down onto the log.

After a minute or two when her crying had subsided Joog hooted down to Amalek, "You need to sort that out, you know," he said gently, "You're the older... you make the first move. We can't afford to fight each other as well as the evil wizard."

Amalek looked up at him and dabbed her eyes with her sleeve, "I know. You're right. It's just so difficult sometimes."

She stood up just as Seph walked out of the trees. He flopped down on the log again and looked at the ground, "Sorry," he said.

"No," Amalek said quietly, "I'm sorry. I shouldn't have said those things."

"Neither should I." Seph buried his head in his hands and sighed, "How can we hope to fight him? We felt his power back at the palace. It's too much! And now he's got Flop and Miriam." His body seemed to shrink and crumple as despair took hold of him. Suddenly it had all become too much for him. He began to shake.

"I feel so cold," he sighed.

Amalek sat down beside him on the log. She felt she would do anything now to turn the clock back, take away the things she had said and make it alright again. She put an arm around her brother's shoulders affectionately. She had always defended and supported Seph whenever he was upset about something or people were being unfair. Now, in this desperate situation, she felt like a rock in her love and loyalty for him. The argument seemed so silly now.

"Seph," said Joog earnestly, "Don't give in to the cold. You mustn't give in. The Dark Wizard is trying to take you. The cold you feel is his power. Do you understand me?"

Seph nodded. After a few moments the Prince's shivering stopped, but he still hung his head in despair.

"Seph," Amalek said affectionately, "You were *so* brave just now. You were the one who confronted Old Howard. You were right... you couldn't have known what would happen. If you hadn't done that it might've been worse," she paused and squeezed his shoulders, "We need you and the Kingdom of Gems needs you. We need you to be brave, as you were. Listen. I don't know if we can do it, but I do know that we have to try. We have to! Think of our parents. And the whole kingdom! All those people and creatures trapped in the spell. He mustn't get away with it, must he?" She paused to let the words sink in.

Seph lifted his head and turned to Amalek, "You're right, of course. I'm sorry, it suddenly just seemed... well, impossible. With Flop and Miriam gone, and I kept thinking of his horrible black eyes... and that cold was just awful, right inside me. But now, yes, I know, I was just being... stupid. Thank you, Amalek."

Amalek looked at him seriously, "You're alright now?" she asked.

"Yes," he replied, with a kind smile. He nodded emphatically, "Yes, perfectly. Thanks to you. And you?"

"I'm fine. We mustn't fight. We must be strong and... well, together to fight against this Troubler... it's ridiculous to fight between ourselves."

"The only trouble is..." Seph continued, smiling as well, "My foot hurts."

"Well," Amalek laughed, "That's your own fault."

Seph nodded and together they reached out with both hands out and lightly touched their fingertips of each others hands three times. This was a gesture they used for their friendship. The air had been cleared and they both felt so much better.

Joog had been watching and listening to this. "Good," he said approvingly.

"Joog," asked Seph, "You know that cold I felt?" Joog nodded, "Does that mean that the Dark Wizard is close and knows where we are?"

"Not necessarily... no, not at all. You could be anywhere and so could he. It's just that... if you weaken you open a door to him, to his evil ways."

Amalek turned to Joog, "What can we do about Flop and Miriam?"

"I don't know, at the moment," Joog turned his head to look at her, "But we must stick together. If only we had not flown off..."

"Perhaps Neville will find him," Seph was standing now, "Are we ready to fight?"

Just then Neville returned, "Nothing," he said, "No sign at all! He seems to have vanished." He glided smoothly down to land on some grass beside them, but just before he touched down he realised he was going too fast and swooped up again. He turned sharply in the air and glided down again looking a little nervous about the landing.

"Wooh!" he exclaimed as one of his great webbed feet touched the grass and he started running as he tried to slow down, his feet slapping the grass in turn. But his feet were too slow and one caught on the grass and he tripped. His head tipped forwards and he stumbled out of control in a flurry of flapping wings and slapping feet, skidding on his chest and neck. He soon came to a halt and as he finally stopped he tipped forwards again and his bill stabbed into the ground. With a shake of his head he pulled it out and looked at the others who had been watching in astonishment.

He shook some bits of grass and earth off his bill, stretched out his wings and said, "I'm down."

"Is that..." began Joog, sweeping his wing through the air to point at the skid mark on the grass, "Your usual way of landing?"

"Well... yes," Neville said as he waddled clumsily towards them, "More or less. Actually that was quite a good one. It's difficult for me."

Joog smiled and shook his head, and then addressed them all, "We are surrounded by food. Look!"

They looked around and realized that they were surrounded by ripe juicy gooseberries which tasted delicious and relieved their hunger and thirst at the same time. They sat in a circle around the bush without speaking a word as they ate sweet gooseberry after gooseberry. Amalek and Seph threw gooseberries to Neville which he caught in his great bill. After a few minutes Joog spread his snowy-white wings, flew into the air and hovered a few feet above the circle of friends.

"We ought to go, you know... and I think the best route is via Butterknowle. We can eat there and then continue," he said, "People there are very friendly." Then his gaze fixed on something in the distance, "Hang on..." and he landed on Seph's shoulder and pointed with a wing, "See, over there. There's some rain on the way. And when it rains... well... it really pours. It's bound to be a really heavy downpour. We need shelter..."

They all stood up and looked in the direction of the Kingdom of Gems. Joog was of course right. The sky was blue and bright, but in the far distance a dark cloud, like a line across the sky, had appeared.

"It can't be that Dark Wizard…" Amalek paused and shuddered at the thought of him.

Seph gazed at the cloud, "It's coming from our kingdom, so it could be."

Amalek shuddered again, "He can't be sending his spell over here, with snow and pepper in that cloud, can he?"

Joog looked anxious, "Surely not," he began, "He can't do that can he?"

"We're protected," said Amalek, then she looked worried, "But what about everything else!"

Seph turned to Joog, "Perhaps he's trying to capture this kingdom too! Quick, check that you've still got magic ink on you," and he looked under his sock for the golden ink. They all checked and found the ink still there.

"But… but does it work in this kingdom?" said Amalek, sounding alarmed.

"I don't know," said Joog.

"What shall we do then?" cried Amalek.

"Let's find shelter," Seph replied. He had grown even more in strength, courage and confidence since the incident with Old Howard and overcoming his despair with the help of his sister, "We need to find shelter. Quick! Into the trees!"

"Quick," cried Amalek, "It's coming!"

"Run," urged Joog, "Run!"

Neville began a slow waddle.

"You need to fly," said Joog, "Amalek and Seph, can you lift him and get him airborne?"

They lifted him up together and ran. Neville spread his wings and then they let go, like launching a toy plane. He dropped first and then floated up into the air above their heads. They sprinted through the trees. The clouds were approaching rapidly. They needed to find a large enough tree to provide good shelter soon but there just did not seem to be one close by, so they kept running. Joog and Neville did not want to leave the others to scout around again as they remembered what happened last time.

"I don't like this!" Joog said, as they gathered around a the rugged trunk of a old elm tree, "Believe me. I've just got a feeling about this. That Dark Wizard Troubler will be trying everything to stop us. I'm sure it's him." He turned to the Prince and Princess and looked at them with his glowing golden-yellow eyes.

"It's not knowing what will happen next," Seph said, "That makes it so difficult. I feel he's watching us but we can't see him."

"Look!" said Amalek, pointing at the approaching cloud, "It's not a cloud, it's something else."

Joog turned in the air, his powerful sight focused on the cloud and immediately he knew what it was, "It's black... black ravens! Look at them all! There must be over a hundred!"

They all saw it now; a large mass of ravens approaching, a huge group of swirling shapes, flying straight towards them, stretched out across the sky and scanning as much of the ground below as they could, moving their heads this way and that, gazing below, searching... searching, frantic to find the enemy and serve their master the Dark Wizard Troubler.

"They're looking for us!" said Seph, "Where shall we hide?"

"Quick!" said Joog, "Deeper into the trees."

They ran to a thicker clump of trees, whilst Joog and Neville glided above them and under the branches. They thought they had made it in time, but then they realised they had been seen because a great chorus of cackling, an uproar of excited noises erupted as the ravens arrived overhead.

"There!" shouted one of the ravens, "Down there in the trees!"

"Attack!" shouted another.

Shadows sped across the grass and darkness grew as the ravens dropped through the air towards the clump of trees. The whole area fell into their shadow as the evil flock came closer. They flew with stunning skill, weaving through the air and in between each other with incredibly controlled twists and turns, one second flying upside down, then with a precise adjustment of their glossy black wings, righting themselves.

The screeching, mixed with the sound of swishing wings which filled the warm air seemed to add to the sense of terrible doom that these black creatures brought with them. Every one of them was cackling, sounding like some sinister laughter, as it trumpeted their arrival and their evil intention, and filled the travellers with icy fear. The great flock of ravens fell like black stones towards the trees.

Down below, gripped with terror, Seph, Amalek, Joog and Neville all huddled together closely under some bushes that surrounded a tree, as if they could protect each other from the imminent attack. They were ready for the attack, or at least as ready as they could be. Seph held the magic drop in his hand - he did not want to be too late this time. He shuddered at the thought of Flop and Miriam being captured, and that if only he had run quicker, got there in time and used the magic drop he might have stopped it happening. But now, this time, he

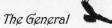

felt he was ready as the screeching ravens descended from above to the tops of the trees.

"Look!" whispered Neville, "They're pecking at insects. They're just eating!"

"So that was what all the fuss was about," whispered Joog relieved, "It was the food, not us! The stupid greedy things."

They all stayed completely still, and smiled with relief as they watched the ravens feasting on insects, their black feathers highlighted with blue, purple and green where the mottled sunlight touched them. The sun was low now, sending its rays angling brightly through the leaves. The ravens hopped around from branch to branch frantically fighting with each other as they stabbed and picked with their beaks and tried to get the most. They were making noises now of "Pruk, pruk" and "Crronk!" Occasionally one would make a deep ringing sound of "Tonk!" Gradually they settled down as their hunger was satisfied. Then one of them opened its long arched bill and spoke.

"As your leader, I think that we should keep searching," he said in a thin nasal voice. He had a black metal chain around his neck with a black compass hanging on it. In the bright sunlight some silver engraving shone out; it was the Dark Wizard's coat of arms delicately worked into the lid in silver and black.

"Who said you're the leader?" snapped another.

"The Master," said the first sharply.

"When? I never heard it," said Gerr, whose cracked bill had lost its shine after he had tried to steal the ruby.

"Well, that's *either* because you don't listen *or* because you weren't there," said the first.

"I'm the leader!" screeched another raven from nearby

tree, jumping up to the top branch.

"I'm the leader!" yet another one screeched louder than all the rest as if this would make his claim overwhelm the others. This sparked off a confused chorus with most of them shouting either "I'm the leader!" or "No you're not, I am!" After a while this died down and the one who had spoken first flapped up to the top of the tallest tree and perched there.

"Listen, males… and females," his nasal voice carried a sense of cruel determination, and they all looked at him and fell silent, "In view of the fact that an army needs a leader, in fact a general, to succeed, and as we are an army, are we not?" there was a cackle of agreement from the great crowd of ravens, "And the Master has ordered us to succeed, correct?" another cackle, "Then I will be your leader and your general. I *am* your general. Anyway, the master appointed me and this compass proves it!" He shook the chain around his neck with his beak and then held it out by clutching it in a clawed foot so that the black metal compass hung freely, swinging gently on the chain. Then he

let   go

with his foot and flicked the compass with a clawed toe and it gave a little ring and spun in the sunlight; the silver of the coat of arms flashed brightly.

"Have any of you got one?" he continued, "No, because he appointed *me*. Got it? And I will lead you to success. Now does anyone want to oppose me?" his voice sounded cold and menacing, and he looked very dominant and strong as they gazed up at him, some of them squinting into the sun. He had no use at all for a compass as he could naturally navigate by instinct, as they all could, but he felt proud of it nevertheless. To him it was like wearing a medal which showed his importance and he puffed out his neck feathers with pride, "If you do want to challenge me, then step up now. If not then be told by me, your general, what to do!" There was a hushed silence. He enjoyed the feeling of power and superiority over the others. Then he continued, "There is no one with the courage, as I thought. So, you will call me 'Sir.'" Silence. Then suddenly he shouted loudly, "Call me 'Sir'!" The ones closest to him jumped with the sudden noise.

"Yes, sir!" they all said together.

"Good. That's better. Here are your orders." He now sounded very matter of fact. "We will continue our search now. We will find the enemy and then... we will kill them. We will split into two squadrons, male and female, and we'll see who finds them first. A little healthy competition to help us along. The females particularly have something to prove as they know they are weaker. And also after all the trouble we had making them enrol in the army to start with. So, I appoint you, Urrg, to lead the females as their Captain, the leader of the female squadron." Urrg puffed up her feathers with pride.

"Thank you sir!" she said.

Then he continued, "We will lea..."

"Shhhh," interrupted an old bird called Crayle who was sitting just below the General. He only had one eye and was turning his head at an unusual angle to look up at the imposing black figure of the General on the branch above.

"Don't 'shush' me," the astonished General exclaimed angrily, "Are you challenging my authori..."

"No, sir," he interrupted. He looked nervous but defiant, "But, sir, be quiet."

"What!?" exclaimed the General.

"I mean... sshh... listen... I ... I think we are being watched."

Immediately they all became completely silent and still and then began jerking their heads nervously in all directions as they looked around. Then Crayle whispered, "I think there's something in that bush down there, at the foot of this tree... sir."

They all looked down with their beaks pointing towards the ground. The General put his head on one side as he gazed below and listened.

"Can't hear a thing," he said quietly but sharply, "Probably your imagination old bird. But I suppose we'll have to check it out just in case. Squadrons, are you ready?"

"Yes, sir!" they all replied.

"Shhhh! Keep quiet," he said softly bringing the tip of his wing up to his beak, "Male squadron... Attennnnnnnn...tion!" All the males got ready, poking their heads forwards as they fixed their beady black eyes on the bush below. The females looked offended and mumbled disgustedly, "Why can't we do it?" and "We're

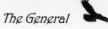

just as good as they are." and "He only picked them because he's a male himself."

"We'll get our chance," said Urrg, "I promise you that…"

"Attack!" shouted the General.

At this exact moment Neville flew out of the bush. The ravens hesitated.

"Stop!" shouted the General, "False alarm!" but four keen young ravens had taken off and had started chasing Neville and snapping at his scarf as it trailed behind him. The sun had now dropped behind the horizon and in the twilight the ravens looked like huge black bats. One of them caught hold of Neville's scarf, but the scarf jerked and threw him off, and he dropped behind the others.

"Come back!" thundered the General, and immediately they gave up the chase and turned to fly back, "Don't waste your energy on that. It's only a silly overgrown seagull!"

"It worked," whispered Seph in the bushes below.

"Yes," whispered Amalek as they stayed completely still in the bush, "But he was heavy to lift!" They had thrown him out of the bush to get him airborne.

The four ravens landed back in the tree.

"That scarf," said one, "Threw me off! It moved by itself."

"Don't be stupid," snapped the General, "It was the wind, and your lack of flying skills. Practice, that's what you need. Practice."

"But…"

"Right," said the General firmly jerking his head as he spoke which shook the chain and made the compass jiggle against the feathers of his chest, "Female Squadron head due east. That's where I really think they are… out towards Lake Burney, Burney's Hill and on to the Becci Mountains. Search thoroughly. Female squadron!" he shouted, and then he turned to Urrg, "Urrg, take your squadron and serve the Master."

"Female Squadron," shouted Urrg, "Let's go! Due west!" The females took off eagerly and flew off towards in a western direction. The General shook his head in disbelief. Then the compass made a little lurch towards the east which made him jump with surprise.

"You're meant to fly east!" screamed the General, "That way!" He turned his head and nodded his bill towards the east. The female ravens turned in an extremely disorganised way and then joined together and flew past towards the east.

"Male Squadron," he said sharply, looking around at the fifty or more ravens that were left. "Now that we've got rid of them *we* can find the enemy," he clutched the chain in his beak so that the compass hung for them to see. He gave it another flick with a claw which made it ring and spin again. Then he released it and let it hang down against his chest feathers once more, "I actually feel sure that the enemy will be heading for Butterknowle over there," and he pointed with a wing, "If they go north they would have to cross the river without a bridge and then go through that great thick forest. No, they will head for Butterknowle where there's a bridge and they can eat and sleep. They'll pick up the road leading to Lake Beautiful and, of course, Elzaphan's Castle. But they won't get that far will they?"

"No sir! They won't, sir!" they answered.

"And why won't they?" continued the General directing this question to one particular raven.

"I don't know, sir!" he shouted back.

"Because we will catch them before they get there, won't we?" he asked them all.

"Yes, sir! We'll catch them, sir!" they shouted back.

"Then we'll show the females who is best. And be in great favour with our Master. So, Male squadron… Attennnnnn…tion!" He checked his compass and again it made a little lurch, this time towards the west. He looked at it for a moment and then shouted, "Male squadron… take flight!"

To the considerable relief of Seph, Amalek and Joog hiding in the bush below, the ravens took off. They headed west with speed and quickly faded into the darkness, led by the General. Crayle and another elderly bird were at the back and struggling to keep up. When Joog was absolutely sure that all the ravens were well out of sight they emerged from their hiding place.

"Thank goodness they've gone," said Amalek smiling with relief, "They give me the creeps."

"Me too," Seph agreed, "But they've gone now, and we know where they're looking!"

"And it's in the wrong place," added Joog, "We're definitely not heading for Butterknowle now! We will go north straight to the Great River Sween. We'll have to find a way to cross which may be a problem, but really we have no choice." He looked up, "Good, here's Neville."

Whilst Neville flew above they moved out of the trees and back onto the path. The last glow of light faded from the horizon and night descended. They continued north where the path passed through Dundonnel Vale nestled between two hills. They tried to keep out of sight as much as possible and were protected in some ways by the darkness of night which now surrounded them. At the same time the dark made them feel vulnerable and they feared that the flocks of ravens could easily change their minds and suddenly be overhead. They felt heavy-hearted about the loss of Flop and Miriam and wondered whether they would ever see them again. This sadness engulfed them as they travelled in heavy silence.

The moon rose and shed a silver light on the slopes of the valley. They decided that despite the danger of the ravens returning they were too tired to travel much further. They would have to find a place to rest and sleep. They began to climb up the grassy slope of the valley.

"Stop," said Seph, "What's that noise?"

They all stopped climbing and listened.

"It's water," exclaimed Amalek with enthusiasm, "Running water. It must be a stream... come on."

Joog and Neville were the first to reach the source of the water sounds. "It *is* a stream!" Joog called back to the others.

Soon they were all quenching their thirst and splashing their faces with the fresh spring water which sparkled in the moonlight.

"We could sleep here," Joog suggested, "Then we'll have water for breakfast. On this grass?" he turned to the others, "I'll keep watch again because I've got the best eyes and ears for the job."

"But you must get some sleep as well," Amalek piped up.

"Yes," Seph joined in, "I'll help keep watch."

"Thanks," said Joog, "I'll let you know if I really need to sleep."

"And I'll sing you a riddle-song," said Neville.

Neville had been paddling in the shallow stream. He clambered out, waddled clumsily onto the grass, settled down and began to sing. It was just what they needed to cheer them up and strengthen their spirits. They lay down, listened carefully to the riddle and put their minds to working it out.

> "We live along the hedgerows,
> where cool breezes blow
> in winter, when we build our dens
> to hide from frost and snow.
>
> "We live along the hedgerows,
> where pools of summer sun,
> lend us the taste of nature's grace
> when freely we can run.
>
> "We live along the hedgerows,
> and carry our defence
> against fierce creatures who try to eat us,
> so we can banish them hence.
>
> "We live along the hedgerows
> and emerge into the night,
> where our round ears listen and our sharp eyes glisten
> under the soft moonlight."

Chapter 10

~ The Phantom ~

After a while Flop stopped struggling. It was doing no good at all and only making the journey more uncomfortable as well as tiring him out. The journey he was on was unknown and all he knew was that Old Howard who was carrying the sack kept walking. This made it a very bumpy uncomfortable ride.

They had been travelling for some hours. The daylight had faded into night, midnight had passed and now the dawn was approaching. There was a little light in the sack from the moonlight which came through the mesh of the material. With his excellent nighttime cat's eyes, Flop could see perfectly. But he was frightened and on the verge of panic. This was really very scary; being carried in a sack by this man who was working for the Dark Wizard Troubler. All he could think of was escape, but how could it be done?

"Flop," said Miriam in his ear which made him jump as he had forgotten about his little companion. They had been too afraid to speak since they had been captured and after Flop stopped struggling Miriam had fallen asleep. She did not know what had happened.

"Where are we?" she asked.

"In a sack! We're prisoners, I'm afraid," whispered Flop, then he put a paw to his mouth, "But shhh, we must keep quiet."

"How did we get in here?" Miriam whispered, looking puzzled and frightened.

"It's Old Howard," replied Flop, "He put us in this sack. He's carrying us and that's why we're bumping up and down."

"Where's he taking us to?" asked Miriam whose whispering voice seemed to be getting softer and softer with fear.

"I don't know and I don't like to even think about it." In fact Old Howard was heading for an old deserted wooden shack at the foot and to the north of Burney's Hill.

"Then we must escape, of course," Miriam squeaked softly.

"That," said Flop, "Is easy to say. Here we are, tied up tight in…"

"Have you forgotten?" interrupted Miriam, "That mice, like me, can bite! We can bite through anything. In my time I've bitten through…" Miriam stopped abruptly as they felt they were falling... and then, BUMP! But even in the sack Flop twisted around and landed on his feet. Now they felt Old Howard picking up the sack and lifting it into the air. A rope rubbed against something above them as Old Howard hauled them higher and then tied the rope. They felt the sack gently swinging to and 'fro. Then they heard voices.

"Leave the cat here… no, you'd better get rid of it first. Then, you must go back."

"No! Oy've caught one 'aven't oy? And that's wha'

yer wanted," replied the distinctive voice of Old Howard. Flop looked at Miriam and mouthed silently, "Who's he talking to?"

"You've caught one, yes, but not the right one." The voice was silky smooth but with a clarity and coldness that sent shivers down their spines, "When I asked for the Prince I *meant* the Prince. The Princess would have done, but not a stupid cat!" Then they recognised it. It was the Dark Wizard Troubler. They had only heard his voice twice before when he shouted at them at the palace, but it was so distinctive that there was no doubt about it. They shook with fear.

"But," whispered Flop, "It can't be the Dark Wizard Troubler! He can't leave the Kingdom of Gems without taking the spell with him and freeing everyone. Unless he's left to come after us to kill us, then he plans to go back and cast his spell again! That must be it. He's so afraid of us, or probably afraid of Wizard Elzaphan, that he's taken a chance and left."

"Then we must all go back to the Kingdom of Gems," whispered Miriam, "That would serve him right! He'd be looking for us here and we'd be back there, free... and waiting for him."

"Good idea," Flop looked serious, "But there's a slight problem. We're trapped in this sack! And, anyway, how do we tell the others?" These facts were undeniable and meant they could do nothing at the moment. Then Old Howard spoke.

"Oy said oy'd catch one... well oy 'ave. Now oy want moy rewards!"

"The cat's no good," the Dark Wizard sounded calm and calculated, "Kill it now. If you had caught one worth catching, like the Prince or the Princess, or that meddlesome owl, or even that mad albatross that is trying to help them, then OK, fine, no problems. But now, now that you failed me, well it's a different story isn't it? Here is your next task. You must stop them crossing the river. Find a way of drowning them... that would do it. And we'll find another way of dealing with the birds. If you kill the Prince and Princess I'll increase your wages."

"By 'ow much?" growled Old Howard, and he gave a tug at one side of his trousers to pull them higher.

"Let's say I'll make it worth your while. That little piece of gold I gave you was just the beginning. Think about it. Much more gold! But... if you refuse," he hissed out the next words, "I shall strike you down!" These menacing words silenced Old Howard, and the two eavesdroppers suspended just above felt the power and the icy chill of the threat, and it made them both feel cold inside.

Suddenly Miriam whispered excitedly, "I can see through, Flop! Put your face against the cloth." Flop put his face right against the cloth and looked through, and sure enough Miriam was right; they could see through. The twilight of the immanent dawn made everything clear to Flop's eyes. There was Old Howard sitting on the ground beneath them leaning against a tree, and they could see that the sack they were trapped in was hanging by a rope from a branch above his head. They could also see the broken-down wooden shack. They looked around but could see no one else.

"Alroight, alroight," said Old Howard who seemed to have accepted that he had to do what he was told, "Oy'll go after 'em once more, but oy'm restin' first."

"I would rather you killed the cat now and then went to do the task," said the wizard, "You can rest and sleep afterwards."

Flop and Miriam looked at the place where the voice came from. Barely visible was the faintest outline, like a ghost which is hardly there and which you can see right through. It was the outline of the Dark Wizard Troubler. The clearest parts were his black eyes and the black stars on his cloak and hat. It was an image of him, just as sinister as the real thing, especially when it spoke as clearly as if he had been there himself.

"Oy'm just restin' first, understand?" Old Howard growled impatiently, "Oy 'aven't slept all noight. Oy'm not yer slave yer know, oy'm 'elpin' yer out," and he lifted a bottle of whisky to his lips and took a great swig of it.

"Have you forgotten our little agreement," the phantom Dark Wizard sneered.

"No, oy 'aven't forgotten our agreement. Oy'll keep moy side an' you make sure…," and he took another swig and then shouted, "You keep yours! Now leave me alone to ge' some rest!"

"Resting later rather than now is far preferable. If you think about it, resting later will be all the sweeter," the cold calculated voice continued, "Especially when the job is done, because then the gold will be yours."

"Restin' later is no good," shouted Old Howard, "Oy'm too tired an' so oym' restin' now! An' that's that!" and he lifted the whiskey bottle and took several long noisy gulps which emptied it. The bottle slipped from his hand and rolled away, his chin dropped onto his chest and he fell into a deep drunken sleep.

They wondered what the Phantom Dark Wizard Troubler would do now and they both kept their eyes fixed upon him. As they watched they saw him shake his ghostly head, scowl in frustration and then to their great relief gradually fade away into nothing.

"Right," said Miriam decisively, "Old Howard won't be troubling us for a while, so let's escape shall we, Flop? We must escape before he wakes," and she began gnawing at the sack. Flop admired her plucky bright attitude. He found it helped to lift his spirits when he certainly needed lifting. It seemed to him that the situation they were in was dire; they were soon to be killed and in the meantime there was nothing worse for a cat than to be trapped in a small place. The sense of panic had stayed with him all the time. But Miriam, although she was tiny, was a source of strength with her positive idea of escape. He just hoped it would work.

However, after ten minutes of chewing as hard as she could she had only managed to make a tiny hole.

"This is tough!" she said, "It's the toughest sack I've ever come across. It's been strengthened somehow."

Miriam kept biting until after an hour, punctuated with little rests, she had managed to make the hole slightly bigger. With encouragement from Flop she kept at it, but it took a few hours before the hole had grown to about half the size of a mouse. After a rest Miriam resumed. It was not until afternoon that she was able to poke her head through. When evening came she was finally rewarded for all her effort.

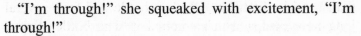

"I'm through!" she squeaked with excitement, "I'm through!"

"Is it big enough for your body?" asked Flop.

"Yes. At least I think so."

There were loud snoring noises rising from below where Old Howard still appeared to be fast asleep. He was no longer leaning against the tree trunk but had slipped down and was lying with his mouth wide open, flat on his back, on the grass. His head was facing straight up which meant that if he opened his eyes he would be staring straight up at the sack. Miriam tried to push her body through, but it stuck and she was left half in and half out.

"Give me a push," whispered Miriam to Flop. He pushed with a paw and sure enough Miriam was through, but before she had time to catch hold of the sack she was falling. As she fell she brushed old Howard's cheek with her tail and a few tiny bits of bitten sack floated down and fell into his mouth. Miriam landed just beside his head on the grass. He woke up straight away.

"What was that!" he said, and he spat out the bits of sack, "Yuk!" he exclaimed and looked around and then up at the sack. As he stared at it Miriam quickly scurried away and hid in the grass. Old Howard scrambled to his feet, hitched up his trousers which had slipped down a little and looked up again at the sack. Luckily the hole was just out of his view. He sat down again, leant against the tree and gazed intently at the place where the ghostly Dark Wizard Troubler had been before. He smiled when he saw there was no sign of the phantom and was just about to close his eyes to resume his sleep when the faint ghostly figure reappeared right in front of him.

"Good," said the voice of the phantom, "You're awake

at last. And rested I hope?"

Old Howard rubbed his eyes and scratched his head. "Yeah," he replied sleepily, focusing in on the ghostly see-through image. Then he suddenly remembered something and slipped his hand into his pocket. Immediately relief spread over his face as he felt the small bar of gold that the Dark Wizard had given him.

"So," the phantom said, "You feel rested and ready for action, I hope?"

"I feel terrible an' all the worse for seein' you, Black Oiys!"

"Well, we are civil and polite, aren't we?" he sneered sarcastically, "That's not the way to speak to someone who's doing you such a great favour."

"Oy don't care!" bellowed Old Howard.

"Now," the voice was slow and precise, "You will kill the cat and then go and complete your task. Let the reward for success spur you on, as well as certain… mmmmmm … shall we say consequences if you fail." This made Old Howard extremely cross. His brow furrowed as he sighed and shook his head, "Now," continued the phantom's voice, "What is your task?"

"To go an' catch 'em."

"Wrong!" the voice shouted back, "Stop them crossing the river and drown them for good luck! Do you understand, you great idiot!" the voice was terrifying with its cutting tone.

"Yes…s…s…sir," stammered Old Howard whose face had turned ashen with fear.

"That's better," the voice was calm again, but hissing out the words with venom, "Time is getting short so go to the Great River Sween, and go fast! They might cross by the Forest of the Fairies, but far more likely somewhere

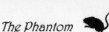

near Butterknowle. But go north first where the river is easier to cross... in fact you'll have to cross two rivers, just before they join. Then work your way along the northern river bank of the Sween. My army of ravens are out hunting... hopefully, they've got them already. But if not, then you will. I'll help you with powers when the time comes, but they *must not* cross the river. If they cross they begin to go out of my power and into Elzaphan's and it will be more difficult, 'though for me, not impossible. Now, go, and don't forget I'm watching you!"

Old Howard seemed to be completely resigned to the fact that he was being controlled and had to do what he was told. He went into the shack and came out carrying a bag which he slung over his shoulder and then he started trudging off.

"What about the cat?" said the phantom as he walked past it. Old Howard turned back and leaping up as much as his short legs could manage with his heavy round body he punched the sack in anger. There was a cry from Flop.

"Take that, you stupid cat! Oy'll deal with yer properly when oy get back!" He turned and as he passed the ghostly figure, barely visible in the sloping rays of the evening sunlight, he swung a fist at its head. His fist passed straight through and he nearly lost balance and then started trudging off once more.

"Now, now," said the phantom calmly, "Temper, temper," and it faded away.

Miriam quickly climbed the tree, ran along the branch and down the sack until her face appeared at the hole.

"Are you alright?" asked Miriam.

"Yes, I think so!" answered Flop, and he licked his side, "But... ow! That hurt. Luckily it was my side and not my head."

"I'm coming in," said Miriam.

"No! Now that you've escaped you ought to go. You're free. Go and find the others."

"I'm not leaving you," Miriam sounded as if she had made up her mind.

"But it'll take ages to make a hole big enough for me to get out."

"As I said, I am not leaving you," she said even more decisively, "And anyway, how can I travel without you? It would take me days and days to go anywhere!" and she began to force her way in through the hole again.

"Well, I only hope we can escape before he returns," said Flop.

After leaving the mountains Tally had travelled along the River Jinny, on the north bank, until he reached Lake Jin. Then he had taken a north-west direction. His land mark was Burney's Hill which he knew would take him in the right direction. Following Hawkeye's advice he was heading for Wizard Elzaphan's Castle to report to the great wizard and offer his services.

Stopping only briefly to rest and eat, he had hopped along with youthful energy all day. The night had drawn in around him and by the time it was dark he began to feel alone and frightened.

Midnight approached and passed.

His fear deepened and he kept thinking that he was being followed. The dark shapes of trees looked like sinister monsters towering above him and he began to panic. He felt too scared to stop and it seemed safer to keep moving and as fast as he could. His hop became a run, his young legs pounding the ground and throwing up small clouds of dusty earth, and soon he was bounding along at full pelt.

Suddenly he heard a voice.

"Tally, it's alright," said the voice, tranquil and strong, "Tally, stay calm. Just remember... KYWAY."

Tally stopped running, skidding to a halt on the grass.

"Gramps," he called out, looking around, "Gramps."

His senses opened out. There was no sign of Hawkeye. But he *had* heard the voice, and it *was* his grandfather. As he gazed into the darkness he realised he was at the foot of Burney's Hill with its dark southern slope rising up above him. He flopped down in a patch of grass. His frantic panic had completely dissolved in the comforting words he had heard. He felt strong again and contented in the knowledge that he had covered a good part of his journey.

As he lay there exhaustion took over. Within a few minutes he had fallen into a deep sleep that lasted through the remainder of night and well into the next day.

The night spent on the slopes of Dundonnel Vale had passed uneventfully. In the morning Joog woke the others and they found they were surrounded by a grey mist which seemed to add to the dull heaviness that weighed upon their hearts. They were already worried about Flop and Miriam and now, with the mist, they could not see if the ravens were coming or not. There was no breakfast but they were able to drink from the stream and splash water over their faces. They were relieved when the new sun pierced the mist and the blue sky began to open up above.

After walking steadily for several hours Amalek and Seph were growing weary. The two birds, Joog and Neville, were fine; they had just been gliding gently in the air.

"Where are we?" asked Amalek, stopping to look down at all the bushes growing close to the ground.

"This is called the Clungberry Fields," replied Neville from above, "Over there," Neville nodded to the east, "Are the Fulwell Fens which cannot be crossed on foot. And just beyond that hill ahead is the river; the Great River Sween."

"So, keep going," said Joog swooping down beside them to encouraging them onwards.

Seph stooped down to look at some bushes. "Joog?" he called out, "Come and look at these."

Joog swooped down and landed on Seph's shoulder.

"Look," Seph said, pointing, "Berries."

"Oh, those are clungberries."

"Can we eat them?"

"You certainly can," he replied, "I should have thought of it myself… but they hide under the leaves. They're very nourishing. If you pick and eat them they will give you strength."

The two children looked around and sure enough hidden under the leaves of the bushes was an abundant supply of the deep red berries. They were small and long like beans and deliciously sweet. The taste was completely new to them. Joog was right about the berries; after eating a few they did feel stronger and enjoying the berries stopped them having fearful thoughts about the Dark Wizard Troubler, the ravens and Old Howard. Once again they threw some into the air which Neville caught in his great bill.

When they had eaten enough they started walking again and with the strength of the berries inside them they made good progress. The sun began to drop in the sky and by evening they had reached the foot of a small hill. They followed the path as it sloped upwards, always keeping alert for the return of the ravens, but they did not come.

All along the path, as they climbed the hill, there grew some fruit trees; there were apple, pear and cherry. They picked fruit, ate them, then tossed the stones or cores away into the long grass. The sun slowly dipped behind the hill as the day drew in and shadow fell on them. Sunset would arrive within a couple of hours so they kept moving because they wanted reach the river before dark.

"Come on, you slow land creatures," called out Joog cheerfully from the air, "We'll have to move faster than this."

Amalek and Seph picked up their pace and soon they reached the brow of the hill. As they walked over they moved back into the sunlight and could see the river ahead. A wonderful view of the northern part of the kingdom was spread out before them. They could see the Great River Sween running along the southern fringe of the Forest of the Fairies. Beyond that the still waters of Lake Beautiful surrounded their destination, the high-cliffed Keill Island with Wizard Elzaphan's Castle on the top. Far away they could see distant mountains, the Daawa Mountain range, fading into blue-grey in the haze of the low summer sun. To reach Lake Beautiful they would have to cut across some fields, cross the river and then pass through the thick forest.

"Is that the Sween?" asked Seph, pointing.

"Yes it is," Joog replied, "It's a wide river and so it's just a question of how you two get across. But we'll face that one when we get there."

In the west the Male Squadron, a large group of over fifty ravens, was circling over the little village of Butterknowle. They had spent the night sleeping in some trees just outside the village near Authen Water which was on a direct line from Gooseberry Wood to Butterknowle. The General had ordered that they took turns keeping watch, and he organised that two at a time would do shifts of one hour. Now they were all airborne and keenly looking for the enemy. They had been searching all day with occasional short rests and were becoming tired.

"Where are they?" said the General with growing frustration, "They should be on their way to here." He had wound up the compass chain to stop the compass from swinging around as he flew and now it looked like a medallion on a short chain around his neck.

"Perhaps they're on their way, sir," said Gerr. He was keen, young and ambitious and had started flying close to the General in the hope of being appointed second in command.

"We've flown the whole route and we've watched all through the night, you duffer," said the General, "Remember?"

"Yes, sir, of course, sir," said Gerr.

"But they can't just disappear. Where are they?" the General asked again, scanning the ground below, not expecting an answer, but just speaking his thoughts aloud.

"Perhaps they've arrived here, sir," Gerr said brightly.

"Look, they can't have got here yet," said the General getting frustrated with the conversation, "Humans don't travel that fast, do they?"

"No, sir, they don't, sir," said Gerr with enthusiasm.

"Well, I'm wondering..." the General began.

"Perhaps they're in Butterknowle Manor, sir," interrupted Gerr.

"Listen, young raven, do you really want to help?"

"Yes, sir, I do, sir,"

"Then... shut up!" the General screamed, "You keep talking rubbish! Can't you think properly! Oh, why am I surrounded by fools? Be quiet and listen. They must have gone north, although I'm very surprised. Or they're hiding like cowards."

"Perhaps they're..." began Gerr, and then he stopped remembering just in time that he had just been told to shut up.

"It's almost as if..." began the General thoughtfully, "Almost as if they knew... but they couldn't... unless..." He adjusted his flight and turned his head to face Gerr, and then spoke quietly to him so that the others could not hear, "Are they all... all the squadron that is... reliable?"

"I think so, sir."

"I want you to tell me if you hear anything, or see anything, anything at all that is, that might expose a spy amongst us. Understand?"

"Yes, sir," replied Gerr, feeling pleased that he had

been trusted and given an important job.

The General rose slightly higher and addressed the whole group, "We'll search the village thoroughly. If we don't find them there we'll sleep somewhere... and then tomorrow we'll follow the river and get them as they cross. By the way, where did Old Howard go? I know my Master is using him, but where is he? We don't want him popping up and interfering." The compass gave a little jump and the General put his head on one side, looked at it and wondered what it meant.

"Perhaps he's..." began Gerr again.

"No! I don't want to hear any more of your stupid guesses," shouted the General. Then he noticed two ravens flying lower than all of the others and dropping behind. He looked at them disapprovingly, "Who are they, Gerr?"

"That's Crayle and Jum."

"Oh, yes," said the General thoughtfully, "Crayle's that old bird with one eye who made that stupid fuss back there about the albatross. He's useless."

"What shall I do about them, sir?" asked Gerr.

"Tell them to keep up," snapped the General.

"They're tired, sir."

"We're all tired. But we've got a job to do."

"But they're old, sir," replied Gerr, "That's why they can't keep up."

"That's no excuse. They're in the army, and if they're in the army they should pull their weight, shouldn't they?"

"Yes, sir!"

"I'm not having indolence in my army." He glared down at them from above, and then screeched, "You two, keep up!"

Crayle and Jum glanced up with surprise. Their feathers looked drab and dishevelled with greying patches here and there. The crisp metallic sheen displayed by the younger birds had all but faded, although the odd glint of purple or blue occasionally flashed in the sunlight. Crayle tilted his head to look up with his one eye.

"What?" croaked Crayle.

"Catch up, you fool!" shouted the General.

"What?" croaked Crayle again.

"Go and tell them, Gerr."

Gerr wheeled around and then swooped down, hoping that the General was noticing his enthusiasm.

Meanwhile Crayle turned to Jum and asked, "What did he say?"

"I don't know, dear," she replied. "He's too far away... it sounded like 'Match up, you two,' but I'm really not sure."

"Well, what does *that* mean?" Crayle shook his head, "That can't be right."

"Well, ask again then, dear."

Crayle was just opening his beak to call out 'What?' again when Gerr arrived.

"Catch up, you two. By the General's command!"

With a great effort the two old birds flapped their wings slightly faster. They rose in the air and gradually caught the others up.

"That's better. Now, squadron! Keep searching for the next hour. If we don't find them then we take some rest and sleep, but not until I say."

Soon after Old Howard had left his shack at the foot of Burney's Hill and was heading north he caught sight of a great flock of ravens flying in his direction. It was the Female Squadron. They too had found some trees to sleep and rest in and had settled in a little wood just north of Lake Burney. In the morning they had resumed their search. After spending several hours scanning the land in between Lake Burney and the Great Crack to the Centre of Ruddha they had flown north, over and past Burney's Hill to look there.

When he saw them coming Old Howard stopped walking and crouched down hoping not to be seen by them, but it was too late. They quickly loomed closer and then dropped out of the clear sky towards him. He watched them descend, squinting into the evening sun with his brow like a furrowed field and his hand above his eyes to shield the sun.

"What are'yer doin'?" shouted Old Howard as he stood up. Urrg was flying in front to lead them.

"Looking for the Prince, Princess, the owl and that cat," she called out, "Have you seen them?" One thing Old Howard knew was that he did not want them or anyone else getting the glory.

"Not 'ere!" he shouted back, "Now get out of 'ere you old bat." He wanted the reward from the Dark Wizard himself.

"Just tell me where they are, will you?" and she swooped past his head making him duck.

"That way, over Burney's Hill," he cried out, pointing, "See that hill with the trees on the top? Over there."

"Then why are you going the other way!" shouted Urrg, twisting her head around, and then turning skilfully in the air to fly towards Old Howard again.

"Ee's given me a different job. 'Onestly, fly over the hill and they're hidin' over there somewhere."

"We've just been over there," shouted Urrg, flying past him a second time and making him duck again.

"Well, you can't 'ave searched properly, can yer?"

"Female squadron! Follow!" screamed Urrg, and the swish of their wings faded as they headed off towards Burney's Hill.

"But, listen," Old Howard whispered, with a rare smile on his round face as they flew away, "You're goin' the wrong way!" he watched them rise up over Burney's Hill to continue their search, "Oh well, suit yerselves," growled Old Howard, "Oy troyed to tell yer but yer wouldn't listen," and then he slipped his hand into his pocket to feel the bar of gold and greedily caress it with his fingers. It was small but heavy and it was this weight that kept pulling his trousers down. He tugged them up again and plodded on towards the river.

Over Burney's Hill, when they were out of sight, Urrg led her squadron down to land in the cluster of trees on the top of the hill. Black feathers shone with blue and green where the patchy red light of the sunset reflected brightly on the ravens' shiny wings. When they were all landed they started preening their feathers and chatting. Urrg had landed high in one of the trees and was looking around at her squadron thoughtfully. Then she spoke.

"Females," she said sternly. Most of them turned to face her, but a few carried on chatting quietly, "Females, I don't trust Old Howard one little bit. And, like most of you I suspect, I don't like or trust the General at all. I think we are being hoodwinked. They are pulling the wool over our eyes and they think we are too stupid to realise. But..." and she raised her voice to make sure they were all listening, "We won't let them do it!"

She had their attention fully now, "*They* want the glory of catching the enemy themselves, don't they? And why... why I ask you... why are they both sending us over here. Now doesn't that strike you as a little suspicious?" There was a chorus of cackling agreement, "The enemy is not over here. So, what are they playing at? Trickery and deceit, that's what it is, and at our expense."

"Trickery!" called out Searle, "At our expense!"

"And deceit," shouted another, "And..."

"We shouldn't allow it," Searle interrupted, "We mustn't allow it any..."

"It makes my blood boil!" Urrg drowned her out as she raised her voice as loud as she could. Silence. She paused and looked around at her captive audience, and then continued calmly, "So what shall we do?" she paused again, "I'll tell you what we'll do. We go where Old Howard was heading. We go where they have not told us to go, OK? And we, the Female Squadron, not them, will kill the enemy!"

They all seemed very excited about this and jumped up and down nodding their great heads.

"Female squadron!" shouted Urrg, "We sleep here... and then, in the morning, at first light, we make our move!"

Chapter 11

~ A Sheet of Ice ~

The four friends had reached the Great Sween and were standing on the grassy bank gazing across. A blazing red sunset painted the sky and was mirrored dramatically in the swirling, gushing waters of the mighty river. Joog had explained how he thought it was wide and deep with a vigorous current that would make it difficult to swim across to the other side. It looked beautiful. The many shades of green from the forest trees on the far side were laid against the glowing sunset behind and the reflection of all this tremored and shook on the disturbed surface. Dotted along the grassy bank were flowers of many colours; there were white daisies, pink rosebay willow herb, red poppies, yellow dandelions and others, and these too reflected in the river making a wonderful display that held the attention of the travellers for a moment. Amalek spoke first.

"It's a shame," she began, "That we can't all fly."

"Yes, I know," Seph agreed, "We'd be across in a jiffy and on our way. As it is, let's face it, we're stuck."

"Yes, this is certainly a challenge," began Joog, "That is a very strong and dangerous current. It's a good thing we avoided those ravens, at least for the moment." He landed on Seph's shoulder. "They're hunting for us over there somewhere." He turned his face towards the west and pointed with his wing, "But sooner or later they'll work out the route that we've taken, won't they?"

Seph nodded, "Yes, but they're bound to spend some time searching over there first."

"I think you're right," Joog agreed, "Let's hope so anyway. So we probably have a bit of time to get across."

"And what about Old Howard?" asked Amalek.

"Well," Joog looked thoughtful, "Now that he's working for the Dark Wizard he has powers. He's dangerous. He may come after us as well. We must be ever watchful and we must find a way to cross. Then we'll have the cover of the forest over there," and he swept his wing through the air to indicate the trees across the river.

"I wonder," piped up Neville from above, "If one of you children held on to my scarf... what do you think? Could I carry you across?"

"Hmmm," Amalek looked doubtful, "You can try, but I think not, we're too heavy."

Neville flew low enough for Seph to grab hold of his scarf. He held on tightly, but Joog was right; the scarf just stretched until Neville was high in the air and Seph was still on solid ground. Then he tried holding onto Neville's great webbed feet as he descended in the air above his head, but again he was too heavy and as soon as he realised that he was pulling the great albatross down he let go. Neville tilted in the air and dipped just above the ground with one wing brushing the grass and the other pointing skywards. One of his webbed feet touched the grass and he took the opportunity and pushed off hard to try and regain his flight. After three one legged hops his wings levelled and he was gliding again. He quickly soared up, wheeling in the air until he was above their heads looking down at them and chuckling with amusement.

"That albatross!" exclaimed Joog laughing, "Put him near the ground and he's more entertaining than a clown!"

The children laughed and looked up at Neville with affection. The spectacular sunset had dwindled to almost nothing, like a dying fire, leaving just a slight glow above the horizon. Darkness was taking over.

"I think we'd better settle for the night," Joog said, "And tackle this problem in the morning. We're all tired and need sleep. But we'll get up before dawn this time and make an early start."

"I'm glad you said that, Joog," said Amalek, "My legs are so tired."

"Mine too," agreed Seph, "What about over there, under those trees?"

"Yes," Joog agreed, "It looks ideal."

"I'll help you watch," said Seph, walking towards the trees, "You need to get some sleep as well, Joog."

"Thank you," Joog nodded, "I'll wake you when you're needed."

Long grass grew under the trees, dotted with red poppies and they found that it was soft and fairly comfortable when they lay down. It was the perfect place to sleep as they were well concealed from any ravens by the trees above and hidden from anyone on foot by the grass. This helped them to relax and fall asleep quickly. Joog perched in the tree above, his eyes alert and his ears picking up the slightest sound.

After a few hours it was Seph's turn and Joog landed

beside him and woke him. Seph walked sleepily to the foot of the tree and sat on a root where he could see above the grass.

"Wake us in a couple of hours," whispered Joog, flying up into the tree again, "Alright? As soon as the sky begins to lighten over the horizon there." He nodded his head in the direction.

"Alright," whispered Seph.

Joog closed his eyes and drifted off to sleep.

Seph was happy being on night watch. He felt he was doing a job that had to be done and enjoyed the challenge of being alert and ready to instantly spring into action if necessary. But as he looked into the darkness he felt the danger they were in. The terrible knowledge that they were being hunted flooded his mind like drops of black ink in water. He wished it was all a dream, a nightmare, which would end and then everything would be alright again, as it was before. But he was not dreaming; they were being hunted and at any moment they could be attacked. It was like have a guillotine hanging over his head and not knowing when it would fall.

Time passed slowly and every so often Seph shifted uneasily as he heard small noises. They were probably just the usual nighttime sounds of nocturnal creatures. Above his head hundreds of stars twinkled in the field of the night sky. The moon cast a pale light softening the blackness of night into shadowy shades of grey, but under the trees behind them, as well as across the river, the darkness was deep. His eyes could not penetrate these areas and this made him edgy. He was not in control.

Time passed, the moon slowly dipped behind the trees and the darkness deepened.

All was quiet now. Seph felt surrounded by stillness

where even the slightest sounds were magnified. Suddenly there was a sound in the trees behind him and he spun his head around. He gazed into the night, through the dark shapes of tree trunks, but the darkness was like a blanket of fog, hiding everything from him. His breath shallowed.

The noise stopped and after a while he turned to look over the grass and across the river. He kept staring into the blackest places, straining to see and he thought he saw something move there. He shuddered.

He glanced above at Joog asleep in the tree, "Joog!" he called out in a half whisper.

Joog woke up immediately. "What is it?" he whispered.

"I don't know," whispered Seph, "There's noises... although it's probably only harmless creatures... through the trees there, behind us. And under those trees over there... it's so dark, but I thought I saw..." He stopped suddenly as there was a slightly louder noise. It was a rustle from under the trees across the river. They both gazed at the place, a little way along the bank and upstream. Then something moved again.

"There is something," whispered Joog, "I saw it. Keep completely still and watch."

For a few minutes they both stared. The sky was lightening with the approach of the dawn and they found that gradually they could see more.

Joog spoke first, whispering. "There's something there. I can see a silhouette. I can see it moving."

"What shall we do?" asked Seph.

"We'll wait and watch."

In the growing light the shape became clearer. But still it was not clear enough to see what it was.

"Perhaps..." whispered Seph hopefully, "Perhaps it's... something harmless." He tried to work out what the shape could be.

"It's a figure..." said Joog, "A person, I think." He kept staring, "Yes, definitely. It's sitting on something, and wearing a cloak with a hood. I'm going to take a look."

"It might not be safe. What if it's Old Howard...?"

"I'm not afraid of him."

"Or it could be... well, we don't know who he's got working for him."

"I can fly silently, you know," whispered Joog, "I'll circle 'round. It's alright."

He was just about to take off when the figure moved. They looked along the river through the shadows of twilight. The figure stood and walked quickly through the trees and along the river bank and away from them. Then it was gone, around a bend in the river.

"It's gone," whispered Seph with relief, "Hasn't it?"

"Yes, I think so," Joog replied, "Just keep watching for the moment."

After a while Joog said, "I'd better take a look now."

Joog took off but immediately landed again when he saw a rowing boat appear from around the bend. In the dim light they watched it glide on the flow of the current. There was a light mist hanging low over the water.

"Wake up the others, Seph," whispered Joog.

Seph moved quietly among the long grass and woke up Amalek and Neville. A few seconds later their heads were just above the grass. The boat moved towards them until it was steered under a group of weeping willow trees which grew down to the water's edge. Now they could see a hooded figure letting go of the oars and standing up in the boat. The figure reached up to a branch, tied the boat and then stepped out onto the bank.

"I don't like this," whispered Amalek, "Who is it?"

In the gloomy light the figure looked ghostly, with the mist hiding its legs and the hood concealing its face. The friends felt they could not move, seized by the fear of who this might be. If they did move now they would give away their position.

Seph whispered, "I don't think we've been seen."

At that moment the figure turned towards them, stood still and then stepped out from the cluster of willows. Then it was walking straight towards them, a black figure with the dawning light behind it. Amalek dropped her head lower and Seph slipped back behind the tree.

"Quick," said Joog, "Into the trees."

As they ran the figure called out to them.

"Do you need a ferry? Or perhaps some food? Or both? Drinking water maybe?"

They all stopped and turned. The figure was standing now, still some distance away.

"Who are you?" called Joog.

"I'm the Ferryman," came the reply. He had stopped walking now, "I can see you're suspicious. Probably wise to be so... but there's no need. Do I sound bad?"

Indeed his voice sounded deep and rich. No one replied. He did not sound bad, not at all, but they were still uncertain. When there was no answer to his question the Ferryman spoke again.

"Do you want to cross?"

"Yes," said Joog, "That is exactly what we do need."

"Do you need food?"

"Yes, we do," said Joog.

"Well, I'll be over there." He pointed under the willow

trees. "You'll have a job to cross by yourselves, unless you walk upstream to where the current is less powerful. You could do that. But there's my ferry if you wish." He turned, walked back under the trees, and then sat down to lean against a trunk.

"I say we trust him," said Seph, looking at the others.

"But," began Amalek, "We don't know who he is."

Seph looked at his sister, "He sounded friendly."

"Of course he does. That's the best way to trick us."

"Yes. I know. But he could have attacked, but he didn't. Why not?"

"Yes," said Joog, "I agree. And also he's left us to go if we want to. Now, that's a good sign, isn't it?"

"It is," said Seph, already taking a step towards the willow trees, "And I just feel that it's safe."

Amalek was nodding slowly now, but spoke cautiously, "I see what you mean... but..."

"Amalek," Joog said flying down to land on her shoulder, "Look, there's a element of chance here, so we keep alert. Alright?" Amalek nodded, "Come on then."

They walked through the fading mist to the willow trees, whilst Neville followed with an ungainly waddle. Amalek hung back slightly from the others, still looking apprehensive. Soon they were standing in front of the Ferryman. He was sitting on the ground leaning against a tree. His cloak was a deep forest green with a hood that hung around his head in such a way that as much as they gazed to see his face it was still hidden. Another rowing boat lay tilted on the grass beside him.

"Well I am the ferryman, and here is the ferry," he waved at the small rowing boat rocking gently on the water, "And if you want I'll row you across. You can have some food and eat it as we go."

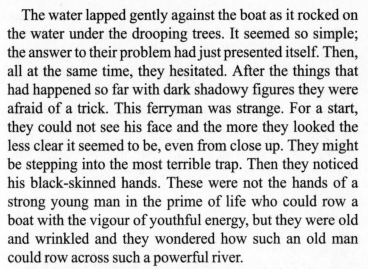

The water lapped gently against the boat as it rocked on the water under the drooping trees. It seemed so simple; the answer to their problem had just presented itself. Then, all at the same time, they hesitated. After the things that had happened so far with dark shadowy figures they were afraid of a trick. This ferryman was strange. For a start, they could not see his face and the more they looked the less clear it seemed to be, even from close up. They might be stepping into the most terrible trap. Then they noticed his black-skinned hands. These were not the hands of a strong young man in the prime of life who could row a boat with the vigour of youthful energy, but they were old and wrinkled and they wondered how such an old man could row across such a powerful river.

"Don't be deceived by appearances, by my ancient body," the ferryman said calmly and softly, reading their thoughts, "You don't think I am strong enough, do you? Didn't you see me row across this morning?"

They nodded.

"Listen, and this is important... very important. Real strength is found within. Never forget this and you will be safe. It is a great great secret - real strength is found within."

As they listened they felt strength flowing into them and they found themselves liking this hooded stranger.

"Well, are you accepting my offers or not?" asked the ferryman and something in his voice made them trust him. It was in the tone; a strength and gentleness behind the words, a sense of limitless kindness that they could not resist.

Nevertheless, Amalek was hesitating, wanting to be absolutely certain that he could be trusted.

"We accept," replied Seph positively, and they got

ready to board the little rowing boat, receive some very welcome food and the ride across the Great River Sween.

Tally was so exhausted from travelling all through the day and half the night that he had slept in the grass right through the next day until the evening light was beginning to fade. He was awoken suddenly by a clear and gentle voice.

'KYWAY.'

It was the voice of his grandfather.

"Keep Your Wits About You," he recollected.

He sat bolt upright and looked around. There was no one in sight. His nose twitched as he sniffed the air and listened, his senses opening out to his surroundings. After a moment he knew what to do next. He would climb Burney's Hill and from the top he would have a view of a large part of the kingdom. It would be like a map to him. He would 'keep his wits about him,' and then plot the rest of his journey.

He set about climbing the hill with vigour. By the time the hill was beginning to level off it was dark. He approached the trees on the very top and picked up a scent. Then he heard voices. He moved slowly and quietly through some bushes to avoid being seen. When he was under the trees he looked up through the leaves of a bush to see the squadron of female ravens settling down for the night.

Tally leant against the trunk of a tree, closed his eyes, and listened to their conversations with interest.

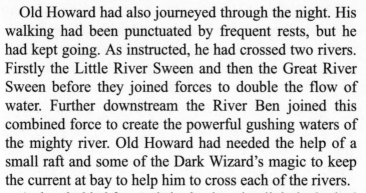

Old Howard had also journeyed through the night. His walking had been punctuated by frequent rests, but he had kept going. As instructed, he had crossed two rivers. Firstly the Little River Sween and then the Great River Sween before they joined forces to double the flow of water. Further downstream the River Ben joined this combined force to create the powerful gushing waters of the mighty river. Old Howard had needed the help of a small raft and some of the Dark Wizard's magic to keep the current at bay to help him to cross each of the rivers.

As he plodded forwards in the dawning light he looked a sad but determined sight, with his shabby trousers wet half way up the legs and his boots squelching with water. One of his hands was in his pocket and gripping the gold bar. He held it tightly, possessively, and occasionally he would release his grip and run his fingers along the edges. Every so often he would take it out to admire it greedily, his black eyes twinkling with covetousness. He would lift it close to his face and stroke it with his grimy fingers. Then he would put it back into his pocket again to keep it safe and give his trousers a tug to compensate for the weight of it.

He moved along the southern fringe of the Forest of the Fairies which skirted the northern river bank and felt more enthusiastic about the 'task' that he had been set by the Dark Wizard Troubler. He had to kill the Prince and Princess who were causing his Master so much trouble. He wondered about the owl and the mystery of that great bird the albatross which he had spotted flying beside the owl when he had captured the cat in the sack. They would be much harder to deal with. It would be no good if they escaped by flying off and sped across Lake Beautiful to Wizard Elzaphan. He would have to think of something.

As he dragged his heavy round body along in the patchy shade of the trees he was blind to the beauty of the river bank. Even in the misty morning light the colours of all the flowers were bright against the green of the grass and presented a rich picture to be enjoyed, but Old Howard was too mean and too distracted by the sinister task he had been given to even notice it. His aim, to kill the Prince and Princess and the animals helping them, filled his selfish mind.

He felt now that somehow the Dark Wizard Troubler was travelling along with him, inside him and looking out through his eyes. He knew that this gave him an amazing sense of strength and power and the feeling that anything could be done. He did not like this at first, but he was beginning to get used to it and even to like it. The best part of it was the enjoyable experience of the power that dwelt inside him.

"Oy can do anything!" he thought.

He was unaware that what was making this happen was the bar of gold in his pocket, his most precious possession which he greedily kept with him at all times. This bar of gold was part of the spell. It had been cut from the square block that was present when the spell was cast and although it was given to Old Howard beforehand it was still invisibly linked to the parent block. When the dark spell was cast it had taken in a small part of the evil presence of the Dark Wizard Troubler. To the Dark Wizard this had been an accidental bonus. He gave the gold to Old Howard to get him into his power and he was delighted to find that after the casting of the spell it began to act as a link. He found he was able for short periods of deep concentration to be with Old Howard, in his mind and thoughts.

Old Howard was facing downstream as he walked and his eyes kept darting along the river and down the far bank where he expected he may see them. The red glow of a bright sunrise lit the scene.

Then he stopped and slipped further into the shadows of the trees where he would be hidden. Taking off one boot at a time, he poured the water out. With great effort he pulled them back on over his wet socks and when he looked up he saw through the dim shadowy light, a little way down the river, a boat rowing across. He watched it cutting silently and speedily through the water. He crouched down and narrowed his eyes as he fixed them on the boat. He could see a cloaked figure rowing forcefully and at the front the owl with the albatross at the back and sure enough the Prince and Princess. A smile touched his lips. He had not expected to find them so easily. The little boat was almost half way across and Old Howard knew that he had to work quickly.

"Stare at the water," said the Dark Wizard's voice in his mind.

He stared at the water. He felt the power of the Dark Wizard Troubler in his mind, acting through him and flowing out through his gaze and into the river. At the point where his gaze was fixed the rippling water became more agitated. The ripples turned into waves and the waves shook and rose as if an invisible dam was blocking the flow of water and building it up like wall. Higher and higher it grew until it was taller than a man and still growing. As the water built up against the invisible dam it crashed into it and the noise increased until it sounded like a rushing waterfall. Meanwhile, along the river where the boat was crossing, the water had stopped flowing and the level was dropping.

Then something distracted Old Howard. Mixed in with the sounds of the raging water were other sounds; sounds of birds that he recognised. He looked up and circling above the little boat was a great flock of ravens, black and angular, loud and raucous as they prepared to dive in for the kill. Then Old Howard realised that his gaze had left the river and the build up of water was falling now.

"Concentrate!" spoke the urgent voice of the Dark Wizard in his head, *"The ravens are on our side too. Work together!"* He obeyed and looked back at the river. Immediately the water began to build again.

"Attack!" shouted the General, but he had been so intent on the boat below which was now more than half way across the river that he had not noticed what was above.

"Attack!" screamed Urrg. The Female Squadron descended upon the males, as the males descended upon the boat.

Old Howard lifted his eyes to see what was happening. *"Concentrate!"* said the voice urgently, desperately, *"Don't stop yet!"* but Old Howard had stopped and the water collapsed and rushed in a mighty torrent, like a huge tidal wave, downstream towards the little boat. The water crashed over the boat just as the Male Squadron was almost upon it and everything, the boat and ravens got carried away in a mass of tumbling water, white froth and black feathers. The Female Squadron who were now right above the massive rolling wave as it sped along, followed it with Urrg leading the flock. The male ravens struggled to free themselves from the great wave, but as soon as they did the females dived upon them and pecked them viciously until they fell back.

"Stop it!" screeched the General who had managed to

get out of the tumbling water.

He rose rapidly towards Urrg, pointing his beak forwards for attack. Urrg was surprised by the General's sudden attack, but just in time she deftly dodged him and he sped past and upwards into the air.

"Our Master will punish you for this!" he shouted from above, and turned to attack again.

Urrg was frightened by his threat. She also realised that he was descending upon her and had the advantage. Frantic panic filled her mind, "Female squadron!" she screamed, "Female Squadron! Leave them! Show pity on the poor weak ones!"

On hearing this the General glided past, giving her a warning stab with his beak.

"A sensible decision," he snapped.

The females stopped attacking the males and gradually they rose out of the wave until all the male and the female ravens were muddled up together and chasing after the wave as one great flock. The whole scene was tinted with the pink glow of the sunrise as the light of the day began to gather.

Old Howard watched this with amazement as the great wave and all that it carried with it disappeared swiftly from view. He felt it had been a success. A great success. He had fulfilled the task; the Prince and Princess could never survive that and he had probably got the two birds as well. If any of them were alive which he was sure they could not be, could not possibly be, then the ravens would get them. He slumped down exhausted against the trunk of an oak tree and fell asleep, whilst the Dark Wizard tried to speak to him in vain.

Meanwhile in the Kingdom of Gems, a few hours earlier during the night before, when Old Howard had been walking to the river to make the great wave, the Dark Wizard had decided to make a journey. He was setting out to do something very important and had decided to assume that Old Howard would be successful. This journey was necessary for the next part of his plan. He had told Jamaar where he was going, instructed him to guard the house in his absence and then had left the house, striding out into the night where snow blanketed everything. Large fluffy flakes flew on the harsh icy wind. He had passed into a copse of trees at the end of the garden and on stepping out of their shelter and heading north he had met the full blast of a blizzard.

He had decided to avoid climbing into the Western Downs where the blizzard would be stronger and the snow deeper. So he turned right until he picked up Charin Road which skirts the Flatsage Farmlands. The road bordered the smooth white fields and the weaving direction of it could still be seen by a low hedge which ran alongside it. The snow had drifted here and there which made travelling difficult and although the wizard was strong and determined he found it hard to force his way along the road at a reasonable pace. The arctic blast was directly against him and he leant into it as he battled along.

As soon as the Dark Wizard Troubler had left Old Howard's house and started his journey through the night, Jamaar had leapt to his feet. His master had told him to be on guard, and when he heard the door close he got up and moved quickly up the stairs, his claws clicking on the wooden steps. In his jaws he carried an oil lamp to see the way. He trotted into one of the rooms, leaving the lamp on the landing so that the light could not be seen from outside the house. He padded over to the window, placing his great paws on the window frame and looked out. As he looked the glass quickly clouded over with his breath so he rubbed an area with his furry head and looked again. He watched as the Dark Wizard passed through the trees at the end of the garden and stride away into the thick falling snow.

He felt a certain freedom now that the Dark Wizard was out of the house. For a while he was not constrained by the strong will of the wizard. He had very mixed feelings about the situation. On the one hand he enjoyed the power of the Dark Wizard and of course the extra strength he had been given. There was also the important benefit of the food he received on a fairly regular basis. On the other hand he often resented the way he was treated like a slave and often bullied into doing exactly what his master wanted. He would like more freedom. Now that the Dark Wizard was out of the house he felt unfettered from his master's control and wandered across the room wondering what to do.

He felt a pang of hunger. He was fed much better now than when he was a stray but he often became impatient and angry when he was kept waiting for his meals. He knew where the food was kept so he headed down the stairs, carrying the lamp in his mouth. He went into the kitchen where he found plenty of food. Hanging up by their legs was a row of dead rabbits. This was tempting and Jamaar licked his lips as he stared at the delicious array of food and wondered whether he should take the risk. He concluded that his master would never miss one from so many and with a huge leap he grabbed one in his powerful jaws and fell to the floor with his prize. He quickly began to devour it.

The Dark Wizard would go out every so often, find some animals that were caught in his spell, then undo the spell and kill them. In this way he had a plentiful supply of food which was very easy to get. Jamaar had soon hungrily gobbled his meal, even crunching up and devouring most of the bones. He was just swallowing the last mouthful when his sharp ears picked up a sound that made him cock his head on one side and listen. It came from the cellar and immediately he knew what he would do next. It was the rumbling voice of Horrik tied by her chain down below and he would pay her a visit.

His meal made him feel content and he walked across the kitchen floor to the door. Glancing behind him he realised that he had not cleared up, so he went back to make sure there were no signs that he had been in the kitchen. He licked the floor where there were smudges of blood and swept some rabbit fur and a few small bones under a cooker until it looked completely clean. Then he grabbed the lamp and trotted out of the room and to the cellar door. He pulled the handle down with his front paws. The door swung open and he stepped in, standing at the top of the stairs and looking down. The room was dirty and smelt damp. He put the lamp down on the top step. His eyes took a moment to adjust to the gloomy room, dimly lit by the pale lamplight and he looked for Horrik.

"What do *you* want?" she growled suspiciously; her deep voice was a dejected groan from the corner of the room. Jamaar looked towards the sound and saw the long body of the komodo dragon in the shadowy corner.

Horrik fixed her eyes on Jamaar. Then she lifted her great head off the floor.

"What's happened to you?" she remarked with surprise, "Your body's grown... you're bigger... and stronger... how did that happen?"

Jamaar just stared back at her.

Horrik opened her massive mouth and roared with laughter, "But you'd still be no match for me in a fight... *when* we fight!" and she laughed again and Jamaar could see her rows of razor-sharp teeth, "I'd eat you alive."

"I haven't come down here to fight," said Jamaar.

"What are you doing here then?" she growled resentfully. Her voice seemed to echo in the great hulk of her body.

"I'm just... well... visiting you,"

"Why?" she snapped crossly.

"Do you want to be set free?" asked Jamaar.

Horrik jerked her head up in surprise. Was this dog helping her, this dog that she despised and hated, this dog that made her seethe with jealousy every time she heard him padding across the floor above?

"Yes," she said cautiously, "But why...?"

"I don't like to see you suffer down here. It must be awful."

"It is," said Horrik dejectedly, shaking her great leathery head.

"It must be just horrible to be shackled down here like this."

"It *is* horrible. So come down and set me free."

"It must be... oh just so... horrible... so humiliating..."

"It *is* humiliating," she interrupted, beginning to get

impatient.

"It must be... it's hard to imagine... how horrible. You, a dragon, but without wings *or* fire... And here am I running around so free. Don't you ever feel jealous?"

She was noticing the sarcasm in his voice now and with a shudder of disappointment she realised he was taunting her. She strained at her chain until it was tight around her neck. She pushed her forked tongue out of her mouth and it snaked in the air.

"If you set me free I could help you!" she said, trying to entice Jamaar.

Jamaar started down the steps, and again her hopes rose.

She added quickly, in a gentle hypnotic voice, "Set me free and I will help you in any way you want."

Jamaar stopped half way down the steps, "It must be completely horrible down there..."

"Listen," Horrik pleaded, "Together we could be strong. We could kill the Dark Wizard and take over ourselves."

Jamaar glared at her as she waited eagerly and hopefully for his response, "It must be... the worst thing possible... ever... to be imprisoned down here. I can't think of anything worse..."

Horrik interrupted him as she suddenly remembered something, "Where's the master?" she asked.

"He's out," said Jamaar, "So it's no good calling out to him."

"I'll tell him about this. I'll tell him what you did when he was out. And I heard you in the kitchen."

"He won't believe you, will he? He doesn't trust you any more... he trusts *me*."

Horrik's anger burst and she suddenly lifted herself up

on her stubby legs, arched her head back on her long neck and with a jerk forwards she spat at Jamaar with all her force. The deadly saliva flew upwards at Jamaar as he scampered up the stairs, but he was not fast enough and it hit him half way down his tail. There was a sizzling sound and a smell of burning and half the tail fell off making Jamaar yelp with pain. He slipped on a step and banged his head on the wall and started toppling down the stairs. Horrik strained forwards, the chain tight as it stretched to the limit. She opened her great jaws ready for the kill; this was the chance she had been waiting for.

Jamaar rolled down and landed on the floor at the foot of the stairs. Horrik's jaws snapped closed, but only managed to catch a small piece of the remaining part of Jamaar's tail. Jamaar yelped again. Luckily for him he had landed on his back legs and he sprang up and onto the stairs again.

Horrik spat out the small piece of tail and it flew past Jamaar's head and stuck to the wall, sizzling. At the top of the steps Jamaar stopped. He felt dizzy from the blow to his head.

"I'll get you!" shouted Horrik.

Jamaar turned and shouted, "I'll tell him what you did!" but as he turned he had knocked over the lamp. He tried to trap it with his paw, but it slipped past and bumped down the steps. Jamaar watched from the top as it tumbled down. When it reached the bottom it smashed, releasing a little flood of oil over the wooden floorboards. There was a plume of fire as the oil burst into flames.

"Help!" cried Horrik.

Jamaar wondered what to do, and it only took him a moment to decide. He would do nothing. If she burnt alive that would be a pleasing result, and she deserved it.

"Help me, Jamaar!" Horrik screamed as she cowered away from the growing flames of the approaching fire.

Jamaar turned and ran out, kicking the cellar door closed behind him. Then he was across the hall and back into the room where his rug lay in the corner. He collapsed down on his rug and licked his wounded tail. He still felt dizzy after the blow on his head and he had lost half a tail, but in exchange for getting rid of Horrik it was a small sacrifice. His mind swirled as he began to drift into sleep. For a short time he could hear Horrik's screams for help, until suddenly, they stopped.

By this time the Dark Wizard Troubler was well on his journey. The Western Downs, dotted here and there with snow laden cottages, had risen on his left as he followed the road. He was the only moving being in this frozen kingdom. Soon he had seen the frozen Blue Lake on his right, snow-covered, a smooth and flat colourless expanse fading quickly away into the grey surroundings of the driving snow. His pale face had become paler still in the deep chill of the biting wind, striking a sinister contrast with his alert black eyes.

He had powered on relentlessly until he reached the bridge across the frozen River Gem. Here he paused, turned away from the wind and reached into his pocket for something. His bony fingers closed around a small piece of gold, a corner chiselled off the same block as Old Howard's small bar. This was now his means of communicating with Old Howard. Through the mirror he could materialise faintly for a while and face the old man, seeing everything dimly and rather indistinctly, but nevertheless being able to frighten him, give him orders and stay in control. With the gold he could speak to Old Howard from inside threading his voice in amongst the thoughts in the old man's mind. He was sure that Old Howard was greedy enough to keep the gold bar with him at all times and so far he had been right.

As he spoke to Old Howard he had carried on walking because he was eager to reach his destination. The dull dawn had broken as he moved. He had not crossed the bridge over the river but had turned left, which was west, and along the river bank. By the time he had reached the Gem Falls, now a great frozen sheet of ice, he had made Old Howard create the great wave. When he had heard that it had tumbled heavily on top of the boat carrying the Prince, the Princess and the others, he felt the thrill of success run through him. The power of the great mass of water had crushed and drowned them and at last he felt free to develop his plans further. He felt exhausted, but still had the strength to give a little nod of satisfaction as a contented smile touched his lips.

After he had tried unsuccessfully to speak to Old Howard, who had fallen asleep leaning against a tree, he dropped the piece of gold into his pocket and stepped towards the vertical sheet of ice until he was two or three steps away. He stopped and gazed in front of him. The light was growing quickly now and dissolving the night into the blue-grey dimness of the twilight. The waterfall created some shelter from the driving blast of the blizzard. The falling flakes were less thick and fluttered down gently, here and there flurrying in gusts of wind. He brushed the snow off his shoulders but immediately white speckles dotted his black cloak again.

He knew that somewhere behind the sheet of ice was the Brinscally Cave and inside the cave were kept the precious Candara Gems. When the two ravens, Gerr and Searle, had returned from their task to find the cave he had hoped they could tell him where, along the stretch of waterfall, the cave was situated. They gave him a rough location by saying that it was near the middle, but now he needed the precise position. He needed to find the cave, enter it and claim the gems for himself. As he thought about this he stood still, beneath the towering sheet of ice, with snow falling on him, and worked out his next move.

There were only a few in the kingdom who knew how to enter the cave; the King and Queen, Amalek and Seph, and Joog. In fact these were the only ones who actually knew that the Candara Gems were more than just a fanciful legend. These few knew where the gems were kept and how to get there.

The Candara Gems had been protecting the kingdom now for about five hundred years since they had been placed in the Brinscally Cave. They were a gift from a great wizard called Candara. He had bestowed them on the kingdom in times of widespread trouble and corruption, when deceit and dishonesty were commonplace. In these times Gugeol, a kingdom in the far west, was beginning its invasion and occupation of all the kingdoms. This was largely successful and created the terrible Thousand Seasons of Night.

The effect of the Candara Gems had taken some years to establish. The great wizard ensured that the inhabitants had to make an effort and play their part in securing goodness and peace. When most of those living in the kingdom had improved their lifestyles then the kingdom began to feel the rich benefits of the energy of the gems. The goodness of the creatures protected the gems and the gems protected the creatures.

Under normal conditions, when the water was flowing, the way to enter the Brinscally Cave was by a small rowing boat. This was impossible for anyone without the special knowledge of what to do. Now the cave was only protected by the frozen waterfall, a great sheet of ice.

The Dark Wizard Troubler was still breathing heavily as he wondered what to do. He looked around for somewhere to sit and chose a snow-covered rock. He badly needed to rest after the tough journey through the driving wind and snow and was relieved to take the weight off his legs. He wanted to gather his strength. He did not mind waiting for a while as he would soon be in possession of a great treasure; the Candara Gems.

He found his mind wandering through his ambitious plans. He wanted success and he thought into the future, imagining how he could now proceed forwards. The first step was to find the gems and steal them and then his plans could unravel from there with the extra power he would gain. He deliberated over what his life would be like with the gems and how he could capture kingdoms and achieve fantastic things.

He sat there for some time, just letting the energy rise in him again. He was patient, because he wanted to make sure that this was a success. Eventually he felt he was really strong again, strong enough for the important task ahead. He stood up decisively, brushed the snow off his clothes and slipped his hand into his pocket. By this time midday was approaching.

He pulled out a black compass by the chain and began swirling it in the air above his head. It whistled as it build up speed. Then, with a jerk in the direction of the ice, he let go. It passed straight through leaving a tidy hole and thudded into the rock wall behind. For two or three seconds there was silence. Then the sheet of ice started groaning and creaking. Cracks appeared, moving out from the hole and quickly spreading until the whole face of ice was covered with an intricate pattern of fine white lines. Suddenly, the whole thing shattered with an echoing sound, like a window smashing, and began to collapse.

The Dark Wizard jumped back, turned and pushed off to get away quickly from the splintered falling ice. His foot slipped and he fell as the shattered ice plummeted into the snow below, sending up clouds of whiteness and engulfing the Dark Wizard. When the snow settled and drifted away on the breeze the wizard was gone.

Then there was a stirring in the pile of snow and ice and an arm emerged, then his head and then his whole body, with his black cloak smudged with snow and ice. He stood up shakily, brushed his cloak and then wiped his face where the ice had left several small cuts. Then he felt a sharp pain in his neck and reaching up felt a splinter of ice embedded there. He clenched his teeth as he pulled it out quickly and held his hand over the cut where he felt the trickle of warm blood. After a minute the pain eased and he took his hand away. The blood dried quickly in the icy wind.

When he looked up over the rubble of snow and ice he saw the great rock face that normally lay concealed by the waterfall. Embedded in it was the black compass with the chain hanging down against the rock. He stared at the compass and it began moving, gradually working itself free from the rock until it was out and flying towards the wizard. He caught it and slipped it back into his pocket.

Then he saw, near the middle, the opening, revealing first a frozen pool and then the entrance to the cave itself. When he saw this his pale face brightened. He walked beside the wall of rock, stepping first over the pile of snow and ice and then out to the middle where he stood cautiously on the smooth ice of the pool and gazed into the mouth of the cave. As his peering eyes adjusted to the darkness inside he saw what he was hoping to see. There was a glow of light at the back, a splash of colour upon which he fixed his eyes, because this is what he wanted. The three gems, the ruby, the amethyst and the sapphire were now in his sight and would soon be within his grasp. Once these gems were in his possession he could use them for himself. He would first take them across the border into the Kingdom of Gliyfild, or even Gugeol, which would complete the total fall of the Kingdom of Gems into his possession. Then he would turn their powers to his benefit.

Still with his gaze unwavering and focused steadily at the coloured light, he passed into the cave. Snow fell off his black boots and powdered the rough cave floor around his feet. In front of him the three gems shone brightly in the deep shadows at the back of the cave, resting in their places in the cavity, glowing in the darkness as they reflected their lustrous colours. There was the deep sky blue of the amethyst with its velvety sheen, the shine of the vivid red ruby and the rich purple of the sapphire tinted with rose flashes. Their colours blended together as the light from each gem met creating many hues and speckling the cave with bright spots of colour.

The Dark Wizard was aware of their extreme beauty

but this just fuelled his greed for them. He was intent on stealing them, of getting them into his own possession; he was completely immersed in his own desire.

He walked quickly towards the shining gems, his footsteps echoing around the cave walls, with his greedy eyes staring into the cavity. Colours painted his pale skin as he looked in glee at the resplendence of the three gems. Excitement rose in his chest and his breath became shallow as the thrill of this moment gripped him. With the gems in his possession, and the power they held, his strength would increase greatly.

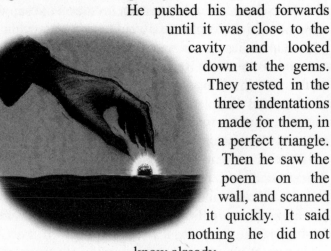

He pushed his head forwards until it was close to the cavity and looked down at the gems. They rested in the three indentations made for them, in a perfect triangle. Then he saw the poem on the wall, and scanned it quickly. It said nothing he did not know already.

He reached out a hand towards the ruby, the gem closest to him.

Then he stopped, withdrew his hand and looked around on the floor for something. He picked up a small stone which he held above the ruby and then dropped. It hit the gem with a clink that echoed in the cave with the ring of a pure note. The stone rolled away and fell onto the cave floor. He slowly lowered his hand and closed the fingertips of his thumb and forefinger around the red ruby. There was a flash and the wizard cried out in pain, pulling his hand away and staggering backward in shock.

"Aaaaaahh!" he screamed.

He clutched his hand tightly with his other hand, as the pain intensified and blood dripped from the wound to splatter on the cave floor. He dropped to his knees half way across the cave and grimaced.

"What had happened?" he thought as he bowed his head and gripped his hand even tighter as he held it against his stomach. He could not understand it. He should have been able to take the gems. The gems protected the kingdom and the people protected the gems, but all the people were frozen and he had just dealt with the Prince and Princess, so the gems should be unprotected. Unless... unless one of them survived the great wave which he had thought was impossible, but now he began to wonder. He tried to think it through but his hand was so painful that he could not think properly.

He freed his hand from the grip of the other and lifted it to have a look and an expression of dismay filled his face when he saw the damage. His finger and thumb were gone and his whole hand was blackened by the sudden flash.

He rose to his feet and staggered to the cave entrance, leaving a trail of dripping blood on the cave floor. Pausing, he reached down with his unharmed hand and ripped a strip off the hem of his cloak and attempted to tie it around his wounded hand. For a few seconds he struggled unsuccessfully with this. The pain intensified. His hand was throbbing now and he fumbled to wrap the blood-soaked material around his shaking hand. After a moment he gave up and held the cloth tightly against the wound.

Feeling slightly stronger now the thought rang again in his mind. *"What had happened?"* Then he suddenly remembered something. The cat was still alive. That was it. A creature from the Kingdom of Gems was still free and that was why he could not take the gems; they were still protected. He had thought it was only people that protected the gems, but now he realised it must be all creatures. Still gripping his wounded hand with the cloth he used both hands to work the piece of gold up until it poked out of his pocket. He touched it with a finger and somehow summoned the energy to shout as loud as he could, "Wake up!"

Old Howard woke with a jerk and looked around in fear. The warmth of the midday sun touched one of his cheeks.

"Old Howard," shouted the voice in his head, "Wake up!"

Old Howard relaxed when he realised where the voice was coming from, "Oy am awake," he replied grumpily.

"Stay awake!" snapped the Dark Wizard Troubler.

"Shut up!" he replied, "Oy need moy rest."

"Not yet!" the wizard dropped his voice to a cutting whisper "Anyway, you've had your rest."

"Oy got the job done so 'oy want moy gold."

"Not yet... soon. Now, I am quite pleased with you, but I have another task. Do not fail me, otherwise you know what I'll do... I'm sure I don't have to remind you, do I?"

"No," said Old Howard, fear rising in him as he listened to the cutting words of the wizard. The Dark Wizard knew he could make him do anything he wanted. Old Howard scrabbled onto his feet.

"I don't want that cat escaping, not now that we've got rid of all the others. I want it dead. Dead, do you hear me? And as soon as possible. So, go back now and deal with it, alright?"

"Allroyt," Old Howard said reluctantly, giving in to the will of the Dark Wizard. Then he asked politely, "After that do oy get moy gold?"

"Do the job well… and you will be rewarded. I've promised haven't I? Now, get on!"

Old Howard struggled to his feet, turned and began the walk along the river. The sun was high enough now to shed a bright warm light and he kept in the shade of the trees as he began the journey back to Burney's Hill.

"I hope," the wizard's sinister whispering voice continued, "I hope for your sake that you deal with this matter quickly. I asked you before and you disobeyed. Do not fail again." Old Howard shuddered with fear as he plodded by the river.

The Dark Wizard released the piece of gold and it fell back into his pocket. He felt exhausted, leant back against the cave wall and tried to gather some strength together. After a while he was filled by a nauseous feeling and the blood-soaked cloth slipped from his hand and fell to the cave floor. He began to feel faint. His legs gave way and crumpled beneath him as he fell to the rock floor unconscious.

Some hours later the Dark Wizard came around with his face squashed against the cave floor. He felt terrible, but managed to get to his feet. For a moment he stood still, supporting himself against the cave wall. His eyes were glazed as he fought to overcome the intense pain in his hand and focus his mind. He looked at his injury and frowned with anger. The cold air had helped the bleeding to stop, but it looked a mess of blackened skin and deep red blood.

After a time he felt some strength returning and became aware of his surroundings. He looked out through the cave entrance at the frozen river resting in the great expanse of the white arctic scene. He had the idea of staying in the cave until Old Howard had killed the cat and then stealing the gems but he decided it was too risky. He needed warmth to recover. He needed to get back to the house as soon as possible to dress his wounds properly. If he stayed here in the state he was in he might die of cold.

With a great effort he made a step, and then another, and soon he was out of the cave and crunching through the thick snow. As he followed his footprints which were not quite fully covered yet by the falling snow, he was seething with anger.

The bitter driving wind was behind him now as he passed Blue Lake, the Western Downs and the Flatsage Farmlands. Evening passed and the light began to fade as he was approaching the copse of trees near Old Howard's house. He walked through the copse, up to the house, stepped in and closed the door.

Chapter 12

~ On Tye Water ~

The huge wave had hurled itself along the Great River Sween until it reached Tye Water, a long thin lake which the river entered at one end and flowed out of at the other. At first the wave had made quite an impact, but with the greater expanse of water it had spread out and settled and soon the surface of the lake was back to normal. It had been slightly lighter here without the shade of the trees along the river and the sun had been just rising above the horizon.

The group of over a hundred ravens had been commanded by the General to land on the water and so they had followed his instructions. They landed tentatively and were pleased to find that they could float on the surface although some tipped over and struggled to stay upright. With some wing flapping and wriggling of their bodies they quickly began to develop the skill. Some tried to paddle along but without webbed feet they hardly moved at all. They looked like a disorganised flock of scavenging seagulls as they bobbed on the gentle waves in the growing light.

"Male and female squadrons!" shouted the General,

and they scrabbled in the water to face him, some being more successful than others.

"Once again," said Urrg who was next to the General, "You are assuming overall command. I would like to question your…"

"You will question nothing!" the General snapped, "No time for that now." He looked furious and puffed out his neck feathers, "And besides, you are in deep trouble after that little demonstration of mutiny back there. I suggest you keep your bill tightly closed." Urrg looked very offended but was too afraid not to follow his order so she closed her bill. Then he addressed them all.

"Males and Females, servants of our beloved Master. We have done well and *he* will be pleased. We have annihilated the enemy. It is certain that no one could have survived that. But we must be absolutely sure…" he paused as he noticed something floating on the water, "Is that the boat over there?"

"Yes, sir!" said Gerr who was once again by the side of the General.

"Go and investigate, quickly." He flew off immediately and returned within a minute.

"It's definitely the boat, sir!" said the enthusiastic Gerr.

"I know that!" roared the General, "We *all* knew that before you left. Any survivors hanging onto it? Or hiding underneath?"

"I don't know, sir!" said Gerr.

"Hopeless! You four," and he pointed with his bill at four other male ravens, nodding his head at each one in turn, "Go quickly and investigate properly!" They flew off.

"If I may say so, sir," said Searle, "We should search the area as soon as possible so that survivors do not escape, sir!"

"Male and female squadrons!" shouted the General, "Attennnnn…tion!" This command made little difference as they just continued floating on the water, although some did lift their bills and point them into the air and some of these toppled over and had to flap their wings to regain balance. "Make a thorough search of the area and report anything you find to me and…"

Some started taking off.

"Stop!" he shouted, "I haven't finished telling you," and the ones taking off fell back, some into the water with splashes and flapping wings as they tried to gain control, whilst a few landed on top of others who cackled and complained. When the commotion had calmed down and they had all settled on the water the General looked at them with a disapproving air and then continued.

"Report anything you find to me, and bring back any evidence of the enemy. Now go!"

They all took off and searched everywhere flying to and fro across the lake. Crayle and Jum, the two older birds, headed straight for a tree to rest. The four who went to investigate the boat returned.

"No one there at all, sir!" said one of them.

"Good!" said the General, "Join in with the general search then."

"Yes. Sir!" they said together and flew off.

When they were gone the General wondered about the albatross and how it had flown out of the bush when they were feeding in the trees. Now he had seen it again on the boat. He knew it was the same one because of the stripy scarf. It began to dawn on him that the enemy must have tricked him then, although he could not work out what had happened. In some way he had been cleverly outwitted and that made him angry, but he was glad that now he had outwitted them. He felt slightly cross about the great wave because without that it would have been his army, the ravens, who would have killed the enemy and he would have had bodies to show to the Master.

After half an hour they started returning with all sorts of things that they had found. They dropped them around the General and then went off searching again. This went on all day until by evening he was surrounded by bits of paper, floating bottles and other rubbish. Then, as dusk drew in, three flew over carrying a dripping wet jumper between them.

"Well done!" the General said, nodding with approval, "An article of clothing worn by the enemy, yes, I am sure. This jumper was worn by the Princess I believe. But no body?"

They shook their heads.

"It has sunk no doubt," he continued, "So we can count this as evidence and take it to our Master. Hello, what's this approaching?" he said, as a group of about twenty ravens were carrying something together, "This looks very promising," and as it came closer, "That is a body, and I recognise the Prince's clothes. Excellent!"

The ravens swooped down with their find and dropped the body in the water by the General. It fell face down and floated.

"Male and female squadrons!" he screeched as loud as he could, "Return!"

They all rushed back and gathered around the General again, landing in the water around him. A few managed to touch down gently whilst most landed with a splash and a panicky flapping of wings. In the dusk the colours of the day were fading and night was descending rapidly.

"All present?" the General asked.

They all moved their heads jerkily and their cackling grew louder as they tried to check.

"All present?" the General shouted above the commotion.

"Yes, sir," said Gerr, "All pre…"

"Except," interrupted Searle, "Crayle and Jum, sir."

The General sounded cross, "They're old and useless. Anyone see them?"

"I did," piped up a young raven, "Asleep in that tree over there," he said nodding towards a tree not far away growing right beside the lake.

The General shook his head, "Go and get them and tell them to get back here at once. Perhaps I ought to throw them out of the army."

They all watched the young raven fly off and return straight away, followed slowly by Crayle and Jum.

"Right," announced the General, turning his head to glare at Crayle and Jum as they approached him to land, "Get back here!" he screeched.

He looked back at his army, all bobbing on the water and waiting for the two old birds.

Some chatter began to rise amongst the mass of ravens.

"What's he doing?"

"He's coming in too low… surely."

"He's got the angle all wrong."

"He's too low… much too low!"

"Silence in the ranks!" boomed the General.

"But, sir…" began one.

"Silence!" he shouted.

They were all looking over the General's head and watching Crayle. With only one eye and weak wing muscles his navigation skills were poor. He often made mistakes and this looked like it had the potential to be one of his worst.

"Look out, General!" shouted Gerr.

"Look out, Crayle!" shouted Jum who was flying behind him.

The General jerked his head around to look behind him. Crayle was just a few feet away and heading directly for his head at speed. The General ducked just in time and Crayle passed over with one foot dangling which brushed the Generals head and ruffled his feathers. A great sigh of relief arose from the mass of watching ravens. Just as the General was lifting his head Jum was there and her feet clipped his head once more. He ducked down again quickly.

Crayle landed in the water with a great splash hitting two other birds who scrabbled away to give him room. Jum followed and landed beside him. It took them a few seconds to get stable and the other birds began to laugh and cackle at the comedy of it all.

"Quiet!" shouted the General furiously.

The laughing petered out apart from a few lingering giggles.

"May I begin now?" the General asked with mock politeness as he glared intently at Crayle and Jum.

Crayle slowly turned on the water so that his good eye was facing the General.

"Thank you," he said sarcastically, "Now that you two have bothered to come back and have shown off your *wonderful* flying skills, perhaps I can begin. I'll deal with you and your ridiculous shenanigans later." He stopped staring at Crayle and Jum and opened his attention to all the ravens gathered around him. He looked slightly comical with the ruffled feathers sticking out on his head and a few of the ravens at the back of the group were sniggering at him.

"We have found," he began proudly and then he paused as the black compass around his neck gave a little jerk by itself. He tilted his head to one side and looked at it. It was now completely still and so he carried on, "We have found a wonderful thing. No, two wonderful things. They are our definite proof, undeniable evidence that the enemy has been defeated by us and we will now return to our Master and present him with these items. One... the jumper of the Princess!" There were some 'oos' and 'ahs' from the crowd as he held the dripping article up in his bill, "And two... the body of the Prince!" There were gasps of excitement from the ravens, followed by chattering. He nodded to the twenty ravens who had found the body, who each grasped some part of it and flapped frantically as they lifted it up for all to see. There was a hushed silence as they all peered at the body through the dim light.

"What!" bellowed the General, "This is a pretend painted face!" He flew up and pecked the body hard. "This is nothing but a dummy, a padded model of the Prince! The enemy has tricked us!"

The thick soft snow lay on everything in the Kingdom of Gems. Everywhere within its borders the land was smooth and white, with lakes, rivers and streams frozen. It was strange to think that this beautiful scene had been the result of such a wicked spell. The Dark Wizard Troubler had used the forces of nature, with all her splendid beauty, for his own selfish ends and cast a subtle darkness across the whole kingdom, in contrast to the bright whiteness of the snow which covered hills and dales. The icicles which hung in long rows off the roofs of the houses like soldiers standing still on parade, sparkled transparently when the sun occasionally came out for a moment or two. Most of the time, however, the sky was heavy with yellowish snow clouds as wave upon wave of snow swept across the land.

When the Dark Wizard Troubler had returned from his attempted theft of the gems he knew something had happened as soon as he entered the house. A pungent smell of smoke hung in the air. He rushed into the cellar, and then came out a few moments later. He glanced into the kitchen and then went straight to see Jamaar.

"Have you been in the cellar?" the Dark Wizard snapped.

After his bump on the head Jamaar had fallen into a deep sleep and woke up with a jerk.

"What?!" he exclaimed. He immediately felt painful throbbing in his head, but worse than this, much worse, was the fear that gripped him as he remembered what had happened and realised that he was in trouble. He almost panicked, but his years of dishonesty immediately presented him with a way to wriggle out of trouble.

"Master," Jamaar said, sounding sorry for himself, "Look," and he showed his tail to the wizard.

"Hah!" laughed the wizard, "What happened to that?"

"Horrik did it, master."

"Horrik?" the wizard looked surprised, and narrowed his eyes, "I need to talk to you about Horrik."

"Oh, she's still down in the cellar," said Jamaar casually.

"What about the fire?"

The wizard was looking at the dog intently and Jamaar knew his story would have to be convincing.

"Fire? What fire?" Jamaar looked up with an expression of surprise, "She spat at me and made me drop the lamp! But... fire? Was there a fire?" The wizard leant down closer.

"What were you doing in the cellar?" The wizard's words stabbed into Jamaar like a dagger.

"I heard her moan, master, and went down to check that she was alright. I thought you'd want me to... in your absence, master. But as I went down the steps she spat at me! There am I looking after her... and she does this. Look!" and he lifted up the remaining part of his tail again and put on an expression of pain.

"Horrik tells the story differently."

Jamaar's heart sank as he realized she was alive. His head was still throbbing.

"She lies," he growled unhappily, "You know she does, master. She spat at me. I had to escape before she spat again."

"Alright," said the Dark Wizard, "Fair enough. But she almost burnt, you know. If it wasn't so damp down there... well, she would never be alive. The fire..."

"She caused fire, master," Jamaar interrupted, looking up with an expression that was a mixture of astonishment and angry accusation, "It's her fault for spitting at me. I had to get away from her... she would have killed me!" Just then he noticed the wizard's injured hand, "What's happened to your hand, master?"

"An unfortunate accident," he hissed, covering his wounds with the other hand, "But you're *meant* to be guarding this house for me. The lamp caused the fire, you stupid dog. You could have burnt the house down. *And*

Horrik. She's a useful asset, you know. She is a killing machine and I'll need to use her later."

He turned and headed for the cellar to talk to Horrik. She had been alarmed when the fire had started spreading towards her and she had started frantically spitting at it as it advanced. Then suddenly, she had stopped.

"Don't panic" she thought, *"If you panic you'll die. Think... think... think."*

For a moment she watched the fire and tried to calm down. Then it came to her. The fire needed the wood to burn. There were gaps in the floor where some boards had rotted away with the damp and in front of her, in between her and the fire, the boards were already crumbling. In several places she could see through holes in the wood. She started spitting again, not at the fire, but at the wooden floorboards in front of her. The saliva fizzed and began dissolving the remaining wood, until the holes had grown to expose a rubble of rocks and stones beneath. She hoped this, and the fact that the floorboards were very damp around her, would stop the fire.

Her plan worked, but not before the heat of the fire had blackened and singed her on one side of her body. Fortunately her scales were thick and were good protection.

The Dark Wizard climbed down the steps, treading on the tail half way down and kicking it to the side. He then jumped over the two lowest steps which were blackened and still glowing red here and there. His feet crunched over the charred floorboards and broken glass from the lamp. He stopped in front of the hole. There was just enough daylight to brighten the glass in the door leading to the garden. In the dim light he could see Horrik.

"Horrik?" he hissed.

Her reply rumbled up from the depths, "Yes, master?"

"You told me Jamaar did it and tried to kill you. Now tell me what really happened?"

"Jamaar did it, master, as I said. It's true."

"Explain," he snapped.

She explained what had happened, but he would not believe her.

"Jamaar has a different story, and I know who I believe. I've looked in the kitchen – he hasn't been in there. By your own foolishness you almost burnt yourself... *and* the house." He paused, then stepped over the hole towards her and kicked her hard in the side. His voice dropped to a harsh whisper as he lowered his mouth close to her ear, "I'll be needing you soon, so this time your punishment will be lenient. I will spare you. But... don't... cross me... again. You will stay living down here until I need you."

He climbed the stairs and slammed the door, leaving her seething with hatred for Jamaar.

Soon after the Dark Wizard entered the cellar again, dragged a basket through the door and stood at the top of the steps.

"I have decided your punishment," he announced, "You will have a special diet for the next three days. After that we need to build up your strength, so you're lucky."

He lifted the basket and flung the contents down towards Horrik and left.

She knew what it was by the sound as they fell. She had eaten them before and she detested the taste; ravens. They were extremely bitter and she hated the thought that she would have the same thing for every meal for three days. To satisfy her huge frame she knew she would have to eat many of them at each meal and the feathers irritated her mouth and tickled her throat as she swallowed. This intensified her loathing of Jamaar. Her anger was ready to explode as she listened to every movement made by him in the room above.

The Dark Wizard Troubler was now slumped in Old Howard's smelly chair. He had carefully washed the wounds where his finger and thumb had been and then he had bound them tightly. He knew that he could not attempt to steal the gems until he was absolutely certain that the cat was dead. He would have to wait, but it was only a matter of time; the cat was trapped and to kill it was easy, even for the bungling Old Howard. Then he would claim the gems for himself.

Horrik had just finished the meal of ravens and had spat out as many feathers as she could in disgust, when she noticed something that gave her a rare moment of happiness. The chain which was fixed to the pipe and had been keeping her bound by her leathery neck like a prisoner, fell off. The metal of several links, where the chain hung down under her chin, had thinned and one was so thin that it had disintegrated allowing the chain to break apart. She stared at them for a moment, amazed, thrilled and elated. At first she thought it must have been the heat of the fire. Then she realised what had happened. It was her saliva... her bacteria-filled, acidic saliva, which dribbled out of her mouth, had eaten through the metal. It had taken time because the wizard had made sure the metal was strong, but he had not foreseen this. She was free. Surely this was the opportunity she had been waiting for and suddenly it was presented to her out of the blue.

Horrik looked around for a way out. Up the stairs to

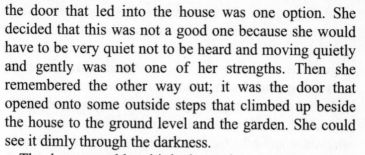

the door that led into the house was one option. She decided that this was not a good one because she would have to be very quiet not to be heard and moving quietly and gently was not one of her strengths. Then she remembered the other way out; it was the door that opened onto some outside steps that climbed up beside the house to the ground level and the garden. She could see it dimly through the darkness.

The door was old and it had rotted away at the bottom where it met the floor leaving an uneven draughty gap. The damp had got into it. With her power she knew she could open this door whether it was locked or not. She lifted her great body onto her stubby but strong legs and walked quickly over to the door. She found it was locked, so she turned and pushed her tail firmly against it. There was the gentle crunching snapping sound of the splintering of rotten wood as the door collapsed outwards and pushed into the snow that was piled up against the steps.

She paused to listen. There were no sounds from upstairs. She had not been heard.

Horrik climbed over the door and began to struggle urgently up the steps, deep-filled with soft snow, with her short legs slipping and sliding. After a few minutes of scrabbling she reached the top. She lay for a moment in the snow, enjoying the cooling sensation on her hot burnt skin. Then she pushed through the thick blanket of whiteness lying in Old Howard's garden.

It was night.

She did not look back until she reached the cluster of trees at the end of garden. Then she lifted her head upwards until she could see the house through the falling snow. There was no movement, no one rushing out to catch her and so she looked around for a good vantage point from which she could watch and think about what to do next.

Inside the house the Dark Wizard Troubler was recovering from his disappointment. He turned his mind to the success of the great wave and his spirits rose. He realised that his failure to steal the gems was only a temporary setback. He had finally killed the little party who had made him so furious when they escaped his spell. Then he thought of Old Howard. He had given Old Howard the bar of gold for two reasons; firstly to persuade Old Howard to leave his house for him to live in, and secondly to make the old man work for him. This had gone well and now he needed to keep holding Old Howard in his power with the promise of more gold. Feeling better he sat up in the chair. Candlelight flickered in the room casting strange quivering shadows.

"Jamaar," he said. The dog jumped up as he always did at the sound of his master's call. The pain in his head had gone now leaving only a sensitive bruise. He wagged what was left of his tail, "There's just the cat to deal with now, do you realise? Then the enemy is gone!" Then he whispered to himself, "Gone forever!"

"It's good, Master," Jamaar's deep growling voice resounded in the room.

"But," the evil wizard frowned heavily with deep concern, "Do you think anyone could have survived that great wave?"

"No," said Jamaar emphatically, "No way."

"I hope you're right," his sinister thin voice, though soft, filled the room and the coldness it carried seemed to seep into the walls, like roots growing into loose earth, "I think not. But I can't help having a germ of doubt in my mind. I need to make sure. Maybe one of them got lucky somehow and did survive. What do you think?"

"No, I don't think so. I'm glad they're gone," growled Jamaar, "But I would've liked to kill them myself, master. You said I could. Remember?"

"Well, dog," hissed the Dark Wizard, suddenly getting an idea, "This is your chance."

"What do you mean?"

"I mean that you can go off hunting into the heart of Summertime Kingdom and if any are still alive you can catch them and kill them. If you find one dead already, then bring back the body, or what's left of it after you've feasted."

"But I'm meant to guard this house, master," said Jamaar who was not so keen on such a long journey; the thought of battling through all the snow made him shudder. And if he survived the snow then he would only find dead bodies or most probably nothing at all.

"There's no point you guarding this house, is there, you stupid dog?" he suddenly raised his voice and spat the words out with a venomous sting making Jamaar jump back in fear, "There's no one here to break in, is there? Everyone is frozen! You're guarding nothing! No, you'd be more use to me going on the hunt. Wouldn't you?" he snapped out the question sharply and then glared at Jamaar waiting for the answer.

Jamaar had learnt not to cross his master or anger him in any way. He had seen, and experienced his dark power and knew he had to be completely servile to him. He was so scared that as soon as the Dark Wizard Troubler raised his voice he would agree and do exactly what he was told to do.

"Yes, master," replied Jamaar, "Thank you, master."

"Good, that's better. Now you know your mission." Suddenly he shouted loudly, "Make sure they are dead!" and then he continued, lowering his voice to a sinister whisper, and stooping down to place his head near to Jamaar's, "I want them dead and out of my way forever. That's clear, isn't it?"

"Yes, master," replied Jamaar shaking slightly with fear.

"From here head north-east." He took a small bag out of his pocket and held it possessively as if it was the most treasured thing in the world. He hesitated. Part of him was reluctant to share this with Jamaar, or anyone, but he knew that to help the success of the trip he had to. He took a black metal compass out of the bag. It hung on a black metal chain just like the one around his neck and the one he gave to the General. He swung it in front of Jamaar's face. It gleamed in the candlelight, "Look, you use it like this," he opened the lid which was delicately and elaborately engraved on the cover with a coat of arms; his coat of arms. It looked just like a pocket watch, but inside, when the hinged cover was opened the directions of the compass were clearly marked under the glass. The needle swung to the north, "See... that's north. Get it?"

"Yes, master."

"Turn the compass until the needle is over the N for north. Then navigate. Understand?"

Jamaar tilted his head on one side as he looked, "Yes, master."

"Good. Keep it around your neck and head north-east until you hit Charin Road. Stay on that road until you reach the border. Then cross the border... cross into the next kingdom," he hung the compass over Jamaar's neck,

"Then... when you're in Summertime Kingdom... head north... due north. Keep the compass 'round your neck *at all times.* Is that clear?"

"Yes, master."

"Never never take it off to show anyone... whatever happens. You see it's... well... it's on our side. I cannot say exactly what it will do... but it will help you. It partly depends on you, but it should nudge you in the right directions. It's a guide in more ways than just journeying. Now, remember. When you're in Summertime Kingdom which way do you go?"

"North, master, due north."

"Good. Eventually you will meet the river, the Great River Sween, where I made the wave and they were carried away. Then search. Follow any scent. Search *thoroughly,*" he paused to make sure the word 'thoroughly' had been heard. Then he hissed out the word again with malice, "*Thoroughly!* When you return you will be rewarded for your efforts accordingly. Now, I'm a fair man, and that's fair, isn't it?"

"Yes, master," Jamaar pretended to look eager and wagged what was left of his tail, but really he was shaking with fear, "Very fair."

"Good." He left the room and returned with a large bowl of food. "Eat this," he said putting the bowl down in front of Jamaar, "You need a good meal before the journey."

Jamaar immediately started wolfing the food down. He was still feeling quite full from the rabbit he had eaten, but he did not want the wizard getting suspicious, so he pretended to be ravenous. When he had finished the wizard took a large bone from the box on the shelf and tossed it into Jamaar's corner.

"When you've finished that, then go," he commanded. Jamaar leapt upon the bone and trapped it under his front paws and began gnawing and crunching on it.

The scene along the Great River Sween where the huge wave had arisen and washed the boat away had returned to normal. The only evidence that a tidal wave had occurred was its legacy of crushed flowers and damaged bushes on the river bank. The waves and ripples had regained their natural flow. The birds, who had been stunned into silence by the extraordinary event, had sung as usual through the day.

At midday Old Howard had been woken by the Dark Wizard and had plodded off with mixed feelings. He was more frightened than ever after the conversation with the wizard, but also he was feeling unusually content that he had done a good job. He would soon be receiving more gold from the Dark Wizard and with this thought he even began to whistle.

He had moved along the northern bank of the river as the day drew in and night arrived. Retracing his steps he had passed the places where the River Ben and the Little River Sween joined. Then he had crossed the two rivers again in the same places as before. It was almost midnight when he trudged, with water in his boots, southwards from the Little River Sween and was on his way back to Burney's Hill.

It was just after midnight when something moved on

the river. From underneath the overhanging willow trees came the slightest of ripples and then the front of a small rowing boat appeared, gliding smoothly on the water. The moon reflected in sparkling lines of silver light on the tiny waves. Sitting right at the front, nestled in the bow, was the Prince, looking straight ahead like a proud statue. The Princess sat at the other end of the boat with the Ferryman in the middle, looking very wet and rowing with long, powerful, sweeping strokes.

Neville circled just above using the breeze to glide effortlessly. Joog was not with them because he had a special job to do. He was following Old Howard. They had all discussed it after they had spotted Old Howard creating the great wave and they had agreed that Flop and Miriam must be found, if they were still alive and then they must be rescued if possible. Old Howard might still have them trapped somewhere. Certainly following Old Howard could do no harm and Joog, with his superb eyesight could keep his distance and out of danger. At least he could find out where Flop and Miriam were.

So Joog had watched Old Howard from one of the willow trees on the other bank and saw him create the wave. When the wave had rushed away down the river he observed as Old Howard fell asleep against the tree trunk, waited until he woke up, and then followed him.

As the boat glided swiftly across the river they felt relieved that they had avoided the great wave. It had been the Ferryman's idea and once it was decided upon he created the dummies with amazing skill and speed. Everyone helped, of course, but he produced everything necessary, using branches, twigs and grass, and producing various things from his bag to colour and create the faces.

"It's always best to be prepared for anything," he had said, "I carry in this bag many useful things. Disguises are a good way of hiding from those you would rather not meet. Every now and then it serves a purpose and saves a life!"

They had all grown to like and trust the Ferryman very quickly. He was mysterious. They still could not see his face because he kept his hood low around his head, but even when they looked closely there seemed to be nothing there. The only part of him that was visible was his hands; they were black-skinned and wrinkled like an old man's and yet he seemed so strong and youthful. They had watched with amazement as he made the dummies, his hands working with remarkable skill and speed.

The boat was almost across now.

"How did you get out of that great wave?" Amalek asked the Ferryman, "We were sure you had been swept away."

"I dived to the bottom immediately," the Ferryman's voice sounded strong but gentle, "I know this river well, every little detail, and I lay in a hollow on the river bed and watched the torrent of water rushing past above me!"

"Well," said Seph, "You fooled them completely. And those dummies we made worked as well! But what will happen if the ravens realise that they've been tricked?"

"First of all," began the Ferryman with a chuckle, "They'll be extremely angry. Then they'll come after us, of course. That's if they find out... but I think they will because when the river broadens into Tye Water the wave will die out and then, as soon as they find just a part of one of those dummies... then they'll know they've been tricked. So we may not have long."

They soon landed on the other side and stepped out of the boat onto the grassy bank. In front of them, beyond the grass, was a forest, with massive shadowy trees rising up towards the rapidly darkening sky. It was the Forest of the Fairies.

Neville called down from above, "They're coming, I think... the ravens, I mean... I can see a dark cloud in the distance! It must be them!"

"Go!" said the Ferryman, "Quickly, run into the trees and hide! Quick," and then, as they ran away, he called to them, "Good luck! And don't come back for me. You must go on. I can deal with these ravens! Go! Go!" and the Prince and Princess sprinted into the trees, with Neville gliding just above their heads.

By the time the mass of ravens were overhead they were well into the forest. They settled in an excellent hiding place behind some undergrowth with an outcrop of rock overhanging them. In the darkness they were safely hidden. Meanwhile the Ferryman had been struggling, despite his great strength, to haul the boat out of the river. He managed in the end and then dragged it up the bank towards the trees, but the ravens spotted him before he reached shelter. They swooped down and landed in the tops of the trees, except for the General who landed on a branch by the Ferryman.

"Oh! I'm glad *you're* here!" exclaimed the Ferryman, his face still hidden by the hood. "It's so good to see you! But are you alright?"

"What!?" said the General sounding surprised. The Ferryman took an oil lamp out of his boat tried to light it with a match. On the second attempt the wick caught and he blew out the match and threw it away. He carefully placed the glass cover over it and the flame heightened and spread a soft flickering light.

"Are you alright?" repeated the Ferryman, glancing at Urrg as she landed on a branch close by, "After being swept away in that huge wave."

"We're fine," said the General, taken aback, "Apart from being tricked. But, if you have any sense," he glared threateningly at the Ferryman, "Any sense at all... then you will help us."

"Of course, of course. You know they tied me up and took my spare boat!"

"Who did?" snapped the General.

"Some young children. Boy and girl. If ever I lay my hands on them I'll... I'll teach them a lesson." The General looked at him suspiciously.

"You're saying they took your boat, are you?" he said. His black compass gave a little jerk as it hung on his chest.

"Yes," said the Ferryman, "And they tied me up!"

"Then who..." said the General slowly. His feathers glinted metallic green in the lamp-light, "Who was rowing the boat."

"It was the boy! He stole my best cloak and put it on. Then he tried to row across looking like me and with those dummies they made. Wanted to make you think they were crossing."

"Then where...?" the General hesitated again as he tried to think the Ferryman's account through and make sense of it, "Where is the boy now? We didn't find him."

"I don't know! Probably drowned. Dead bodies can sink you know. Sometimes they don't come up for weeks."

The General's compass jiggled against his feathers, "I still don't get it," the General looked puzzled, "Because, when he had crossed, he would have been on one side and the Princess on the other. And the owl, *plus* that stupid looking albatross in the stripy scarf, all left behind as well! Although they could fly across of course. But the Princess, stranded and left behind! Funny sort of plan that is!"

"Yes!" said the Ferryman, "Then when you'd gone hunting for them in the forest he'd have crossed back in the boat and they'd go by another route and fool you – that was their plan. Of course he didn't expect your attack so soon. They thought you weren't close enough, but that you'd just see from a distance and then follow into the forest. Then he'd row back and they'd be off together due east to Burney's Hill, and then north from there. But you spoilt their plan. The girl, though, with the owl and the albatross, is still over there... and they'll go east. They'll be travelling right now."

"I don't know," said the General, weighing it up and shaking his head as the compass jiggled again, the silver coat of arm glinting momentarily in the glimmering light of the lamp. The Dark Wizard had told him that the compass would help him and guide him, but were it's movements in agreement or not? Did a jiggle or jerk mean he was doing the right thing, or the opposite? He decided to assume that a movement meant agreement. He continued, "It doesn't quite add up somehow. It's too complicated. Too clever. No no... I don't believe it."

"Don't be silly," said Urrg, "It makes sense. It explains everything..."

"Be quiet!" snapped the General, jerking his head to look at Urrg, "Don't interfere again...You've made a mess of everything so far." He jabbed his beak in her direction as a threat and she jerked back. Then he turned back to address the Ferryman again, "If he stole your cloak what is that you're wearing?"

"This is my spare cloak. Not as good as the other I admit, but it's all I've got now."

"But it's wet!" shouted the General, "How did that happen!"

"Of course it's wet," he retorted, "They threw me in the river and kept dunking me under the water until I said I'd do it."

"What!" exclaimed the General, "Two children holding a man down! They wouldn't be strong enough."

"But I'm old," said the Ferryman, making his voice sound shaky and weak, "Look at my old hands," and he stretched out his old wrinkled black hands to show the General.

The General nodded slowly and doubtfully and then waved a wing at half a dozen rugged looking ravens who were perched together on one of the trees. They looked sinister in the dark; black silhouettes shifting restlessly on a black branch. They flew down and landed in a row next to the General.

"Not you," the General nodded his beak at Gerr who had not been picked but had enthusiastically joined the selected six. Gerr reluctantly flew up to another branch and sat there looking disappointed.

"I don't think," the General began, "That this man knows how to tell the truth." The compass was moving more and more, as if it could hear the conversation and was telling him he was right. Urrg looked at him and shook her head.

"You stupid bird," she blurted out, "Here is this man helping us, telling us where they are, and you're..."

"Shut up!" he shouted at her and the ravens perched

beside him jumped at his loud voice, "I've warned you. Let me handle this!" He turned to the six evil looking ravens who looked eager for some action and were glaring down at the Ferryman, "I think he needs some encouragement to tell the truth, don't you?"

"Yes, sir!" they said together.

"Well then, encourage him!" One at a time they jumped off the branch and glided towards the Ferryman. He ducked to avoid the first and nearly fell. He looked old and frail and he staggered as the next one swooped. This time he did fall and cried out as he landed face down.

Then the others followed and landed on his back. They started pecking him hard with their large bills.

"Aahh!" he cried loudly, "Have mercy on an old man. Stop. Please stop! I'll tell you the truth!"

"Leave him!" commanded the General and they immediately flew back up to the branch. The Ferryman just about managed to sit up. His hood was still over his head and hid his face.

"Now," said the General with authority, "I thought I could loosen your tongue, old man. But I didn't expect you to give in so soon. You're ready to talk? Or do you want some more?"

"No! I'm ready!" the Ferryman sounded terrified, "They wanted me to tell you that they were heading east to Burney's Hill, but really their plan was to head *west* to Butterknowle and *then* north-east to Lake Beautiful. Of course now that you killed the boy it's just the girl and the others... and they'll be travelling now," and he paused to take a deep breath, "There I've told you. Now let me go."

The compass jerked around even more now. The

General looked at Urrg, "There! What did I tell you? *That* is why I am the General and you are not! Don't forget your station in the future!" he glared back at the Ferryman, "And you... trying to deceive me! I don't like that at all, old man. If you beg for forgiveness I may soften your punishment."

"Please forgive me, sir," the Ferryman's voice sounded desperate, "Please, please, please, sir. Please forgive me."

"Pick him up," he said to the six ravens sitting next to him, "And throw him in the river... in the middle where it's deep and the current is strong. He won't survive."

"No! No!" shouted the Ferryman, "I can't swim!"

"All the better," said the General. The black compass was moving again and even spun around a complete turn as it hung on the chain. The General took this to mean that he was definitely doing the right thing. The compass was guiding him with its approval. When he saw that six ravens were struggling to pick him up, he shouted up the tree to some of the others, "You help as well. Come on! Quick! Get rid of him!"

It took a great mass ravens, clutching different parts of his cloak to slowly lift him into the air.

"Help!" shouted the Ferryman, "What are you doing?!"

The General watched as they carried him towards the river, then he turned back and faced Urrg.

"Now," he continued, "You are sacked due to insubordination. You challenged me by attacking the males... *and* by constantly interrupting me as I speak. As if you knew better than me. *And* you disobeyed me *and* argued with me in the line of duty."

"But, General!" Urrg was furious.

There was a loud splash as the Ferryman was dropped

into the river and the remaining ravens jerked their heads around to look. In the darkness they could hardly see him, but they heard the frantic splashing as he struggled and panicked. Then there was silence as he sank under the surface. The others returned and they all stared and listened to see if he would come up again, and after a while, when he did not, the General said, "He's gone. Don't say I don't provide you with some entertainment. Now, where was I... Oh, yes. Cleaning up my army." He looked at Urrg who had hoped he had forgotten about her.

"You can't do this to me!" Urrg snapped.

"I can and I have!" he said emphatically, "Now, who to replace you with..." and he looked up at the great gathering of ravens perched in the trees, "Searle, come down here." Urrg was seething with anger as Searle flew down, "You did well before... finding the gems for the Master. Yes, I appoint you Captain of the Female Squadron. Let me know immediately if Urrg gives you any trouble... any trouble at all." Urrg glared at him whilst Searle held her head up high as if she was queen of a whole kingdom.

"I will, sir," said Searle, "Thank you, sir. I won't disappoint you, sir."

"Good. You had better do a better job than the last captain," and he glared at Urrg.

The General paused to think. He was almost expecting a jerk of approval from the compass but it was now still, "The Male Squadron will fly back across the river and then west to search for the girl. The Female Squadron will cross the river too and then fly east, just in case it's a double bluff and they've gone that way. If we search thoroughly we are bound to find her. Then bring the body to me. OK?"

There was a great cackle of agreement.

"The girl's body will be my evidence, my proof of success for the Master. We *must* succeed. I received certain information before we left that our master is dispatching an elite group of ravens, just a few, three or four I think, with special powers to penetrate deep into this enemy kingdom. They can go where we cannot... all the way to the castle. So they have an advantage over us, which is... most frustrating! Now, we don't want them to get the glory do we?" there was another cackle of agreement, "*We* must get the enemy!" he screamed, "Male and female squadrons, attennnnnn...tion!" he shouted, "Male and female squadrons... take off!"

They all flew off across the river and then split into the two groups. In the dark their black shapes could hardly be seen as they sped through the warm air. One group flew east led by the General with Gerr flying close behind him while the other headed west with Searle, the new captain, in front.

As soon as they had gone the very wet hooded figure of the Ferryman climbed out of the water and fell onto the river bank gasping for air. After a minute, when his breathing had almost returned to normal, he stood up, walked to his boat which was just under the trees. He sat down on a moss-covered log. From beneath his wet hood a gentle chuckle could be heard as he sat down to dry in the warm nighttime air.

He was totally unaware that he was being watched. In a nearby tree, with his head tilted to one side and his one beady black eye staring, was the aged Crayle. Leaning against him, in a deep sleep, perched Jum. She had her head resting on his wing, whilst he leant against a branch to stay upright. Unknown to the other ravens they had been left behind. After all the travelling and flying about of the last few days they both felt exhausted and had been finding it increasingly difficult to keep up with the younger birds. During the conversation with the Ferryman Jum had fallen asleep. When all the others took off Crayle had made a quick decision not to follow them. He felt they badly needed the rest, especially Jum, and he knew that the General never made any allowances for their age. But also he was suspicious. In his cunning old mind he was not convinced by the Ferryman's words and when he heard the sounds of splashing water and then saw the Ferryman emerge from the river he knew he was right.

He had watched intently with his one eye as the Ferryman walked up the bank and sat down on the log.

"Jum!" he whispered, moving his wing to wake her, "Keep quiet and wake up."

Jum opened her eyes and blinked. For a moment she wondered where she was. Then she remembered, but she had missed most of the conversation with the Ferryman and Crayle knew it.

"Through there..." he whispered, "Look... down there... see that man... that's a ferryman..." Jum peered through the branches into the darkness, "That ferryman tricked the General and they've all gone looking for the enemy over there across the river." He jerked his beak in the direction.

"So, they've all gone?" Jum asked.

"Yes."

"What shall we do?" whispered Jum. She sounded worried.

Crayle looked thoughtful. After a while he said, "Look... it's OK. Don't worry about anything. This is our big chance, isn't it? We'll watch. See, I've got a feeling that the Prince and Princess are close by... they must be. If he sent the General over there, then they must be over here somewhere, yes?"

Jum nodded.

"So we must find them," continued Crayle, "Then we will be the heroes of the army."

This amused Jum. They were the oldest of all the ravens in the army and she knew that the General thought that they were useless. She did not like the way he shouted at them. Here was their chance. She began to chuckle.

"Shhh," Crayle lifted a wing to her beak and whispered, "We mustn't be heard. Listen... first, we'll watch for a moment. He might lead us to them and save us a job. If not, we'll soon find 'em, OK?"

Jum nodded,

"OK,"she whispered.

A short distance away, just north in the Forest of the Fairies, Amalek, Seph and Neville huddled in the dark under an overhanging rock. They had listened to the General screeching his commands and stayed completely still and silent, expecting at any moment to hear the frightening swishing sound of their feathers cutting through the air above. They were relieved that the sound did not come and they relaxed, feeling safely hidden behind some thick undergrowth.

"They must've gone the other way," whispered Seph after a while, "The Ferryman is too clever for them.

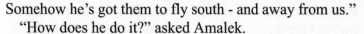

Somehow he's got them to fly south - and away from us."

"How does he do it?" asked Amalek.

"I don't know. But he's great at disguises isn't he?"

Amalek and Neville nodded.

I hope," began Neville, "Well I just hope that he's alright."

There was a pause as thoughts of concern for the Ferryman flashed through their minds. The urge to go back and see if he needed help, or if he was even alive, was strong but they remembered what he had called out to them. He had told them to keep going to the castle. They could only hope that he was alright.

"What next?" asked Amalek.

"Well... we're through," whispered Seph, "We've got past them all. We escaped from the Dark Wizard Troubler. Now we're past the ravens and they don't know where we are, otherwise they'd be looking for us here, in the forest. Whatever the Ferryman said to them has sent them another way. *And* we've tricked Old Howard... *and* we've crossed the river."

"You mean, the rest of the journey should be straightforward?" asked Neville.

"Yes," Seph nodded reassuringly, but then he added, "Well, let's hope so anyway."

"What about Joog?" Amalek looked concerned, "And Flop and Miriam? We must look for them."

"Yes, I feel the same as you, but we can't go back, can we?"

"But..." began Amalek.

"Listen," Seph interrupted, "If we go back we might all be caught and then what would happen to our kingdom? We've got this far we must carry on to Wizard Elzaphan now. We're almost there. It would help Flop and Miriam more, and Joog, by getting Elzaphan's help, wouldn't it? So the best thing is to finish the journey."

Amalek sighed, but she knew that her brother was right, "I feel so tired," she said.

"Yes, and so do I," he agreed.

They began to feel their bodies aching and they realised how weary they were. The escape from the Kingdom of Gems and the following journey through Summertime Kingdom, had been tough. They had gone through so much in a short time and now they needed to rest and gather their strength ready to continue. Seph and Amalek yawned together.

"We'll sleep here and rest and then carry on tomorrow," Seph said, speaking with a comforting authority.

Neville shook his wings without unfolding them. His white feathers ruffled and then settled flat.

"Good night," he said and turned his head to tuck it under a wing.

"Good night, Neville," said Amalek.

"Night," Seph added.

"Neville?" asked Amalek. He drew his head out from under his wing and looked at her, "As we go to sleep could you sing us a riddle-song, please?"

"Of course," replied Neville, "I have one that suits the situation perfectly. But you should get comfortable first."

The two exhausted children tried to get as comfortable as possible in their earthy hideaway. They still felt their minds turning with images and thoughts of the past few days. So much had happened. The journey had been filled with danger and their meetings with the Dark Wizard Troubler and his great hoard of ravens left a numbing cloud of fear in their hearts. However, they had found that an inner strength had somehow arisen in them to meet the challenge that had been thrust upon them. They were determined to fight and not give up in the face of the dark power which had struck at their kingdom.

There were plenty of dried leaves which helped to soften the hard ground and so they swept them into piles with their hands and arms. As they settled down for sleep they found that they could look out and up through the entrance at a star-spangled sky above the trees. This beautiful sight began to soothe their restless minds.

"Ready," asked Neville.

"Yes," replied Amalek, and Seph nodded.

Neville took a breath and began to sing.

"When everyone is sleeping
and the silver moon glides by
and the lord of night turns the stars of light
to decorate the sky,

"And when the deepest shadows
fill alleyways and glades
you may see me, on wall or tree,
in my cloak of many shades.

"You'll need to look with care
else you may be deceived
and only see a wall or tree
or a pile of dying leaves.

"For me a candle's danger!
and here's a mystery -
I wake at night, but love the light
which attracts me endlessly."

The song acted as a lullaby. They felt too tired to work out the answer and by the time he was on the third verse they felt their minds beginning to drift into slumber. In their leafy hideaway they were safe and by the morning they would be refreshed enough to carry on and finish the journey. They were soon all asleep.

Close by, in a tree within listening distance, a flash of purple glinted in the moonlight. Two black ravens, Crayle and Jum, perched on a branch, watching and waiting.

...CONTINUED IN BOOK 2 OF THE TRILOGY ~ THE SILVER WELL

Acknowledgements

In the writing of Candara's Gift I have been supported and encouraged by many people. This wonderful help kept the project going until it finally reached completion and found its way into your hands. Without this support I am certain that an early A4 draft version of it would be sitting on a shelf somewhere in my house growing dusty. So I owe a great debt of thanks to all the positive thinking people who had the vision to give me the very special gift of encouragement.

Firstly, my family. My wife Sarah, daughter Rebecca and son Joseph have been three excellent sounding boards. They were ready at the right time to read the book through and litter the margins with their comments, such as 'he wouldn't say that', 'lol', 'this bit needs working on', and even 'delete this'. They have also been always willing to listen to newly written extracts and offer their thoughts. They played a major part.

There have also been financial sacrifices which they have happily taken on board for the sake of the book. They have continually expressed their enjoyment of Candara's Gift and have been unceasingly enthusiastic about it.

Rebecca and Joseph were the first inspiration when it was told as a short bedtime story about eleven years ago. They kept asking for it until I decided to write it down. I started writing some each evening and then reading it to them. It is amazing how things grow from small seeds.

Almost two years before the publication of Candara's Gift the whole Kingdom of Gems trilogy was one third shorter than Candara's Gift. At this time it *was* sitting on a shelf growing dusty. I have to thank a friend, Spiros Alexopoulos, who insisted that I fished it out and got back to work. He even phoned me up regularly to make sure I was doing it. This was a real turning point from which I never looked back. Thank you Spiros.

Thanks also to Spiros' son, Orpheas, who was the first to read it outside my family. The fact that he enjoyed it so much made me realize I should try to publish.

There is a wonderful family, the Milnes, who have always given me a lift each time I have shown them the latest versions and illustrations. They have shown continual interest and their wholehearted encouragement has been invaluable. Thank you Stephen and Martha, and their children Katy, Ben, Emily, Rosie, Ellie and Peter. Special thanks to Emily who actually read the book three times at various stages, giving me very useful feedback each time.

Finally, Debbie and Julian Newby who proof read the book and offered some excellent advice on the text and about other publishing matters. Their positive comments about the book gave my confidence a real boost.